ONCE A SPY

ONCE A SPY

ROBERT FOOTMAN

DODD, MEAD & COMPANY / New York

Copyright © 1980 by Robert Footman
All rights reserved

No part of this book may be reproduced in any form without permission in writing from the publisher Printed in the United States of America

1 2 3 4 5 6 7 8 9 10

Library of Congress Cataloging in Publication Data

Footman, Robert.
  Once a spy.

  I. Title.
PZ4.F6895On   [PS3556.O64]   813'.54   80-15748
ISBN 0-396-07864-8

Part One

1

It was a good wedding. The champagne was not mucky sweet—just sweet. The shrimp was fresh and crisp; the cheese ripe and rich; the punch adequate and safe; the bride lovely and happy; and best of all, the parents at peace and numbly euphoric.

And he turned to congratulate Jean and there was Carter talking to Mr. Bernhart, father of the bride.

Jean had seen his mouth puckering into a beginning smile, so he smiled. "One of your best, my dear, one of your best."

His wife's grim face may have smoothed a trifle; but she merely shrugged. "I try. Harry, I think Mr. Bernhart wants to catch your eye. There's someone with him. He doesn't act like a guest."

Jean Ryder could spot an interloper. With two to four weddings on each of forty weekends, she knew more about weddings than anyone in Contra Costa County. (On the weekends with four hitches Harry handled two of them for her, one in the morning and one in the afternoon. It wasn't difficult; Jean had every kind of wedding tape-measured to the last detail. For organizing ability he knew no one like her.) And James Carter was an interloper if ever there was one, the worst kind of interloper,

3

one from a past utterly dead these five years.

Turning as if to find Mr. Bernhart, Harry faced directly away from the father of the bride and James Carter. He only had five seconds to think before Jean pointed him right, but those were a long five seconds.

The impertinence of the son-of-a-bitch. The unmitigated gall. To barge into the midst of this peaceful, joyous scene, with over a hundred reception guests babbling wedding nonsensicals, to barge in and force a confrontation. The son-of-a-bitch of a bastard. A clever bastard. Anywhere else, he could have slammed a door on Carter, cut off the phone, torn up the letter unread, if necessary punched him in the nose. Well, hardly that. Carter would break his arm if he tried any rough stuff; Carter had always been a master at martial arts. But regardless, he would not have had to listen to one word. Not one. But here he was trapped. And knowing that, he turned again and strode toward his host.

"This is so nice of you, Mr. Bernhart," Carter was saying. "Hello, Harry, I was just explaining to Mr. Bernhart that I was driving down from Sacramento and I have to catch a plane for a Washington meeting and so I asked at your office and they told me I would find you here and it's good to see you, Harry, after all these years. Thank you again, Mr. Bernhart."

He didn't bother to tell Carter he was lying. Carter should know his own lies. "Have some champagne, James."

Carter's Cary Grant face registered horror. "God, man, you have gotten out of touch. Is five years really that long?"

"Here, take the champagne. Regard it as a cover. What do you want?"

"You weren't ever as good an operative as you made everyone think, Harry. You were always too blunt. Maybe that accounts for the trail of bodies that seemed to accumulate wherever you popped up."

The garden was spacious. A hundred people were able to hold fifty private conversations. They themselves were isolated against the trunk of a giant oak tree; a foot-thick limb went horizontal to the ground and they draped their shoulders over it. In spite of himself, Ryder looked up into the branches and Carter laughed delightedly.

"So five years isn't all that long. I told him it wouldn't be. I told him I'd find you as flat-bellied as ever. The same round chubby innocuous baby face that suggests fat and sloth and idiocy and conceals reflexes of a cat and the brain of a computer. Over fifty and looks barely forty. Management consultant. . . . Well it's happened before. The cover becomes the reality. The Hollow Man. The perfect company tool."

"Him?"

"Oh, you didn't think I would come myself if he hadn't sent me, did you? I told him it would be a waste of time, but what choice did I have?"

"Him?"

"Oakland, Harry. Junius Oakland. Who else? The man you admire so much. He's now in charge of the Far East Desk. You could have had his job, Harry. I've always wondered why you didn't take it. And don't tell me you wanted to come in from the cold. The Far East Desk provides ample heat. Warm enough to thaw out the memory of those five commie thugs in Frankfurt—you were in or near Frankfurt about then, weren't you, Harry? I've always wondered. . . . Well, so you're a management consultant now. And on weekends you cater weddings for your wife. And you make three times what you made with the company. Well, well, I can't knock it."

How many man hours had been spent researching his bucolic suburban life? That didn't matter. What did matter was that he had been quite unaware of the investigation. Had he slipped that much? Worse, was it possible Junius Oakland had reneged on the unspoken truce? Was Orinda, California, no refuge from the past? Ridiculous. It was 1977 and five peaceful years had gone by. Nothing had happened to galvanize Oakland into action. Oakland was safe as far as he was concerned; ergo, he should be safe as far as Oakland was concerned. Should be.

"What does he want?"

"Not him, Harry. It's a State Department caper. He's just a go-between, or a catalyst, maybe. Our hands are clean—ah, Harry, this must be your wife."

He looked at Jean. She showed her years. And her disapproval. Her lips were pursed, censorious, grim, and her eyes betrayed a most unhappy woman. Had Carter found out that they slept in the same bed and hadn't touched each other in three years?

"James Carter, my dear. My wife, Jean. I used to work with James on that oil deal in Iran."

"That was twelve years ago." Jean's statement was uncompromising, suspicious, full of distaste. Why should she care? He had left the Agency; why should she care if the Agency had not left him? She had insisted on making her home in California. "I don't want Peter growing up in that phony Georgetown hothouse, the poorest kid on the block. I won't divorce you, Harry. You're the only man in my life; but I don't like what you've gotten into. It didn't sound then the way it's turned out. So when you're back from Tokyo, Bonn, Teheran, Santiago, wherever, stop by in California. I've got a career picked out for myself, and when I get located I'll tell you where your home is." And he had not objected. Peter had turned out well, taking medicine at Columbia College of Physicians and Surgeons, no less; and as for the normal amenities of marriage, well, that had never particularly concerned him. Abroad there had always been women for men like him —and of course a man for women like them—and it hadn't mattered all that much. Perhaps he lacked normal sex drives; perhaps at fifty-two he had left what little he had behind him. For certainly he had not missed sex these past three years. The fact that Jean lay like a log on her side of the bed, while he lay equally stiff on his side, had not bothered him. He simply had not wanted to touch her even to say good night; and Lord knows she didn't want to caress him. This was the way they lived and he did not lack, nor did he sense, any need to pursue other women. Had Carter's investigation—his spying—turned any light on this happy little marriage?

"You're right, my dear. Twelve years. That's a long time in the past. The utterly dead past."

If he had wondered if Jean would rejoice when he returned prematurely, he had been quickly disillusioned. "You quit at forty-seven. In three more years you would have received the special early pension for field men. I've supported myself handsomely here without you and I don't relish carrying both you and Peter. Two Ryder male drones are too much for me. I expect you to carry your own weight. I have my career. You find yourself your own." She hadn't rejoiced then, and she didn't rejoice now.

"Mr. Carter is not here to talk about the utterly dead past. If you go with him, Harry, don't come back. I put in twenty-two years with that utterly dead past. It killed me after the first ten. I was a dead woman in ten years. Expecting a visit every day when you were away.... I could see them, two men in grey at the door, each carrying his hat in his hand. 'May we come in, Mrs. Ryder? ... We're friends of your husband.' Oh yes, I knew the speech and I had mine all ready. 'You may not come in, gentlemen. If my husband has friends like you, I wonder what kind of enemies he had.' It was a good speech, don't you think? I was really sorry I didn't get to use it. Good-day, Mr. Carter."

"Well," said James Carter.

"Well," said Harry Ryder.

"Nice wedding," said James Carter. "I've never seen a more beautiful bride."

"Thanks for stopping by, James. Have a nice trip to Washington."

"What do you mean 'nice trip'? We haven't finished our discussion."

"You heard the lady. We're finished."

"It's the Philippines, Harry. Manila, maybe Leyte even. Old homeweek. Watsonville revisited. Leyte, I have returned. And not us. We shake hands and I'm gone and Oakland is gone. It's you and the State Department, Harry. A modern hero. All for the good and glory of his country. The rarest of all assignments, Harry—a heroic job."

The clever bastard. Watsonville revisited. How carefully Carter had studied the personnel files. No one else in the Agency had ever tied Watsonville and Castroville, California, home of the apple and the artichoke, with the Visayan Islands, home of the coconut and the banana. The Watsonville connection.

"Sorry, James. I'm no hero. In 1943 I was a hero. For about two days. Thanks old chap. Give my regards to Junius. Here, have another glass of champagne. See you twelve years from now."

On Monday morning, Mrs. Swinton handed him an envelope.

"It was under the door when I opened up. See, it says, 'Confidential. For the eyes of Harry Ryder only.' What a peculiar way to put things. 'Confidential' is enough, I should think."

He looked at the stern Mrs. Swinton, at the envelope, at the door sign which read, "H. Ryder & Company, Management Consultants." He didn't have to open the envelope. But Jean's greeting at breakfast formed into capitals before his eyes. "I don't know whether I'm glad you're here or not, Harry. I made a resolve to myself years ago I would not leave you until Peter was on his own or you went off on one of your ridiculous missions. I really hoped you would be gone this morning, because then I would be free. But I see you're still here. So be it. See you tonight."

"Thank you, Grace. I'm meeting with the developers at eleven this morning. I think the project will pay out in three years and I imagine they'll want to go ahead. So let's have Plymouth gin, Cutty Sark, and Jack Daniels at twelve-thirty."

Her eyes stayed on the envelope, which he kept flipping against his thumb. He said, "You know, one thing bothered me about the wedding yesterday, Grace. It still bothers me. The grass was green. A bright green. In this time of drought. The Bernharts must have wasted a couple of acre feet of water on that lawn. A bright green. Just like the Leyte green."

"Leyte green?"

His window faced toward the Coast Range separating Orinda from Berkeley and the bay. He swiveled his chair to look up at the wild California oak trees. Live oaks. What is a dead oak?

> Dear Harry. Sorry you wouldn't talk to me. But you wouldn't have learned much. Just a name: Maricar Macasieb. He's in the San Francisco phone book. He's got the message for you. As I said, it's State Department all the way. Only the DCI and DCID are in. And of course the State Department and maybe some others. I don't think our mutual friend knows any more than I do. So what can be wrong with anything this hush-hush?

There was no signature. Only a P.S. "I'm told to tell you there's $50,000 tax-free clear for you. And that or more in expenses. With no accounting. Heroic patriotism at a profit. Hail Nathan Hale."

One hundred thousand dollars or more. Just like that. A fortune by Agency standards, when five hundred dollars a month would buy chiefs of staffs throughout much of the world. One hundred thousand dollars. He rolled the figure around, wrote it on a scratch pad, doodled with it north, south, east, and west. It always came out the same.

The Plymouth gin, Cutty Sark, and Jack Daniels were duly sampled at twelve-thirty. The builders and their lawyers were astonished to see him take not one but three gins over the rocks. Ralph Levison said it for all of them. "I've never seen you drink during business hours, Harry. Almost never at any time. Are you all right?"

"It's a big deal, Ralph. Just say I'm celebrating."

Celebrating what? Not a hundred thousand dollars. He didn't need one hundred thousand dollars, he didn't want one hundred thousand dollars. He did want freedom. From Jean. From that pursed, censorious, reproving grimace. From her rigid, unresponsive body logged beside him in bed. Was that what he was celebrating? A decision to take her at her word? "I really hoped you would be gone, because then I would be free." Well, that worked both ways. All he had to do was go home, pack, move out. And celebrate.

And he did not have to phone Maricar Macasieb. He knew the number. He had looked it up in the phone book —492-8203. He did not have to phone 492-8203, because freedom did not lie in that direction. Freedom meant simply facing up to his ridiculous, demeaning, and demeaned way of life and getting out. Did Jean have someone on the side? Wouldn't that be something? For a moment she had looked almost pretty, until she had seen him at the breakfast table. His suspicious antennae went pointing around Orinda and he instantly knew who it was. The great spy scores again. Gulled for three years and none the wiser. "I made a resolve I wouldn't leave you." Not,

"I wouldn't find another man." Not, "I wouldn't sleep with widower John Sweeney," whose daughter she had married off three years ago, who was one of the really attractive, really nice middle-aged bachelors around the country club, who was always being coupled with each new divorcee or widow or importee, and who had remained resolutely single. But not unattended.

"Well, I'll be hanged."

The phone rang. Mrs. Swinton called him on the intercom. "I know it's after hours, Harry." It was five-thirty. The live oaks were in shadow. A dulled, blackened, green shadow. "But the call is from Washington. He wouldn't give his name. He said, 'Just tell him Nathan Hale rises again.'" Her voice was reproving. Her boss had never had secrets from her before. She considered him a thoroughly ordinary, mediocre, uninteresting country club hanger-on. His biggest excitement, as far as she could see, was his weekly Friday domino game. She sniffed so Harry could hear her sniff.

"Harry, I'm calling on my own. J. O. says you'll go for the deal. You're normally greedy. But I know better. Know you better. You've already turned it down, right?"

Silence. A laugh from James Carter. "The silence of pure innocence. You know it, Harry? 'The silence often of pure innocence persuades when speaking fails.' But not this cynic. You don't persuade me. So I'm calling to say one thing. I worked out my one-liner all the way to Dulles."

"And that is?"

"It costs nothing to listen."

The phone clicked.

Grace Swinton came in. "I'm going home, Harry."

"Good night, Grace."

"Is there anything you want to tell me?"

"Good night, Grace."

He sat until the live oaks merged into the black shadows. It was after seven. He dialed 492-8203.

11

3

Fog blanketed the City. (When San Franciscans call it the City, both speaker and listener hear and see the capital C. All northern California recognizes only one city. Even as a boy in Watsonville, Harry knew where grown-ups were heading when they trekked off to the City. It was a shock to him later on to find that people east of the Sierras and south of the Tehachapis used the word to designate places like Chicago, New York, Los Angeles. How could that be, when there is only one city in our country?) The Pyramid and Bank of America buildings were shrouded in fog from about the thirtieth floor. Wisps of fog even dodged through the streets of Chinatown. The restaurant he sought was on the edge of Chinatown. The Philippine Gardens.

And a garden it was not. Unless one counted a few green potted plants in the corners of the room. It was a long, thin structure. Half-walls broke up the rectangle into a kind of maze, so that one zigzagged through the dining room, which was about three-quarters full. Each table had a Queen Kaahumanu chair at the head. The tables and chairs and walls all seemed fairly dirty, though an examination of any particular square inch revealed no sign of dirt or stain. In short, the Philippine Gardens was just like any of a dozen restaurants he had seen in Manila —even to the sinigang soup and adobo and kare-kare dishes he spotted. The bar was about halfway down the maze. It had five wicker stools. He was the only customer.

"A Plymouth gin on the rocks, please."

"I'm sorry, sir. We do not have Plymouth gin. Would Gordon's do?"

"Excellent. Would you please put the ice in a separate glass?"

What silly nonsense. How many silly years he had devoted to this sort of thing. "Carry the London *Times* open to page three." "Ask for a package of Players and a Dutch cigar." "Go into the small bar off the street at the Vier Jahreszeiten, order two glasses of Enzian and spill one of them." Everyone did it, even Filipinos a half-block off Kearney Street in little old San Francisco. Where did they learn such rigmaroles? Or was covert guile a natural way of life with all human beings? It began with childhood: secret caves, hidden passageways, code words, invisible inks, the works. Where did children learn this? No adult taught them; and from childhood games to an organized intelligence apparatus was an effortless transition.

A Filipino leaned over the bar next to him and ordered a San Miguel beer. While he was waiting, he spoke straight ahead without looking at Harry. "Go past the men's room. There is a door. Open it and go upstairs." He took his beer and went back to his table. Harry poured the ice into his gin, drank it appreciatively—Gordon's was a fine gin, no question about it—went past the men's room, opened the door, trudged up the dank, dimly-lit wooden stairs. A saintly-looking Filipino welcomed him at the top of the stairs.

"I am Maricar Macasieb. Thank you for coming. This way please."

He did not ask Harry his name. Harry did not volunteer it—to him or to the eight other Filipinos seated at the rectangular table and against the walls. He studied each man carefully, impersonally. High-cheekboned faces, round Tagalog faces, a trace of Chinese heritage in one of the men. Some scowled at his stare, others shifted their eyes. He recognized two of them: an auto dealer and a photographer. They ran regular large space ads in the *Philippine Free Press,* which he received weekly along with the *Hokubei Mainichi* and the *Sing Tao Jai Pao.* Pete Zarnora, your friendly Ford dealer, and Ernesto Caragan,

13

who captures the true Filipino spirit for you in his portraits.

Macasieb gestured. "Please be seated. Were you followed?"

The whole scene was incredible. Was he followed? How could he be followed? He had come straight from Orinda after calling Macasieb. What kind of game was this—why the grim, almost murderous expressions on some of the faces? Maybe not murderous—disapproving. They disapproved of him, of this whole operation.

"I was not followed." (There had been a car that pulled right behind him into the parking lot at Pacific and Montgomery. Two men had gotten out. He had waited until they disappeared up toward Broadway and Sex Nude Encounter Parlors. Training, training, training—anything James Carter and Junius Oakland were involved in called for training, the trained response.) "No, I was not followed."

"Good. Why do you think you are qualified for this job?"

Macasieb had an unusual face for a Filipino. It was the face of a seventy-year-old medieval French monk. A saint's face, with its smooth skin, white halo of hair, and gentle, kindly expression. He was plainly a superior man who led by spiritual strength, not by the brutality and cruelty so visible in the others.

"I can't answer your question. I don't know what job you are talking about. So I don't know what qualifications are called for. I came here to listen and decide if I want to help you."

A crashing babble of voices broke out. Visayan, Tagalog—and when they wanted to talk to each other, the southerners and northerners used Spanish. They took it for granted that he could not understand them. They shared that familiar universal contempt for the parochial, insular American, too ignorant to do more than speak his own language and barely that. Harry kept his face blank as he listened. The gist of their complaints was that the whole idea was a mistake. The American government could not be trusted and God knows this baby-faced old man was not the one to help them. They didn't want a man who might be almost forty to do this job; they needed someone in his twenties, certainly no one in his late thirties, so let's throw this bum out and do the job ourselves. Harry was delighted about the late thirties. His baby face had been a severe handicap in his twenties; but now it was beginning to pay off.

Macasieb paid no attention to his ranting colleagues. He was studying Harry thoughtfully.

"This is rather a stalemate. Perhaps it's just as well. Obviously the people who sent you think you have the right experience and qualifications. We're rather at their mercy. But what did you mean, 'decide if you want to help us'?"

"Exactly that. I'm a free man. I'm not here under any compulsion. I can see your problem. You have to take me on faith. But my problem is equally real. I don't have to take you at all."

The room was silent. Their anger was almost palpable. Macasieb turned to the others. "I don't believe there's any point in talking Visayan or Tagalog or Spanish. I believe this gentleman understands every word you say. Am I correct, sir? Did you learn our languages in the Philippines?"

"Tagalog and Spanish, yes. Visayan, no. I learned Visayan in California. I grew up near Watsonville. I spent a great deal of my childhood with people from Leyte and Cebu. They taught me Visayan songs. I learned to play their guitars and gradually I learned a child's vocabulary. The rest followed."

Everyone in the room sighed. A chubby little man said in Visayan, "I am from Hinunangan. Have you ever been there?"

"Briefly, but I operated mostly in northern Leyte and southern Samar." He also used Visayan. "I was landed in

Leyte near Dulag in the fall of forty-three. I organized a reporting system on Japanese installations and troops and ship movements. I worked mostly through a man named Alex Ayalin. And of course with Colonel Kohleon."

Another sigh. The man from Hinunangan nodded. He switched to English. "I know who you are. You are Harry—Harry the American. Your Visayan is good. Only a little accent. But then you must be older, much older than you look."

"True, I am ancient. Perhaps the memories of Leyte help keep me young."

They thought of Leyte or of Cebu or Samar or Mindoro or Luzon or any and all of some seven thousand islands ravished by the Japanese. They thought of beheadings, torture, rape, simple massacre. They thought of one million dead Filipinos. They thought of Americans operating in the jungle—Colonel Wendell Fertig in Mindanao, Harry the American in Leyte, Chuck Parsons in Luzon. Each man there had relatives—men, women and children —whose lives had been lost on these islands; they had others whose lives had been saved by these and dozens of other strange Americans who blended into the jungle like incarnate Tarzans.

Macasieb broke the silence. "I take it, my friends, we can accept Mr. Harry's qualifications." The eight men nodded. "Then let me tell you what this is all about."

Harry raised his hand off his lap, the slightest of gestures.

"Before you do, let me outline the risk you take. If I refuse to work with you, your plan or purpose or scheme or whatever is compromised. Someone outside this room will know what you're up to."

And once again Harry looked at each of the eight men. Only this time, just like the old days, his antennae functioned, the Spiderman tingle seeped through him, and he knew there was danger in this room. Danger to him and to Macasieb and the "loyal" members of this nucleus. There had been no need for some mystery person to follow him. He had walked right into a trap.

"And I'll say one more thing. I'm not concerned if you trust me. I am concerned that I don't trust you. Please, don't overreact. Nothing I'm saying can surprise you, Mr. Macasieb. For it's obvious, isn't it, what's going on? You're up to some plot or other against President Raymundo and General Maximus Cruz and their sadistic hatchet man, Colonel Calixto Calugas. And if I'm correct, I can assume that at least one of you is on the payroll of either Cruz or Calugas or both of them.

"Please, let us not be hypocrites. I know Filipino politics. I know what you represent. I also know how Colonel Calugas works. So let me lay down certain terms. First, I will not give you a reply tonight. There's much for me to think about. Second, I will not give my reply to anyone in this room. If I accept, I'll call you, Mr. Macasieb, and tell you the way I'll operate. I promise you, you'll find it satisfactory. Third, if I accept and if I carry out your mission successfully, my name or person will never be mentioned, certainly not publicized. I do not exist, I have never existed."

4

Harry Ryder stood by the front door of the Philippine Gardens. It was the swinging kind that opens in the middle. He could see up and down Clay Street. Innocent Clay Street, well lighted even in the lowering fog. Innocent Clay Street, with almost no pedestrians, not since the recent spate of nighttime Chinatown murders perpetrated by teenagers from Hong Kong. Innocent Clay

Street, and someone not at all innocent was waiting out there to kill him.

He considered. His car was parked four blocks away. Should he go down to Montgomery or up to Kearny? Kearny was better lighted, had more traffic, more people. Montgomery, the financial street of San Francisco, was quite dark, with no traffic to speak of, and with dozens of dark doorways, crevices, and alleys suitable for ambush. The prudent man would go up Kearny to the light. Harry the American would choose the way of darkness. Hit 'em where they ain't.

He considered. Could he be imagining things? Had he been away from the action so long that he saw bogeymen now? Was his fear of betrayal without foundation, a sign he was no longer capable of a reasoned response? Certainly Macasieb had been outraged by his mistrust. Once again he saw Macasieb's fiery face, no longer so saintly— though, come to think of it, the saints he had read about were also apt to be a quite choleric lot.

Macasieb had snapped it out. "That is the most insulting speech I have ever listened to. I see no reason to carry on this conversation. I don't care if you're the best-qualified man in the world, I want nothing to do with you."

Harry nodded and rose to go. He tried to keep every man in his sight. He was not armed, unless a jackknife impaired his virginity. What could he do with a knife against eight men? But it was not a question of eight men, not even of one traitor, now that he was no longer their candidate.

The chubby little man from Hinunangan pushed his chair back and stood up. He was not impressive, not assertive anyway, but he did have grace. So many Filipinos had it, had grace. Maybe that was why Harry loved this gentle, fiercely proud people. Maybe he was being more sentimental than usual. But grace was worthy of sentimentality, and of sentiment, too.

"I don't agree. Americans have a saying. They say, 'I'm

not running a popularity contest.' Well, we're not running a popularity contest, either. In fact, in the Philippines we're decidedly unpopular. Not a man in this room can go back there. I say, not a man. I don't agree with Harry the American. I know there are no traitors in our midst. I don't blame Mr. Harry for thinking what he thinks. There are plenty of precedents. In fact, I respect his caution. He doesn't know us. He should be cautious. If he wasn't cautious, he would not be the man we want. Mr. Harry survived among a hundred thousand Japanese troops. This time he'll have to survive among a hundred thousand Cruz storm troopers. I do not want to be popular. I want to be successful. I say, let's put our trust in a man we know has been a success in our country against unbelievable odds. That's what I say."

Each man ruminated. Each man, Harry thought, was in a difficult position. Each man had to ask himself, if I were a traitor would I support Mr. Harry or oppose him? Each man, that is, except the traitor. He knew what he would do. And Harry thought he would opt for support of Harry the American, because then he would know whom to destroy. Perhaps the chubby man from Hinunangan was that traitor, because he had spoken first. And Harry watched each man work out these choices and laughed inside. The old days again. Hope and treachery, the Scylla and Charybdis of his profession. Was it possible he, Harry Ryder, the happy management consultant, had truly missed all this?

Macasieb nodded. "Very well. I can rise above personal feelings, if that is called for. Very well, Mr. Harry the American. I will tell you what this is all about. And I'll accept your conditions."

A dirty window—this window really was dirty—could be seen over Macasieb's shoulder. It looked out into a lighted stairwell toward a mongrel Chinese alley hotel. A row of fish—miserable, bony, scaly, white fish—was strung out to dry across the stairwell. A dingy geranium pot sat under the fish. He could have been in a back alley of Hong Kong or in the Binondo district in Manila.

"Do the names of José Manzano and Emerenciana Manzano Darang mean anything to you?"

"They do. They're one of the most famous brother and sister acts in the world. In the Philippines, José rates as a political extremist. He believes in democracy. He's made it clear General Cruz has only two choices: to kill him or lock him up. They can't exile him, because he'd promptly set about organizing a revolution. And Emerenciana is a poet. A poetess. She only writes one kind of poem: an anticipatory paean of victory for the revolution her brother will lead.

"The two of them have the best kind of credentials in the world for leading a revolution. They're rich. Or were once rich."

"Once rich indeed. And do you know where José and Emerenciana are now?"

"Certainly. They are in Fort Malolos prison. Have been there for several years."

"Guests of General Cruz. The Philippine government has taken everything away from the Manzanos and Darangs. A vast banking empire stolen."

"Not stolen, sir. The government paid a couple of thousand dollars for that billion dollar bank."

The Filipinos jumped angrily, then laughed sheepishly. Macasieb said, "You are indeed informed, Mr. Harry. Yes, the government promised to pay for the bank, but they have not yet contributed one penny. There is no one in all history worse than the tyrants who terrorize our country."

"All history?"

"Pardon me, Mr. Harry. We are Filipinos. We think of Filipino history, of Filipino problems. There is no one worse in Filipino history. These tyrants have taken a great nation, a nation struggling on its way to become the first genuine Third World democracy, and have subverted it into a police state, a ruthless extortionist torture-ridden police state. Even Yamashita was more honorable than our own blood brothers."

Harry could have provided a few insights into General Tomoyuki Yamashita. But he remembered the wart incident. Once as an adolescent he had been cleaning a stable yard with an illiterate handyman from the South. He had picked up a frog and showed it delightedly to the man, who had backed away and said, "Don't touch that there frog, man. He'll give you warts." A hot argument about warts had ensued and it was only halted when the owner of the stables, a white-haired gynecologist, had whispered to Harry, "Don't waste your breath trying to convert the ignorant." How often that piece of wisdom had steered him through maudlin controversy.

"And I suppose you want me to rescue José Manzano and Emerenciana Manzano Darang from maximum security Fort Malolos?"

Macasieb nodded. The eight Filipinos nodded. He nodded.

"You mean you will do it? Rescue them?"

"I mean I understand what you want. I mean I understand what you want is sheer stupidity." Not just stupidity from an intelligent rescuer's point of view, but stupidity on the part of his government. Why should it get involved in Filipino politics? And to ask the question was to sense an answer, a host of answers. Subic Bay Naval Base. Clark Field. Military aid. Long-term treaties. Revolution. Human rights. Friendly power. China. Russia. Japan. Maybe even simple justice and idealism, though one's training, everyman's experience, called for a cynical horselaugh at this thought. Certainly one hundred thousand dollars was a lot of loot to pay for justice and idealism.

"It can be done, sir. We've given a lot of thought to it. No prison is escape proof."

"Why don't you do it, then?"

Macasieb's face fell. "We don't know how, Mr. Harry.

We can communicate with José Manzano and his sister. Through their families. They visit them. You understand?"

"I understand."

"So we can get things to them. To help them escape. But . . ."

"But you don't know what things. And if you get them out, you don't know what to do next."

After forty minutes of protest and harangue and bombast, they fell silent and he left them. "I will call you, Mr. Macasieb. I will let you know my decision."

And that was a bit of bombast in its own right. For even as he left them, his antennae told him he was in trouble. Perhaps it was a betrayal from somebody in this pathetic group of amateur plotters. Perhaps it was worse than that —a gift from James Carter and Junius Oakland. In which case, he was truly in a world gone mad. The CIA didn't operate that way, couldn't operate that way. And therefore, he was imagining the whole thing and he could walk out the front door, go down Clay Street, turn up Montgomery, get his car at Pacific and Montgomery, and go home.

And if that was all there was to it, then he would phone Maricar Macasieb and tell him the truth. He was not the man for the job. He wasn't a forty-year-old has-been; he was a fifty-two-year-old has-been. He saw bogeymen where none existed. He put his hand on the swinging door and slipped into the fog. How silly of him. His dreadful Frankfurt experience must have gotten to him. That night had not been foggy, but it had also started with his departure from a restaurant in the darkened financial district, from "Das Börsenbericht."

He stood outside the door and shivered. From the April fog? From overwrought nerves? He slipped off his shoes and held them in one hand. Now he could identify the cause of his shiver. Simple cowardice. Scylla and Charybdis indeed. Pathetic amateurs, plotters forsooth. Who could be more pathetic than Harry the American, padding down Clay Street in his stocking feet and swinging up Montgomery Street and ducking to his knees between two parked cars, the overflow from the North Beach restaurant lots? And he prepared to wait and had hardly got into his crouch when two small men darted around the corner, slipped into the black entrance of an office building, and fell silent. He felt like laughing hysterically. He almost stood up and cried out in relief, "Here I am, come get me."

He set the shoes down and carefully pushed them under the rear bumper. He got out his jackknife and opened it. He could hear Jake Twillers's laconic lecture. "Remember this, you are always armed. A pen or pencil is a weapon. A wallet is a missile. A shoe is a club. A penknife? A penknife qualifies you for the commando squad." What would Jake say to a jackknife? He knew what Jake would say because he had had to memorize his speech. "With a jackknife you can take out two men armed with handguns. The first in the back, the second at twenty feet if necessary. Remember. One, two—with no delay. If you delay, you'll get a slug between the eyes. One, two—don't delay."

His nose to the ground, he watched the doorway from under the rear wheel. In less than a minute—less than thirty seconds—he saw one man dart across the sidewalk to the front of the parked car. He couldn't see the man in the darkness of the doorway, but a gun barrel glinted for a moment. He slid to the street side of the car and shifted his knife to his left hand. This was awkward. He could stab with his left hand, but even Jake Twiller would not have expected him to throw with it.

The man on the street inched along the car, his shoes slapping, his gun before him. And Harry slashed the wrist upward. The gun flew into the air, the man screamed and Harry's knife thrust right up his stomach and into his heart—left-handed at that. The classic thrust and he swung into the street, pushed the man upright over the trunk of the car, pulled his knife out with his right hand, placed his head behind the victim's head and threw the knife over the body's shoulder. There was a gasp from the doorway and the man slowly slumped to the sidewalk. One, two—don't delay. Jake Twiller was right again.

He ran over to the slumped body, kicked the gun out of its hand, turned the body over, pulled out his knife, wiped it on the man's sweater, cleaned it and put it away. He skipped to his shoes, put them back on, gave one last glance at the two would-be assassins—Filipinos, both slight fellows, both wearing dark sports shirts and black or blue sweaters. He wanted to go through their pockets, but this hardly seemed the occasion. And furthermore, he felt as if he were going to throw up. Upon which, he did throw up; in the gutter. He managed to miss the corpse in the street. What a hero he was; what a cold-blooded killer. His stomach gave a few more convulsive heaves as he staggered up the street, keeping close to the buildings so that car lights wouldn't pick him up. He strolled casually into the parking lot, paid the attendant, not looking him in the eye, drove his car carefully along Pacific Street, heard not a sound. His bodies were still a-smolderin' on Montgomery Street.

It was ten minutes to midnight when he pulled into his garage. Not a light was on in the house, not even the porch light, which went on automatically at seven in the evening. Crickets were serenading one another. A frog added a basso counterpoint. A distant car radio blared for a second and was instantly turned down. Lover's Lane. None of the night noises helped him resolve his problems.

The note was waiting on the hall table.

> Harry. I expect you to be out of here tomorrow. I know you have gone back with those people. I called Grace and she said you had talked to Washington. I'm

with friends. Don't look for me. I will see that all your things get stored in Bekins. When I sell the house, you'll get your share. I'm filing for divorce immediately. We should have done this ten years ago. Good luck.

Scylla and Charybdis. James Carter and Jean Ryder. There seemed only one direction for his ship to go.

5

He slept hard but not long that night. At five in the morning he was making breakfast, smoking a cigarette, waiting for the *Chronicle* to arrive. It usually came at quarter to seven.

At six-thirty he left the kitchen and climbed to the attic and unlocked an ancient cabinet. It held three rifles and five pistols. His Colt forty-fives, both automatic and revolver; his Webley 455; his Smith and Wesson Bodyguard model thirty-eight; and his little prize, the Walther PPK. (Prize literally. He had won it in the massacre in Frankfurt. Five pistols on the ground, one of them this dandy.) He picked up the Smith and Wesson and four boxes of cartridges. He had not held a gun in his hand for five years.

He set it on the kitchen table. A gun, even a handgun, seems monstrously large on a kitchen table. He thought conscientiously about guns for the next ten minutes. About the merits of revolvers versus automatics for field men. (Automatics were recommended; he simply liked the aesthetics of the revolver and its history. Who ever saw John Wayne twirl an automatic?) About the intricacies of shooting a handgun. (It was difficult, most difficult.

It had taken him six months of hard practice to hit a man-sized target every time at twenty-five yards; another six months to hit a moving target at all. He was no Hopalong Cassidy.) About the problems of carrying a pistol on an airplane when he had no official status. (In the Frankfurt case, he had traveled from Zurich to Vienna to Munich to Leipzig to Frankfurt. He represented the California Laser Corporation. His mission for them was to analyze potential business in each city, with the Leipzig Fair serving as the central point for interviewing Iron Curtain prospects. His mission for the CIA was to meet an East German scientist at the fair and receive a vial of poison gas. In each city he was issued a Smith and Wesson by the local station chief and relinquished it just before his departure. As plain old Harry Ryder, there was no way he could go traipsing through an airport with his handy little equalizer.) About how thinking about guns kept him from thinking about Jean Ryder and James Carter and Precy and Adoring Raymundo and General Maximus Cruz and Junius Oakland and Maricar Macasieb and José Manzano and Emerenciana Manzano Darang and two bloody nameless Filipino corpses on Montgomery at Clay. (It almost worked.)

At six forty-five the paper thudded against the front door. The little bastard. He had been told over and over not to hit the front door. Every time he did so, the paper left a black ink smudge. Maybe the little bastard knew Harry Ryder wasn't going to be there anymore to tell him not to hit the front door.

His first quick glance spotted nothing on the front page. Then he saw a small box.

MURDER ON MONTGOMERY STREET.

The bodies of two murdered men were discovered at eleven o'clock last night by a passing motorist. Full story on page 6.

Page six added very little to the headline.

Driving home at eleven o'clock last night from a dinner with his wife, John Quigley felt his front and rear right wheels run over a bump in the street. Investigating, Mr. Quigley found that he had run over the face of a man's body. Police were called and they discovered another body on the sidewalk. The two men were Filipinos. Each had been stabbed. Police were unable to find any identification. Inspectors Graham and Tedeschi have been assigned to investigate the fatal stabbings. They request any witnesses to call them at the Homicide Section, 415-553-1145.

Before he could read further, the telephone rang.
"Well, well, well," the familiar voice said. "You do work fast. Not even in the game yet, and two hits already. Quite a batting average. What will you do when you sign up to play full time?"
"Fuck you," Harry said and hung up.
The phone started ringing before he picked up the paper. He let it ring.

Mr. Quigley of 1183 Prenth Street, San Francisco, said the experience "was a terrible shock. At first I think I've run over a guy. Right over his face. And then I see the blood on the street. Man, I'm so sick I heave all over the place. A good dinner at Vanessi's—just like that. Man, this is no way to celebrate an evening with your wife. Thank God for the police. They came right away —none of this delay stuff like you always hear about and they were just wonderful."

He picked up the phone.
"Temper, temper, temper," James Carter said. "What did the paper say? Read it to me. I know you've got the

paper. It arrived at six forty-five. It's six fifty-two your time."

Harry was silent. Carter said impatiently, "Don't worry. Your phone's not tapped. This is a secure line."

"You think of everything, don't you? What toothpaste do I use?"

"Crest, old boy, Crest. Now read."

Now Harry knew what had happened. They had pulled a full-scale psychological profile on him. "How's he taking his retirement? Has he gone flabby? Is he a lush? Has he lost his drive? Is he dissatisfied, happy, at peace, resentful, morose, calm, active, overcome by acedia, by hyperthyroidism? Will he respond to patriotism, antipatriotism, appeals to the team spirit, or to rebellion, to money, to fame, to praise, to blame?" On and on and on. The works. Why Crest toothpaste? "Because he lives by his essential training in anonymity." What is more anonymous than Everyman's toothpaste?

He read the story aloud. "Good," Carter said. "Our friends in the Bureau cooperated beautifully. They didn't like it. But we assured them there would be no further action in this country. So they got the police to keep quiet on the guns. The Philippine consul will also keep quiet once he's told about the arsenal."

"Consul?"

"Yes. The two enforcers were traveling on a Filipino passport. Their names were Antoine Arejedos, journalist, and Ruperto Soriano, lecturer in economics. Incidentally, you left no traces. You lucked out there."

"Calugas's men?"

"The good Colonel's, no less."

"Thanks for the information."

"Don't go away. A question. Two questions. First, how did you know you were in trouble?"

"I don't know. I've asked myself the question a hundred times. I think basically I decided at my meeting last night that you had set me up. The whole affair stank.

Half those fellows would have done me in right there. Did you?"

"Did I what? Oh, set you up. No. Second question. What is your decision?"

"I want the expense account and wages deposited at Wells Fargo Main, San Francisco. Make it one hundred and twenty-five thousand. This will be expensive. I'll keep an accounting and whatever's left over you'll get back. But I want it all now, just in case."

"Well, I'll be damned. Someone tries to kill you, and you find the proposal irresistible. Let me make one thing clear, Ryder. I did not recommend you for this job. I thought you were overrated in the old days. In my mind, you were the all-American goof-off. Luxury hotels, the big expense account, fancy restaurants, and geisha girls—like a goddam Arab sheikh. I still think you're overrated. Last night was luck, just sheer paranoid luck. You always were paranoid, weren't you? When I'm not there to be the straw man you hate, you'll fall to pieces. Okay. Okay. So much for me. The money will be deposited. I'll have Sommers get together with you and work out details of the help you'll need."

"You'll do nothing of the kind. You are not my case officer. I have no case officer. I work alone on this. Don't you forget this, James, my friend. This is the last communication you'll have from me until I walk into your office with my mission complete. Or wherever you want me to walk."

"Alone? The State Department and the Director—and God knows who all—and you'll work alone!"

"And I'll also work slowly. Nothing will happen for three or four months."

"Now you're trying to set me up. I don't know anything about this caper, but I know three or four months are out of the question."

"If the money is not in the bank by two o'clock this afternoon, no hard feelings. And I still won't talk to you.

Not to an idiot who thinks I ever touched a geisha girl. I just wish I had."

He hung up, picked up the revolver and the cartridges, drove to a remote valley in the Coast Range near Dublin, asked his cattleman friend and client if he could target-practice on his property, and proceeded to shoot at Campbell soup cans silhouetted before a newspaper at twenty-five yards' distance. He fired from the standing, crouched, kneeling, and prone positions. In the prone position he hit the cans four out of ten times. In the others he was uniformly two out of ten. He was terrible. However, this much could be said. Each shot hit the newspaper somewhere.

6

The Man at the Southeast Asia Desk looked at the blinking light with distaste. He did not want to pick up the phone and talk to that dreadful CIA ghoul. But he was caught squarely in the middle. He had no choice.

He reached his left hand forward, a quizzical frown on his face. What would great-grandfather have said to this? A member of his family fomenting revolution in the Philippines! Well, if not fomenting, at least acquiescing in preparations for a possible foment. (This thought was no idle self-pity. The Man at the Southeast Asia Desk tried to be a democratic sort. But when he and his wife went out to a spur-of-the-moment quiet dinner, it didn't make any difference how many senators, ambassadors, lobbyists, and millionaires were cooped behind the velvet bar, the headwaiter took one look and jumped to let them through. And no one protested. No one admires an aristocrat more than a democrat, and though the Man would never be a Supreme Court justice like his great-grandfather, a senator and the most powerful man in his nation next to the president like his grandfather, and though he was painfully shy and stuttered at odd times, he was one of Washington's genuine aristocrats; his family name rested on his head like a crown or halo. And great-grandfather, who as adviser to the Philippines had nursed that country into the twentieth century and helped plan its democratic evolution throughout that century, would unquestionably regard that crown as tarnished and that halo as cracked.) He cradled the phone and said, "Yes, Mr. Carter."

"Yes, Mr. Carter! Christ, between you and the idiot in San Francisco, I don't see why I have to take this shit. I know, I know, I'm caught in the middle and I have no choice."

For the first time the thought crossed the Man's mind that James Carter might also be human. "I th—th—th—think we're all kind of caught in the middle in this one."

"You betcha. For once our hands are clean and you Ivy League boys are playing the heavy. Not a nice feeling, is it? Okay, so we're both gargling soap. I called to say our man has accepted. But he has two provisions."

"Oh?"

"Yes, oh. The first oh is that he will only work alone. He refuses any support, not that we are prepared to do much of anything, but a hand to a drowning man, you understand? And the second oh is that he wants three or four months to do the job. What, sir, are your instructions?"

A wild hope flamed through the Man at the Southeast Asia desk. Work alone. Marvelous. The whole Philippine government could collapse in three months. There could be a revolution or maybe the clowns who run that mess could get run over by a truck. Or, at worst, the treaty might be resolved and there would be no need to gargle soap any longer.

"Mar—, I mean, y—y—y—yes. Those terms are acceptable. Y—y—y—you may proceed."

He hung up and smiled a truly happy smile for the first time since the Chief had told him what he must do. He smiled until a sudden, sodden thought struck him. If the idiot in San Francisco was working alone, how could he be stopped if all bets were called off?

7

"Who killed our enforcers?"

The minister's face was suffused with blood. A few more degrees of rage, General Calixto Calugas thought, and Cruz would have himself a genuine, old-fashioned apoplectic stroke. However, another thought flitted through the dour colonel's mind. Was Cruz really infuriated over the death of two loyal Filipino servants of the State, or was he enraged because his evening golf game at the Palace Course was delayed?

And, in fact, the minister had unconsciously—or at least unself-consciously—taken out his putter and began to ease balls into a green contraption at the far end of the enormous Persian rug. Calugas shuddered. God bless the Philippines. Well, as the Americans say, it's a living.

"His name is Harry Ryder. You may recall him as Harry the American. In Leyte."

Cruz totally missed the ball. The blood receded as if his heart had stopped. His brown, round, well-fed, well-oiled face seemed white or freckled. He nodded. "I remember."

"Here is a photograph. That's when he was number two at the CIA station here. Subsequently he was transferred to Washington and we lost sight of him."

Cruz studied the photo. He saw a man with a round face

not unlike his own. Eyes and nose and ears and crew-cut hair all seemed harmoniously nondescript. It was not an easy face to remember. It was not a face to fear or respect or admire. A nothing face on a nothing man. "He looks plumpish. Is he?"

"As I recall, yes. He was a bit on the chubby side." There was a little note of satisfaction in the colonel's tone. At sixty he was lean and hard as a club and a thousand times more dangerous. "But he does know his way around our country."

Cruz thought a moment, addressed the ball, and this time stroked it into the green target. Still bent over, a pleased expression on his now normal, self-satisfied face, he said, "Kill him when he arrives. But do it so that José is killed, too. Not Emerenciano. Remember that. Kill him as he tries to escape. Before impartial witnesses. You understand?"

The minister picked up his bag of golf clubs and strode to the door. He paused and looked back at Calugas. "You can trust your source?"

"Totally."

8

When Harry returned from target practice, he could hear the phone ringing. It rang steadily. A determined, patient, unrelenting ring.

He sat in the car and listened. He went inside the house and sat by the phone and listened. Every four seconds. Ring. Four seconds. Ring. Four seconds. Ring. Four seconds.

He picked up the phone. He heard, "Now listen, Harry old buddy, don't get huffy with me. I'm glad I caught you.

Your conditions are okay by the powers that be, but they're tough on me. It's not easy to transfer a certified hundred-twenty-five-thousand-dollar check just like that. Take my word for it. There are transfer banks, agent banks, and correspondent banks and computers, and God knows what all. So if the money's not there precisely at two o'clock, don't get huffy. It's on its way. Harry? Harry, are you there? Damn, have I been . . . ? Who is this?"

"Don't shout, James. I heard everything. Now a question. A matter of timing. When was the decision made to go ahead with this?"

"Two weeks ago. But I suspect the usual preliminary ebb and flow went on. Four weeks or maybe more. The usual."

"When did my two snakes slither ashore?"

"One week ago."

"The timing stinks, James."

"When you put it that way, old buddy, truly it doth stink."

He hung up and immediately rang his office. "Sorry I did not call sooner, Grace. But I was tied up. And there's been a new development. I'll be away for four months. Yes, four months. I'll send you a check covering your pay for the next four months. Please, Grace, please listen to me. I am under time pressure. You can do anything you want. Come into the office every day. Go on a four month's vacation with Tom. Run the business yourself, if you want. Have some cards printed up and call yourself vice-president. You know as much as I do about consulting."

At this point she broke in. "That's nonsense. I only know what to do after I've watched you do it. How will I reach you?"

"You won't. You can't. Four months. Have fun."

He packed two light sports jackets, three pairs of slacks, five sport shirts, and all his identity papers. He sat by the bed and wrote a note:

Dear Jean,

You don't have to save any of it or share the proceeds with me. It's all yours. You're right. Ten years ago would have been about the time. At least we did have Peter. That's a good thing. Have a happy life with John. He's a good man.

He did not go to the bank at two o'clock. Instead, he registered at the Fairmont Tower, had lunch at his room window overlooking the Golden Gate, the bridge, Alcatraz, and a portion of Treasure Island. A few sailboats idled towards Sausalito. Near him a grey, lengthy Navy transport headed toward the bridge. Number 1184. Tank landing ship. Newport Class. Give him five weeks sitting at a window like this and he could form a mosaic of the Navy's Pacific operations. The Russians had a consular building on Green Street with twenty windows like this. Did it occur to them to keep tabs on Number 1184? Keep tabs? They knew the kind of bread the rats liked on Number 1184.

He sat at the window until nightfall. Nothing in the bay answered the questions he kept asking: "Why did they pick me for the job?" "Why, exactly, did I accept it?" "Who set me up with the two thugs?"

As darkness fell, he dialed a number. "Mr. Macasieb, I have decided to accept the assignment."

"Ah, Harry the American. You were busy last . . ."

"Mr. Macasieb, please. This is an open phone. If you have any surmises, please keep them just that. My concern is security. I think you'll agree there's been a certain lack of that . . ."

"Who were those two men?"

"Please, Mr. Macasieb, please. What two men? I do not know anything of two men. You understand, don't you? No surmises, no post-mortems or pre-mortems, for that matter. And because of the security situation, I'll deal with only one man."

"Ah, of course, I understand. I'm at your . . ."

"And that man is Emilio Lanante."

"Impossible. Lanante knows nothing of our plans. How could he? He's a public figure. He's a professor of international law at UC Berkeley. Why, he's the last man we'd want involved in a thing like this."

Harry kept silent. He could hear Macasieb breathing heavily. "Mr. Macasieb, let me explain something. Emilio Lanante was a skinny kid of fourteen in Leyte in 1944. I was vastly his senior, I was nineteen. Emilio Lanante was my chief messenger to and from Alex Ayalin or Colonel Kohleon. Twice he was stopped and questioned by the Japanese. Twice he talked his way out of it. We called ourselves the teenage terrors of Tacloban. Sorry, it was funny in 1944. The point is we go back a long time. We know how to work together. So please clue Emilio in and ask him to be ready to meet me at five-thirty tomorrow afternoon. I'll phone him where to meet me. Trust me, Mr. Macasieb. I do know what I'm doing. And please don't feel you'll be slighted. I'll need your help. You and your friends. At the crucial stage of this affair, in about six or seven weeks, I'll pass the word to Emilio for your people to get cracking."

"You are a very hard man, Mr. Harry. I will hold you to your word. We must play an active part. This was our idea. Your people have sanctioned us. But it is our idea."

"I understand, Mr. Macasieb. And I respect your position. Your idea is a great idea. Its time has come."

9

Wells Fargo Main opens at nine in the morning. He was the first customer. He made out a withdrawal slip. For a hundred twenty-five thousand dollars.

He handed it to the teller. "I'll take the money in one thousands, if you please."

The teller was a pretty Chinese girl. A Cantonese. Shirly Ng. Her slant eyes grew as round as Bette Davis's. She punched up his account number on the black terminal. She read it, glanced swiftly at him, saw his eyes on the terminal, instantly snapped it off. "Surely, sir. It will take a few minutes." She waved her hand at her cash box. It showed a conspicuous lack of one-thousand-dollar bills.

She walked toward a man in a grey sharkskin suit at the right rear. She whispered to him. They both looked at a nearby terminal, glanced at him, turned their backs while the sharkskin suit man whispered instructions. She nodded and disappeared. The man in the sharkskin suit picked up a telephone, dialed, and talked rapidly. He looked pleased with himself.

Fifteen minutes later Shirley Ng returned carrying a packet of money. Her black button eyes were snapping with excitement. She counted out one hundred and twenty-five bills. They were crisp and clean. They were numbered consecutively. They made a package about an inch thick. Miss Ng watched him walk all the way to the front door.

In a straight-line distance of some twenty downtown blocks—on Columbus, Grant, Montgomery, Sansome, California, Pine, Bush, and Sutter—there are thirty-four banks. Six Bank of Americas, one Bank of California, one Bank of Canton, one Bank of Montreal, one Bank of the Orient, one Barclays, one California Canadian, two California Firsts, two Chartered Banks of London, two Crockers, one First Enterprise, one French Bank, one Hibernia, two Hongkongs, one Lloyds, one Philippine, one Redwood, one Sanwa, two Security Pacifics, one Sumitomo, one Toronto Dominion, one United California, and three Wells Fargos. (Another ten blocks would add another twenty banks. This does not include thirty or so savings and loans next door to the banks.) He left Wells Fargo and went next door to the Bank of California. He exchanged two one-thousand-dollar bills for twenty one-hundreds. These were not numbered consecutively. He went from there across the street to California First Bank and then, by three o'clock, to a total of twenty-four bank offices. He had exchanged forty-eight of his large bills. His pockets were bulging. At five-fifteen he deposited five hundred and fifty-seven bills in a Fairmont Hotel safe-deposit box. At five-thirty Emilio Lanante knocked on his door.

The once-skinny kid was now a roly-poly little man, much much too fat. They embraced unaffectedly. Lanante's fat did not conceal the gun in his shoulder holster. "How long has it been?" Harry said. "Since your daughter's marriage? Annaliza it was. How about the others?"

Emilio beamed and chortled. "Two more will get married this year. That means five will be married, three girls and two boys. Three babies are still in high school and college."

He poured Emilio a Scotch, himself a gin. He gestured to the chairs by the window. They talked about this and that until the second drink. Emilio's eyes were alert and amused. He turned the subject to business. "Maricar briefed me. He was outraged by your high-handed dictatorial tactics. After all he had gone through. Gone to Washington himself. Seen his great and good friend in the State Department. Been turned down cold. Oh yes, Harry, turned down. Your government has had enough Bay of Pigs. But then out of the clear came the word to expect a mysterious savior. You. Dear me, he was mad. A shame he couldn't head off this tripe. Did you see it?"

He tossed the *Philippine Free Press* to Harry. An enormous black headline jumped out at him. "Tragedy on Montgomery Street. Filipino tourists slaughtered. Outraged civic groups get no help from San Francisco police."

"Filipino tourists, indeed. Maricar swears no one in his group betrayed you. They're loyal. They're fanatics. I believe him. Fanatics and foolish."

Harry sipped his gin. It was Gordon's. His lucky gin for the duration. "I'm going to help them, Emilio. I want you to help me. I don't care if they're loyal or fanatic or foolish. There are nine of them. Can you imagine how long we would have lasted on Leyte if we had to deal with nine others?"

Lanante bobbed his head like a village idiot. He was his own best cover. No one could take him seriously. Nevertheless his constant grin concealed a razor-sharp military mind. Lanante had risen to colonel in the Philippine Army, when he and his doughty wife fled before they were jailed. If there were to be revolution in the Philippines, José Manzano might be its leader, but Emilio Lanante would command all the invading forces. He poured himself a third drink. "I know. I know. And I will help, Harry. But I am puzzled. This is not like you. You're not doing it for money. Certainly not for patriotism. You've made it very clear to me, you think we're not any better than the present government. We'll set up a tweedledee dictatorship in exchange for a tweedledum."

"Your questions are lucid and logical. Surely you've worked out an answer."

"Yes, I have, Harry. You're doing this for personal reasons. We're fighting a battle for freedom so you can settle some personal score. Solipsism, thy name is man."

"Someone wants to kill me, Emilio."

"Someone? Colonel Calixto Calugas. Yes, that's someone."

"Maybe. Maybe Calugas is just an agent in another war. My war."

"I don't understand."

"I don't either, Emilio. Maybe I'm imagining things. But listen to this. Most CIA men—even the toughest covert boys—go through their whole careers without ever using or even needing a gun. That was my career until my last three years. In that period I killed eight men, five of them at one blow. Like Grimm's tailor, no?"

Lanante grinned and smiled his idiot smile. "You were being set up?"

"I was being set up. Thrown into dangerous situations, the Christians and the lions. Unnecessarily dangerous situations. Nothing that time and discretion couldn't have solved. Worse, situations that did not call for violence, but there I was right in somebody's line of fire. That's why I got out."

"And you're being set up again?"

"I'm being set up again."

"You know who it is?"

"I know."

"Why not just walk away from it. Like you did five years ago?"

"Walk where?"

"Then attack now."

"Stroll into the front door at Langley and blast away?"

"So our war becomes your war."

"I've got to play out the hand as it's being dealt. I don't understand the sudden urgency. What's happened after five years to make death and destruction necessary?"

"The statute of limitations never runs out on murder."

"Or kidnapping."

"Or kidnapping. All right, though I don't understand. What can I do for you?"

"Provide six or seven things. First, this." He handed Lanante a torn dollar bill. "The old matching dollar bit.

When I make contact in Manila, we'll match our torn halves."

"Done. What else?"

"Now the old code bit. I want a phone number in Manila. Preferably an unlisted number. When I call, I'll say 'The Cry of Balintawak.' I expect to hear back 'The Liga Filipina.'"

Lanante smiled and chuckled. "Just as appropriate today as they were in 1896. We're always revolting against someone, aren't we? Only now it's not against the Spanish or Americans, it's against ourselves. What else?"

"I want false passports for José Manzano and his sister and complete profiles on the two of 'em. Their health, their strengths and weaknesses, their history, their character, their personality. Everything you can find out. Even what toothpaste they use."

"Toothpaste? Oh, I see. All right. This will be harder. But we have people who have known one or the other or both. I'm not Intelligence, Harry. But we'll do our best. What else?"

"I want a sewing machine delivered in the next week or so to Emerenciana Darang. She is to say she wants to sew clothes for herself and the other prisoners. They won't let her write. But she has to let her creative powers have some outlet. With the machine will be two or three bolts of cloth. They will have these items in it. He handed Lanante a list. Emilio read it and looked quizzically at Harry.

"Maybe you're being set up, but I can see you're the right man for the job. Remember that Japanese prisoner? How you cornered him? It was . . . but pardon me. I understand. Pliers. Wire cutter. Twelve-inch-pipe wrench. Small crowbar. Screwdriver. Hacksaw. Glass cutter. It will be done." Suddenly he frowned. "I wonder. You know, Macasieb hasn't thought this through. If your plan works, this will be the end of visitation privileges for political prisoners in the Philippines. The constabulary will go out of their minds. I don't know that it's worth it."

"If José Manzano is to be president of the Philippines, he won't do it from Fort Malolos. Trade-offs, Emilio, trade-offs."

"Very good. What else?"

"After I phone my contact in Manila, he will meet me at noon the next day at the bench under the dapdap tree in Rizal Park. Noon the next day, mind you. He will bring two things: a map of Fort Malolos and surrounding grounds. And a minute-by-minute timetable showing what the prisoners do each week. Their daily schedules. All this will be in a copy of *Shōgun*—hollowed out, of course."

"*Shōgun?* Oh. Okay. Then what?"

"Send the phone number, passports, and profiles to General Delivery in Los Angeles. Under the name Peter McClaren. You have three to four weeks. One suggestion. Whoever you send to Manila with the dollar bill, do not tell him a word as to what this is all about. That person is the weak link in the whole operation."

"Harry. Harry. How do you think I've survived these last ten years. On the international law level I've been quite a thorn in the government's side. So at first they tried to endow a chair at UC, providing I was fired. For one million dollars. Can you imagine it? Emilio Lanante from Tacloban with a million-dollar bonus on his head. Then they tried to assassinate me. That's why I carry this." He whipped out the forty-five automatic from against his ribs. "Fat has its place. My jackets have to be ample, don't they? I didn't think you had spotted it."

He didn't disabuse Lanante. "You're right, I didn't. I've slowed down, don't rub it in. And thanks for everything. And for two more things. First, would you mind calling Jean tomorrow and asking her to pick up the car in the garage downstairs? The parking will be paid for. And second, if I am killed, please read this document and do whatever you think needs doing. I'd suspect the FBI and the *New York Times* would be good bets. Maybe Arlo Thomasson at the FBI would be best."

10

Behind the Ambassador Hotel in Los Angeles there lies a square mile or so of Raymond Chandler country. Small stucco bungalows; three- or four-story brick or stucco apartment houses, each with fifteen or twenty two-room units, furnished and unfurnished; retirement homes; retirement hotels; mom-and-pop grocery stores run day and most of the night by indefatigable Lebanese; laundries; drugstores; and everywhere dispirited lawns, never robust and now in drought-time a sickly, crumbling brown. Harry Ryder walked a half-mile into this wilderness of hopelessness until he came to the Kingsley Crown. Like every other apartment house, it had a vacancy sign. Unlike every other, it had an elaborate shield on the side, presumably the Crown of the Kingsley. It was irresistible.

"The rent is two hundred forty dollars a month." The scrawny landlady was still in her pink bathrobe. Her hair curlers struggled with hair as stringy as the lawn. She was not irresistible. "There's a twenty-dollar cleaning fee. All payable in advance. Don't you have any baggage?"

He did. His suitcase was checked at the Ambassador, where he had gone by city bus from the Greyhound depot. If Maximus Cruz or Junius Oakland were trailing him, it wasn't on the Greyhound. He was the only San Francisco to Los Angeles passenger under sixty-five on the bus. His revolver certainly seemed overkill amidst these white hairs and wrinkled faces. Seventy-year-old secret agents were not the stock in trade of either the CIA or the Philippine National Security Intelligence Agency. Nevertheless, he found himself as alert and observant as a bird near a cat. Maybe he was not up to Olympic condition, but he was getting there. Fear was a remarkable conditioning agent.

And, as he sat in his meagerly furnished apartment, he knew that he was afraid. It didn't matter if he could rationally tie Junius Oakland to Colonel Calixto Calugas. They were tied together all right. Oakland nominates him to effect a Philippine rescue and Calugas tries to kill him. A strange alliance this, but ineffective as their first at-bats had seemed, Harry could not assume the two putative partners had really struck out. Oakland could not use CIA facilities to tail him, but he could use a private investigator, as Harry had employed one to uncover Oakland's kidnapping caper back in 1962. Because of that possibility Harry had taken two hours to walk his half-mile. There was no way he could have been tailed. No way, except that at any minute Calugas's men might burst through the plywood door and blast him to bits.

However, as one day followed another and became one week, he had to assume he was running free. Calugas would be waiting for him in Manila. After all, Harry could wander the face of the earth, but sooner or later he would have to appear before the fences of Fort Malolos. The yellow stucco fences as he recalled. When that happened, Calugas would pounce—if he could spot Harry the American. And that was the first problem. To effect a disguise. The second was to secure a cover. And the third was to plan the escape. Of them all, the disguise had to be the most difficult and most painful.

For two weeks he sat in his room or, rather, slept in his room. It was best to sleep, for that way he could ignore the hunger pains. His diet was right out of Mahatma Gandhi. One glass of orange juice in the morning, plus vitamin pills. By the third day his stomach howled for food. He had a constant vision of meat and vegetables and bread and desserts. He could see feasts piled on the plastic kitchen table. He preferred the banquet that had both white and red Napa Valley wines, preferably Stony Hill whites and Louis Martini reds. By the seventh day the pangs had subsided; he was numb and torpid. Sleep was not an escape, but a necessity; he couldn't stay awake if he wanted to. Not until the tenth day did he touch solid food—and then it was one slice of American cheese a day. At the start of the third week, lightheaded and trembling, he went outside for the first time. He had taken off twelve pounds, almost a pound a day. His weight was now one hundred and seventy-three. His slight paunch had vanished. His round cheeks had begun to hollow out. A budding moustache accentuated his nose, giving him a faintly hawklike look. His brown crew-cut hair was long enough to be combed—and its true colors were revealed. Brown streaked with grey. The crew cut had minimized the grey and had helped create the youthful effect. There was no getting around it now, Harry Ryder looked his fifty-two years. Or maybe only forty-seven. Why did he like looking forty-seven? Who was he trying to impress? Harry the womanizer. That was a laugh, if he could have summoned up the strength to laugh.

Slowly, pausing to rest every few steps, he walked to the Ambassador and took a cab to Fifth and Olive. He rode up to the sixth floor of the ancient building. The office door read "Holst Secret Service." There were three people in the waiting room. He gave his name to the sympathetic motherly receptionist.

"Do you have an appointment, Mr. McClaren?" She smiled encouragingly, but her eyes were hard and cold. Her name plaque read "Mrs. Margaret Layton."

"No, Mrs. Layton. But I hope Mr. Holst will have a minute or two for me."

"Does Mr. Holst know you?" Her hand went under the desk unobstrusively. She had punched a button to tell Jacob to look at the television monitors. There were three scanners in the waiting room. Head shot and both profiles. "Let me call him."

She said the necessary, listened a while and then smiled apologetically. "I'm sorry, Mr. McClaren. Mr. Holst is tied up and all these people are waiting. Perhaps Mr. Carlisle would do. I believe he's free at the moment." Her eye lingered reprovingly at his waist. So the scanner had picked up the revolver.

Harry looked at the three people along the walls. They stared back at him with hostile looks. A fat man, a thin lady, and a man wearing painter's overalls. The man and lady were legitimate clients. The painter had the same cold eyes as Margaret Layton; one of his hands was in his overalls; obviously Mrs. Layton had tipped him off about the pistol.

"Please give Mr. Holst this name. Li Ngor Sheung." He spelled it for Mrs. Layton. She repeated it on the phone and a look of surprise flashed across her face.

"Mr. Holst can't see you right now, Mr. McClaren." In spite of herself her voice had a faint tinge of respect. "But if you'll wait inside, I'm sure Mr. Carlisle will see you. Please follow me."

"Of course."

She led him down the hall and stopped abruptly and pushed against the wall. It became a door. She stepped back and he walked in.

"Hello, Jacob."

Jacob Holst was a tall man. His face showed the ravages of alcohol. Jack Holst was a member of Alcoholics Anonymous. He scrutinized Harry Ryder. "Sit down, man. You look like you're going to collapse. I didn't recognize you at first. But now I see how you did it. You carved yourself out."

"Just a start, Jacob. I've got thirteen more pounds to go."

"With that moustache you look like a movie star. John

Gilbert. Omar Sharif. Has Li Ngor Sheung surfaced again or was that . . . ?"

Ryder shrugged. "Li Ngor Sheung might well be in it. Except now he's gone way up the ladder. Very close to the top, near to Chien Chung-Yao no less. Maybe over him. We never could tell exactly the names and positions of all the players. Not since K'ang Sheng's day, anyway. So I can't see myself rubbing shoulders with Li Ngor Sheung again."

This was a lie and Jacob Holst knew it for a lie. He switched off the television sets. He rubbed one of the splayed blood veins on his cheek. "I thought you had retired."

"I have. Let's say I'm serving as a consultant. Entirely on my own. With no help, no resources. Just money."

"Ah, just money. What can I do for you?"

Harry put an envelope on the desk. "Here's five thousand dollars. As a retainer. Simple research. Not like last time. I need the names of two or three television production houses. Ones that aren't doing too well."

"That's not five thousand dollars worth. That's one phone call."

"There'll be more. Mail the names to this address. Under the name Peter McClaren. Oh, one more thing. Where will I find Tony Giambruno?"

Holst grimaced. "You do have money." He handed Harry a Hollywood Boulevard address. "Be careful, Harry . . . uh . . . Peter. Tony forms an intersection point. Be careful."

11

Carmelita Pinson Manzano greeted the prison guard with a genuinely warm smile. She would have greeted the devil with the same smile. Carmelita Pinson Manzano liked everyone. If fate forced a man to become a monster, she made him feel that monsterdom was one of God's necessary and chosen professions.

"Ah, Mrs. Manzano. You brought your children." The guard nodded at the two boys, José, Jr. and Manuel. They were skinny lads of fifteen and thirteen. They shuffled their feet self-consciously and leaned on the sewing machine and bolts of cloth they had lugged in.

"Yes, Sergeant Duldalao, Mr. Manzano complains he doesn't see his sons often enough. And of course Emerenciana has gotten permission to do some sewing. Thank the Lord for small favors."

Beaming, she let herself and her entourage be led to her husband's cell. José Manzano was, if anything, skinnier than his sons. With the Manzano males it was not prison food that produced the starved look. They simply lacked fat. Manzano greeted them, his astonished eyes on the sewing machine and bolts of cloth.

"Darling, here's the sewing machine Emerenciana asked for. Boys, you take it next door and give it to her." Her practiced eye swept the stark white room and she clucked disapprovingly at the ill-made bed. "Wait a minute, Manuel, before you carry those things away, help me with this bed." She chuckled. "There's a saying with my family: 'People who can make a bed together can eat bread together.'"

The guard chuckled in response and left them. Carmelita put her fingers to her lips and her husband nodded.

They talked family talk for an hour until the uneasy boys were allowed to depart. José eagerly undressed his wife. Prison diet did not affect his sexual appetite either. He had to make up in one bout for six days' abstinence. He was very good at that. He took off his wife's bra and panties and admired her grandly. The Pinson family did not suffer from lack of fat. Carmelita Manzano was plumpish and roundish, her breasts were magnificent mounds and her stomach a pneumatic pillow. After he had sunk into it two times and was pausing for a third venture (she had been a most enthusiastic collaborator; she had a way of wrapping her strong legs around Manzano's behind and pulling him even deeper into her), she whispered in his ear.

"The bolts of cloth contain tools. The escape is finally on. One whole year of planning. There's someone from San Francisco coming to help us. In a couple of months, I think. We've picked Pilar to be his contact."

"Pilar." Manzano took his mouth from his wife's nipple. Then he nodded. "She's the most innocent person in the family. Good choice." He went back to a breast but drew back and chortled. "Why did you make the bed just now?"

12

The company's name was Commercial Los Angeles. It occupied three rooms in a small business mall four blocks off Hollywood, three blocks off Vine. Jacob Holst had recommended it as one of dozens of television production houses living in either feast or famine luck. The problem was, as Harry Ryder could see from outside, Commercial Los Angeles was swarming with people. There seemed to be more feast here than famine.

Sighing, he entered the mob scene. If Jacob's choice was bad, he had two other companies to visit. No one was at the reception desk. He waited by the desk and observed the crowd. Ten men and three women. And all talking at once, waving their hands, striding up and down, banging papers at each other and acting thoroughly miserable. This was no place for him. He turned to go, but one of the women disengaged herself from the contestants.

"Sorry about this. What can I do for you?" Her eyes took in his ill-fitting clothes—everything was four sizes too big now—but she still managed a smile.

He took off his sun glasses and replaced them with regular glasses, nonprescription, owlish glasses that he had picked up at a Thrifty Drugstore.

He opened his mouth. She helped him. "Are you buying or selling?"

"Buying."

"Then you sit right there. Read *Daily Variety* or *TV Broadcast* or something." She was about thirty-five, with a neck like a football lineman's. Her name seemed to be Molly Bernstein. He felt as if he were in a scene from Baudelaire, or better, *Faust*. "That's a candidate for city attorney. Primary's two weeks off and they're in a panic. Politicians are always in a panic two weeks before election. They want to throw out all the commercials they've already made and produce a complete new set. At no extra cost, of course.

"This won't take long. We'll calm 'em down and in a few minutes they'll go away and if it weren't for you I'd be counting my freckles again."

Freckles she had to count, that was for sure. He sat and pretended to read while he listened in amazement to the altercation. As far as he could make out, half were demanding more close-ups and the other half were arguing for larger titles. He welcomed the rest. It was now the twenty-second day since his diet had begun. The fat was dropping away at less than a half-pound a day. He still had seven pounds to go to effect the final transformation from round-faced Harry Ryder to hawk-faced Peter McClaren. One of his accomplishments since giving Jacob Holst five thousand dollars was to open an account at Bank of America. He deposited ten thousand dollars in a checking account, kept ten thousand, put twenty-three thousand in a savings account. (The remaining seventy-seven one-thousand-dollar bills he put in a safe deposit box.) He applied for overdraft privileges and a Visa card with a ten-thousand-dollar limit. With a checking account and a Visa card, he had taken his first step toward establishing his new identity. And sanctifying it. Money is sanctity. And sanction. And sanctuary.

Molly Bernstein was right. In twenty minutes the whole crowd went to lunch, clapping each other on the back over their wisdom at not changing a single second in the commercials already made. She sat down and heaved a sigh. "Okay. What do you want to buy?"

"I would like you to make five phone calls. For this I will pay you one hundred dollars per call." He put the money on her desk. She looked at the five bills as if they were beetles crawling out from under a rock. "They are real. And payment in advance."

"What am I supposed to do? Call Buenos Aires by way of Leningrad?"

He laughed. "They are ten-cent local calls. To modeling agencies." Her eyebrows went up. "I would like the names and photos and biographies of five or six girls—models, actresses, whatever—who can fly private planes and have licenses covering a Cessna 310."

"Cessna 310? That's a twin-engine six-passenger job, as I recall. Don't look surprised. We use private planes and helicopters all the time in our work. People want their commercials shot in the darnedest places." She thought a minute and her face grew doubtful and disapproving. "What are you running? Guns, people, or stuff?"

He laughed again. "Nothing that would be illegal in our country, I promise you." The truth, that; but a limited truth to say the least and he saw that Molly Bernstein had caught the limitation. But now the five bills no longer looked like insects, they looked like rent and telephone and gas and electricity payments and maybe even a lunch or two.

She picked them up and patted them affectionately. "Come back in three days and I'll have the mug shots for you. By the way what's your name?"

"Peter McClaren. M-C-C-L-A-R-E-N. Thank you, Molly Bernstein. Three days it is."

13

"The end and aim of spying is knowledge of the enemy." So said Sun Tzu in 500 B.C.

Conversely, the end and aim of the person being spied upon, Harry Ryder had thought when he first read Sun Tzu's *Principles of War* during indoctrination, would be to deny knowledge to the enemy. Or distort it. The time had come for a little distortion.

The evening before he was to call back on Molly Bernstein, he went to a street phone booth and called a residence in Alexandria, Virginia. It was, he knew, an unlisted number. He put in four dollars worth of quarters. "I don't want to be interrupted, operator. I'll hang up before the money is used up. You keep the change."

The phone rang three times. A man's voice answered. Harry Ryder said, "Arlo Thomasson, please."

"This is Arlo Thomasson."

"And this is Harry Ryder, Arlo." He could picture the square-jawed FBI man. He would be in shirt sleeves. He would have set a martini on the sofa end table. An old-fashioned three-to-one martini. His briefcase would be lying next to the martini. He wouldn't open the briefcase until after dinner or four martinis, whichever came last. "I'm calling from Los Angeles. From a phone booth."

"Phone booth? Harry, what's up? Phone booths. Harry, you're retired. Phone booths should not be your style."

"I've been unretired, Arlo. On a one-time assignment. But it's no different than in my last five years. Nothing's changed."

"You mean the assignment is really you?"

"Exactly. And it's a rough game. On both sides."

"Somebody's going to get killed, Harry."

"Somebody already has gotten killed. I take it from the way you're talking you've got an untouched phone."

"Like a virgin, Harry. What can I do for you?"

"I'll lay it on the line, Arlo. You owe me one. Agreed?"

And there was some hesitation. Good man, Arlo Thomasson. "Agreed. I owe you one."

"I want you to place a phone call at precisely three minutes before noon tomorrow. Your time. I want you to ask for a spur-of-the-moment lunch. If your party is in, you'll set up the lunch. If he's already gone off to lunch—and he normally leaves precisely at eleven fifty-two—then you say, 'Oh, I'm sorry. I didn't see how late it was. Please ask him to call me when he gets back. I'd like to chat informally about a few matters.' And you hang up and at three minutes past noon I'll phone you again to see what happened."

"Who do I call, Harry?"

"Junius Oakland."

The expected pause extended beyond expectations. Well, Arlo had a lot to think about. True enough, Harry had done him a favor. When the Chinese decided they needed Mok Bing Goon of Cal Tech in China, they could not use their usual inducements—blackmail or money or high position or flattery or all four because Mok Bing Goon was a third-generation American citizen with minimal ties to the mainland. (They wanted him because no one knew more about computers than Mok Bing; the Chinese are a bit unbalanced on the subject of computers.) Nor would they mount another kidnapping, as with Yung Song Hom back in 1962. They couldn't make a kidnapping stick, not with Mok Bing Goon. So K'ang Sheng turned the problem over to Li Ngor Sheung and his plan was simple. The FBI in the United States and the CIA overseas began getting tips that Mok Bing Goon was a Chinese spy. Li Ngor expected the FBI to drive Mok out of the country, as it had done before with the two men who brought China into the nuclear age—Jue Sik Kwan of Cal Tech and Yu Yuen Chee of UC Berkeley. But Harry outwitted Li Ngor. He provided Arlo Thomasson with complete details of Li Ngor's scheme and, instead of being ostracized, Mok Bing Goon was honored with a presidential citation. Harry had enjoyed that battle of wits with Li Ngor Sheung, while Arlo Thomasson had gotten a major promotion. But major promotions can become major disasters with one false move. And calling Junius Oakland was not only a false move, it was potentially disastrous.

"That's putting it right to me, Harry. I'll have to make this phone call look awfully good. But I know. That's my problem. Call me at twelve-three tomorrow."

14

Harry stood at the phone booth a block from the Ambassador and watched the time. It was unseasonably hot in the booth and seemed hotter, thanks to his disguise. He had embellished his stomach with a small pillow. He had stuffed foam rubber into his cheeks so that they puffed out like a squirrel's—or like the old Harry Ryder's. His Vandyke beard itched and his wig of wavy black hair forced the sweat to stream down his neck. He was amazed there was any sweat left in him.

He placed the call. "Well?"

"He's gone to lunch."

"Thanks, Arlo. Now I owe you one. Things have to be kept in perspective."

He took a cab to Hollywood and Cahuenga. Tony Giambruno's store was called "The Dandy." The salesman who minced toward him was precisely that—the dandy, Hollywood style. He wore an elegant silk shirt open at the collar and to his navel, incredibly tight slacks, a two-inch Gucci belt with matching Gucci shoes. He was lean, rugged of jaw, exuberantly masculine. He was beautiful in a dark Italian manner—and obviously disconcerted by the stoutish, middle-aged, professorial type in this place for male underdressed youth. "May I help you, sir?"

"I hope so. Is Mr. Giambruno in?"

"I don't know." The dandy picked up a phone. "We'll find out. And your name is?"

"Roger Hiller. Tell Mr. Giambruno Junius Oakland sent me."

Tony Giambruno was an intersection point. Indeed he was. Harry had never used him, but the Agency had from time to time when they wanted an outside source to provide a convenient passport or driver's license or safe-cracking kit or whatever. Giambruno served as a kind of technical services division for the West Coast Mafia. The basement to the Dandy was built like a miniature fortress. Within its foot-thick concrete walls were, he knew, printing presses, exotic papers and credit card stocks, a chemical laboratory, standard and microphotography equipment, cameras, telescopes, binoculars, an arsenal of small arms, burglar's tools, wigs, costumes, electronic bugging equipment. All the goodies that a modern criminal might find useful from time to time. Giambruno's craftsman did excellent work. And Junius Oakland knew that Harry Ryder knew of their existence.

"Mr. Giambruno is tied up for a few minutes. If you could wait? Perhaps you'd like to look around. We have the finest clothes in Hollywood."

So he looked. He held up a sexy leather jacket before a mirror. His revolver at his waist did not show. But the man with the Polaroid camera did. He was shooting Mr. Hiller's reflection in the mirror. The Polaroid man turned and went through a door. To the basement, obviously. The time was nine-fifty. Ten minutes to one in Washington. The call was being made. "Sorry, Mr. Giambruno. Mr. Oakland is out to lunch." "I don't care if he's out to confession. You reach him and tell him a man calling himself Roger Hiller is here to see me. He doesn't look like the description Oakland gave me. This Hiller fellow has a Vandyke beard, lots of black hair and maybe more fat than I'm told to expect. I'll stall him for ten minutes. Have him call me back and give me the word."

He put the jacket down. "Love to wear one of these. But I guess it's just not my style."

The Valentino look-alike choked back a guffaw. "No, I guess . . . oh, I see Mr. Giambruno is ready. If you'll just follow that gentleman there."

The gentleman looked precisely that. No sports coat, no leather jacket or plunging neckline here. The gentleman wore a grey business suit, just a trifle too tight, perhaps, because his shoulder pistol harness wasn't too well concealed. Maybe it wasn't supposed to be.

Ryder went over to the gentleman. He grunted, opened the door, and followed Ryder down. The back of his neck cringed. He could feel the pistol cracking down on his finest Feinstein wig. But he was still alive and conscious when they reached the basement door. The gentleman inserted a magnetic card and punched a button to some code and the door swung open. Ryder couldn't help gasping. Tony Giambruno's office was right out of MCA in the days of Mr. Stein. Antique furniture so beautiful even he recognized their beauty. Persian rugs. Tiffany lamps. And on the walls Picassos, Klees and Miros. They were not prints. Giambruno's desk was a rococco explosion of marquetry of colored woods and gold mounts. Louis XV would have felt at home behind it—and in the arm chair that Ryder's escort preempted. He seemed to disappear in it. Only his beady, cocker-spaniel eyes that fixed themselves unwaveringly on Ryder betrayed life. His jacket was unbuttoned. His right hand rested on his chest.

Ryder finished his sightseeing and looked at his host. "An incredibly beautiful room, Mr. Giambruno."

His host grunted. He was a handsome man of fifty-five or sixty. He had the same lean face of the dandy salesman upstairs. His wavy hair, however, was grey. He could have served as a model for a Cadillac ad. He suddenly proved he could do more than grunt. "What can I do for you, Mr. Hiller?"

Ryder did not like his voice. It was not so much high-pitched as off-pitch. It had a crackle to it, the bark of a man who expected his questions to be answered, his commands obeyed.

"I have done a few services for Junius Oakland." He sat carefully in the frail Dutch side chair. His jacket was also unbuttoned but his right arm was not near the opening. "He suggested if I needed help, I could come to you."

"What kind of help, Mr. Hiller?" Giambruno's eyes

57

flashed to the paneled wall near his beady-eyed watchdog. So that was the door to the technical services division.

"It is necessary for me to go to Mexico City. And beyond. For that I need a passport. Unfortunately, I have allowed mine to lapse. And it would not be becoming for me to apply for a renewal."

"Passport? Me? Mr. Hiller, I don't understand. There must be some mistake. I run a men's fashion store."

"Dear me. I must have misunderstood Mr. Oakland. He did say that ten thousand dollars might be required. I can put my hands on ten thousand dollars. But of course . . ."

And at that moment the phone rang. Giambruno cuddled it to his ear. "Giambruno." He listened with a stone face. "I see."

His eyes flicked over Ryder's left shoulder. The latter flung himself to the right onto the floor. His revolver was out and pointing at the Louis XV armchair. Its occupant barely had his hand inside his jacket. A blackjack—a genuine LAPD blackjack—whistled down on the Dutch side chair. The seat cracked in two and the chair folded, taking the blackjack and its holder down with it. The holder was a stocky pugilistic type about five feet eight. He seemed astonished at his own strength.

"Tut, tut," Ryder said. "That's no way to treat an authentic irreplaceable antique side chair. Mr. Giambruno, please hang up and tell Louis the Fifteenth to bring his hand out. Otherwise I will have to shoot a finger off. And of course I might miss the finger."

The fingers were withdrawn. Ryder went behind the sprawled figure and removed his handgun. He did the same to the ex-watchdog. He made them both lie flat on the floor. Giambruno shook his head. "I don't carry a gun." "Ah, but a man must look." He looked. "An honest man. But how could an honest man like Tony Giambruno say he knows nothing about passports?"

He looked at the pugilist. "How did you get in here so

quietly, my friend? Well, it doesn't matter. The question is, how do we terminate this discussion? I could end it by terminating you. That would make five men in five weeks. That's a high batting average—if you can suggest another solution?"

The two employees looked at him with hate—pure, absolute, unmitigated hate. Tony Giamburno just looked. Ryder sighed. "Is there a closet here, Mr. Giambruno? I hope there is. Because then we won't have to face anything drastic, will we?"

Giambruno thought a long moment, then pointed. Ryder nodded. "You open it. And be very careful. Because if it is not a closet, if it is a door, say, then I will have to put a bullet through your brain. I prefer the brain to the heart, Mr. Giambruno. Very few men survive a brain shot. And then they are liable to be paraplegic."

Giambruno rose slowly and went to the paneled wall. He walked with Cadillac model grace. He flicked open a door. It was indeed a closet.

"And how do we lock it, Mr. Giambruno? That is very important. How do we lock it?"

"I am reaching in my pocket to get my keys." He reached. "It is this key."

Ryder made the recumbent figures crawl into the closet. Giambruno walked into it. The closet had several sets of clothes on hangers and two suitcases on a shelf. It might have a concealed rear door. Well, a man can't have everything.

He locked the door, but before he did, he saw that this time even Giambruno's solid black eyes were flaming red. "Tut, tut," he said and went upstairs. He waved to the bare-bosomed dandy. "Someday maybe I'll be able to wear your remarkable clothes. Thank you for your courtesy."

The dark Italian face registered surprise as it looked for Ryder's gentleman escort. "They let me find my own way out," Ryder said. As he went out onto Hollywood Boulevard, the salesman grabbed the interoffice phone. Ryder walked briskly to the Hollywood Holiday Inn, dropped Giambruno's keys into a waste can, took a cab to the Ambassador, walked to the Kingsley Crown, undisguised himself, and took a cab back to Commercial Los Angeles. He was six blocks from Giambruno.

Molly Bernstein handed him four eight-by-ten glossies. "That's all the candidates I could find. And I had to call ten agencies to get them. Those Cessna requirements are a bit stiff. No extra charge for the extra calls."

She put them in an envelope and he started for the door.

"Do me a favor, Mr. McClaren. When whatever you're doing is all over, come back and tell me how it all came out, will you?"

He stopped and looked at her and smiled.

She said, "I wouldn't be so curious if your clothes fitted better. You understand, don't you?"

15

This time Mrs. Layton took him right in to see Jacob Holst.

"Lordy me, what have you done to yourself?"

Ryder pirouetted. "Like it? I stopped by at the Gap and bought five pairs of Levi pants, three jackets, a dozen shirts, five ties. They didn't have leather jackets, though."

"Leather jackets! Where's my Yale Ivy League company man gone to? What is this, change of life?"

"Peter McClaren has incarnated. Here, earn your five thousand."

He tossed the envelope on the desk. Holst pulled out the glossies. He saw four remarkably beautiful women. Two of them looked like Farrah Fawcett-Majors. One looked like Dorothy Hamill. One had long hair down over her shoulder blades. She looked like a girl with long hair down over her shoulder blades.

Holst read their names. "Dawn Meredith. Heather Harper. Mary Jane Rickert. Terry Jefferson. What do I do with these?"

"Complete profiles. And fast."

"One week okay?"

"One week okay. If any of them are married, go no further. And one more thing. May I borrow one of your cars? Until my new driver's license is ready."

Holst nodded. He picked at a vein near his nose. "Did you see Tony Giambruno?"

"I saw him. I told him Junius Oakland sent me. He wouldn't give me a passport. I told him I had to go to Mexico City."

"Did he believe you?"

"I doubt it. But he's got something to think about."

Holst's eyes bore into him. "Any bodies?"

"Almost. But we parted quietly. I parted quietly."

Holst sighed. "You learned bad habits in the Philippines. You always think you can cut it fine and not lose a thumb."

The car was a beige Dodge Dart. He drove to Kingsley Crown, put his purchases away, packed a suitcase, drove to Oxnard, and took a room at the Holiday Inn. The next morning he drove to the western part of the city and stopped before a printing shop on Bella Vista. There were two signs, one in English, one in Spanish. They both read "Printing, Photocopying, Sign-making." The shop was no different from hundreds of other Spanish-language stores in Ventura County, except for a notice in the lower corner of the window that had Tagalog along with the English and Spanish: "Gus Gutierrez—owner."

He went in. The office seemed pitch dark after the hot Oxnard sun and the blinding-white stucco cottages and buildings. He shut his eyes, replaced the sunglasses with the plain ones, blinked, and made out a round-faced, shapeless Mexican lady sitting behind a counter. Her desk and the counter were cluttered with handout sheets, proofs, bills, invoices, brochures, posters. They were all jiggling slightly as a heavy press thumped behind the dirt and oil-speckled door. The air reeked of printer's ink. The lady rose and smiled at him with that ineffably polite smile of the native-born Mexican. Ah, what a people. He could live to be a thousand and never achieve such courtesy. This would be Maria Sanchez Gutierrez from the town of Uruapan in Michoacan State, Mexico.

He tried to speak as politely as she smiled. He spoke in English. "Is Mr. Gutierrez in?" He said "Geteris."

She winced slightly, said, "He iz in the back, sir. Helping wiz the blue ink. It comes out green, no, and he . . ."

"I'll be glad to wait. I'm Peter McClaren."

"I weel tell heem you are here."

He sat on a green wooden bench. She came back, smiled politely, and went to work on the invoices. After about fifteen minutes a stocky Filipino came in. He was like any other Filipino except that he had blue eyes. This was impossible, but there they were, blue as a Viking's.

"How do you do, Mr. Geteris? I'm Peter McClaren and you have been recommended to me by some Filipino friends. From Baguio. They tell me you should be able to print up some typical NPA leaflets—like the ones they post on light poles in Baguio and Manila and throughout central Luzon. I'm making a study of underground literature throughout the Third World."

Gus Gutierrez blinked his blue eyes, but that was his only emotion. "NPA? I do not know what this is, this NPA."

He was examining Harry Ryder critically. But no sign of recognition crossed his face. Harry the American did not exist. Peter McClaren stood in front of him. Peter McClaren, with hollow cheeks, pointed chin, moustache, thick frame glasses, frizzled, grizzled hair. (This frizzled part was a new development. After his crew cut reached about an inch and a half long, it had started to curl; the top of his head now looked like a dry mop.)

Time for one more test. Using flawless Filipino Spanish, he said, "But you can forge green cards for citizens of Michoacan, Senor Gutierrez. Why can't you forge a document of the New People's Army for me?"

Now shock on their faces. Maria put her hand over her mouth as if he had struck it. Her husband leaned forward and stared even more intently. "You are not of the Immigration. What are you?"

And now the final test in Tagalog. "So I help you escape from both the Huks and the Philippine Constabulary. I set you up in an honest printing business in California. Almost honest. Once a paper man, always a paper man. And this is the way you receive me?"

Now a startled comprehension, but still no recognition. Maria had not understood the Tagalog; she snapped her head toward her husband. He waved a hand at her like a symphony conductor quieting a bass drum. "I understand the words, I do not understand why you say them."

"Because I am Harry the American, my friend." He took off his glasses. But Gus still shook his head doubtfully. "Perhaps," he said. "Perhaps. Prove it."

"Very well. When you found out Pedro Camagdan had betrayed you to the P.C. in order to save his wife from torture, you hitchhiked from Baguio to Manila and phoned me at the embassy and said, 'Harry the American, I saved you at Bambang. You save me at Manila.'"

And now recognition and a delighted smile. Gutierrez sprang forward and embraced Ryder. "Maria" (this in Spanish) "this is the man I told you about. Harry the American. After his work in Leyte, they sent him up into the mountains of Nueva Vizcaya to work with us."

Twenty minutes later Gutierrez said. "So much for the past, my friend. You didn't come by here to talk about old times. Not looking like a survivor of a concentration camp. What can I do for you?"

Ryder spread his papers on the counter. Driver's license, airman, radio and medical certificates, logbook, Social Security card, passport. "I need these in the name of Peter McClaren. With these numbers, these visas, these dates, and these photos. And a separate passport in the name of Roger Hiller. With this information. And my old Harry Ryder passport updated with these visas and dates."

Gutierrez fingered the documents absently. "As you say, I do make green cards. To get by Immigration. For Maria's friends and relatives. That covers just about everybody in Michoacan. California is the chief source of income for Michoacan, did you know that? Thanks to Maria. But I haven't done this kind of work. Not in twenty-five years. I don't have the stock. And your passport—I can touch it up, but not the new ones. The new ones are not grey. They're smaller and they're purple. To make two purple ones—that's impossible."

Ryder put another envelope on the counter. "There's five thousand dollars. Maybe that will help make it possible."

Maria picked up the envelope and pulled out the hundred-dollar bills. She looked hopefully at her husband and he laughed. "Maria is the practical one in the family. She keeps the books and provides for our old age. All right, I'll see what I can do. I'll need time."

"You have two weeks. Most of that stuff will cause you no problem. Just the passports. And if you look at it carefully, you'll see you only have to change a couple of pages in each one. Same with the logbook. You can work with anybody's passport. Maybe some good Michoacan U.S. citizens."

So much for the disguise. Now for the cover.

16

He parked in the Channel Twelve lot. In a reserved slot. This was it. Make or break.

He walked to the front door of KCAX-TV. The brown stucco building was in need of repair. KCAX-TV was in need of repair. A sad little independent that did nothing but make money. It ran reruns and reruns of reruns; and according to Nielsen, someone out there actually watched these shows. They certainly bought the products advertised on them.

The girl behind the glass looked at him. "I'm late," he said. "I'm with the Happy Tonic crew. With Terry Jefferson in studio two." Jacob Holst had said she'd be here.

The girl waved languidly at a smudged plywood door; he went down a grimy corridor, pushed open a rusted metal door and eased into Studio Two.

It was as dirty as the rest of KCAX-TV. A large, warehouse-type room. The control booth on the mezzanine. Two cameras focused on a bedroom scene. Gaffers struggling with aluminum screens. Electricians stringing cable. A make-up lady dabbing at the forehead of a woman in a nightgown and bed jacket. A beautiful woman. With long black hair down over her shoulder blades. Terry Jefferson.

He eased himself onto a metal table along the wall. No one paid any attention to him for an hour. A cheapie television commercial for a cheapie product in a cheapie television station. During a break, a girl in jeans and bandana suddenly saw him.

"Are you with the client?"

"No. I'm here to talk to Terry."

"Oh, from her agent." She went over and whispered to Jefferson, who glanced at him, said nothing. He could understand her self-control after reading her dossier.

"Heather Harper and Mary Jane Rickert are married," Holst had reported. He had set their photos aside. "So we did nothing on them. Here's the dope on Dawn Meredith."

Ryder noticed the protective air with which Holst's hand hovered over Terry Jefferson's file. He shrugged, looked at Farrah Fawcett aka Dawn Meredith, read her biography.

"Dawn Meredith, born Esther Regelstein. Grew up in Chicago. Aged twenty-six. Father a millionaire-plus shopping-center developer. Flies a Lear jet to developments. Daughter learned to fly at fifteen. Has private jet license, but no longer flies. Graduate of University of Arizona. Studied at Pasadena Playhouse after graduation. Bit parts in three movies, four television shows, many commercials. Recently became mistress of producer Sol Benjamin. Rumored to be in line for second lead in Benjamin's next movie, *The Kibbutz*.

"Evaluation: Miss Meredith is smart, cautious, ambitious. She has no acting talent to speak of, but every penny she makes is invested in shopping-center developments. She already owns three Safeway leases. She is determined to show her father she's as good as the son he never had. When she is financially independent, she plans to take over her father's business. Summary: a walking computer in a very attractive body which she uses as an additional profit center."

"You don't like Miss Meredith, Jacob. She's not exactly the gal you'd want to share a desert island with, is she? What about Miss Jefferson?"

He took the biography.

"Terry Jefferson, born Gayle Elliott. Grew up in Chico, California. Age twenty-eight. Father died when she was eleven. Mother supported her and two brothers as clerk in Allis-Chalmers distributorship. Boys became mechanics upon graduation from high school. Miss Jefferson went to UC Berkeley. Worked her way through as catering maid for parties in rich homes, progressed from there to call girl. Clients: the men in the rich homes. Maintained attractive apartment on Telegraph Hill in San Francisco, serviced seven or eight men regularly. When rivals charged a hundred dollars a trick, she charged two hundred; five hundred for the whole night. Customers thought she was worth it. One of them taught her to fly. Has twin-engine airman's certificate and over five hundred hours logged time. Another taught her to shoot.

"At graduation, with honors, changed her name to Terry Jefferson, entered UCLA Drama School, used a hundred fifty thousand dollars savings to buy Van Nuys apartment house. Cash flow from that twelve thousand dollars. No movie roles yet, but is in fairly regular demand for television commercials. Owns a Cessna 150 and takes off occasional weekends for Arizona, New Mexico, Baja California. Speaks Spanish. Likes to drive fast cars fast. She's also a member of the Southern California Rod and Gun Club. Competes in National Rifle Association match courses—both single gun and three gun. Has never won but placed several times. Much desired by male pistol nuts and Hollywood swingers, but apparently no visible affairs with people in her profession or hobbies. She lives quietly, almost secretively, in three-room apartment in Hollywood hills.

"Evaluation: Miss Jefferson is an athletic, smart, totally self-reliant woman. She takes life as it comes. If she has ambitions, they are simply to excel in whatever she does —from acting to shooting. Much better shooter than actress.

"Summary: She is a force."

"You do like Miss Jefferson, Jacob. So do I, I must say. How do you learn facts like these?"

Holst shrugged. "Routine. Neighbors. Where she worked as caterer. Talking men. Hell, they wanted to talk. She's the best thing that ever happened to them. Most of them wanted to divorce their wives and marry her. To that, no thanks. As for the shooting, we simply followed her to the Gun Club and watched her shoot. As to her original name, she had to take out a mortgage, didn't she?"

"She is a force." So she was, as he knew when she came over to him at lunch break. He sprang from his table. She was almost his height. He couldn't focus on her face, which he already knew was beautiful, because her solid black eyes—El Greco eyes—impaled him.

"You are not with my agent."

Her voice was round and mellow, altogether pleasing. "I didn't say I was." What did his voice sound like? "I didn't say it, that girl over there did."

Terry Jefferson snorted and turned to go.

"Please, I do want to talk with you. Not here. About a business proposition." He felt like a teenage schoolboy summoning up courage to ask the beautiful girl at the desk in front of him to share a candy bar. "Three weeks' work. Adventurous work. You can fly a Cessna 310, can't you?"

"That kind of work."

"That kind. With acting ability required. May I make a suggestion? Can you have lunch with me two days from now? At the Polo Lounge?" (A bit of glamor this—and bravado. With the Polo Lounge, Hernando Courtwright wrought an image and a myth that has bemused Hollywood for forty years. Courtwright could go on to the Beverly Wilshire, but the Polo Lounge was—is—greater than its creator. It was also Junius Oakland's home away from home. If he were to come to Los Angeles after the Giambruno intersection, he would be staying at the Beverly Hills Hotel. He would be eating in the Polo Lounge.) "My name is Peter McClaren. I can also fly a Cessna 310."

"How did you get my name?"

"From Blum's Modeling Agency. But they're blameless. I had the request made through legitimate channels."

Terry Jefferson's black eyes bored hypnotically into

him. She was still wearing the nightgown. Her nipples and breasts were quite distinguishable, he knew. He would have liked to look at them, but he didn't dare waver from her eyes. They measured him. They accepted him.

"Very well. Polo Lounge. At twelve-thirty. Two days from now."

17

He was in a panic. He had not counted on this. On sex, his reaction to sex, his fantasy about sex, his need for sex. His need for Terry Jefferson. And his fear of Terry Jefferson —of his lunch with her in two hours.

It was quite one thing to seek out a girl for cover and quite another thing to discover that said girl is not Junius Oakland or a Filipino assassin or a Mafia goon. He could hold his own with such ilk. It was even more startling to discover that he was all man, with a man's desires. Damn it to hell, he mused, this was no way to start a purely business relationship. Further, he was almost twice her age. There is nothing more obscene than a dirty old man. And further further—and most telling—he was terrified of this one-time professional love-maker. Sex-maker. Orgasm-maker. What did he have to offer her? He was a fifty-two-year-old one-time professional spy, and in spite of popular myth he had never once had occasion to use sex as part of a mission. An oversight, that.

He arrived at the Beverly Hills at noon. He watched the boy take the Dodge Dart away and stood for a few moments at the portico. There was no Junius Oakland in sight. In fact, he was the only Occidental. The hotel entrance and lobby swarmed with black-suited Chinese. They weaved and whipped around him and into the lobby. Large labels proclaimed the purpose, People's Republic of China Trade Mission, with the names printed in oversize typewriter type.

At twelve-thirty sharp she walked into the Polo Lounge bar. She wore a simple white blouse, black Russian-type trousers, and high boots. The boots fit her legs tightly and were not crinkled. She was stunning. He started to gasp, repressed it. She didn't conceal the twinkle in her eye. She knew quite well what she did to men.

"We have a table outside. Under the Brazilian pepper tree. Is that okay?"

He did not look at her, he didn't dare look at her until he had his Gordon's on the rocks at his lips. She saluted him with her iced tea. He refrained from saying "Cheers," though he felt like cheering. For, now that he could look at something besides her eyes, he knew himself awed. Her face was narrow, her chin somewhat long, her cheeks hollow, her nose tilted slightly upward. Bare facts to catalog bare beauty. She shook her head, brushed her hair back so that it fell behind her shoulders. The black hair framed her face and he looked, now, into her startling black eyes and he knew why all the men wanted to marry her.

"Thank you for coming, Miss Jefferson. Would you care to talk business before or after lunch?"

She considered. She was no machine-gun talker; she thought a moment before any reply. No intuitive, she; probably Jung's sensation mind. "Let's enjoy the lunch. If we can't agree on the business, I'm sure we can agree on the food."

She ordered cold poached salmon with cucumbers, so he did likewise. She ate only the salmon, he did likewise. "Why did you order the cucumbers if you're not going to eat them?"

"I like to give the chef a chance to employ a little artistry. Salmon alone lacks a design quality."

They talked about her business. As consultant to several large corporations, he had learned something about the writing and producing of television commercials. "That's how I secured your name. Through a TV production house."

"Am I the only one with a twin engine license?"

"There were three others. But two are married and I don't want to approach them."

"And the other one?"

"She looks like Farrah Fawcett-Majors."

Terry laughed. It was a genuine, right-from-the-diaphragm laugh. "All right, lunch is over. Business time."

A dash of cold water, that.

"Miss Jefferson, I'm masterminding a somewhat complicated deal. It requires the use of a plane. But if I go around flying this plane all by myself I will be very very conspicuous. Certain people will take a good look at me and may suspect what I am up to. If that happens, your humble mastermind becomes a humble stumblebum."

He lit a cigar. He loathed cigars. Harry Ryder loathed cigars. Peter McClaren would like cigars if they killed him. She was thinking hard while he manipulated the cellophane and tip and match.

"I believe this is called 'providing a cover'?"

"It is."

"People who provide covers for themselves are criminals or government agents. Police, narcs, spies."

He was tempted to say, "Or ordinary citizens who want to make a fresh start." But Terry Jefferson would instantly think of Gayle Elliott. Not yet. He said, "I am none of those. I am a business consultant. I have been called in to consult on this deal."

"But you are not keeping your distance from it. Good consultants say 'you do this.' Not 'I will do this.'"

"Touché. I am consultant and operator, too."

"Is there danger in this job?"

71

"Why do you ask that?"

"Because, Mr. Peter McClaren, you look to me like a dangerous man. Polite, soft-spoken, deferential. The gentleman's code. The gentleman killer."

"Killer?" He thought of the two Filipinos on Montgomery Street. The five East Germans outside the Börsenbericht. "Strong word, Miss Jefferson. Many men my age have killed, but that does not make us killers."

"Yes, you are old enough to have been in the war. You look about forty or forty-two, but I think you're older."

"I'm fifty-two." Somehow it was important to lay that fact on the line. "Old enough to be your father."

She laughed her hearty laugh again. "If I had a dollar for every father who raped his daughter, I'd be very wealthy. Rich.

"Anyway, you said the other day this will take three weeks?"

"About three weeks. Maybe four."

"How much will you pay?"

"Ten thousand dollars."

She shook her head. "I don't make that much in three weeks. But I do average about seventeen hundred. In five or six months I've got my own peaceful ten thousand. Without covers. Without danger. Without killing. Don't shake your head. You did not deny me earlier. You weren't the least bit shocked by what I said."

"Fifteen thousand."

"You know all about me, don't you?"

"Not all about you. The broad outlines, yes."

"All right, what about sex?"

"You are an astonishing woman. Does the gentleman's code cover that?"

She snorted.

"Then let me say something else. Confirm something, if you will. I have not slept with a woman in three years. Well, there was a once. A meaningless once. But sex, I'm sorry to say, is not one of the highlights of my life. Anyway, this is a business proposition, Miss Jefferson. And your intelligence, beauty, athletic ability, and apparent fearlessness are very real plusses. I need no other."

"Mission Impossible."

"What?"

"Hollywood kitsch, Mr. McClaren. I think in terms like that. Mission Impossible. That's what you're up against, isn't it? In a foreign country, I'll bet. Am I right?"

"I feel all of my fifty-two years, Miss Jefferson. Yes, in a foreign country. No, it's not at all impossible."

"Just difficult and dangerous. What is the danger for me?"

He thought of Maximus Cruz, Calixto Calugas, Junius Oakland. Of bullets flying around wildly. Of a plane crashing.

She said, "I can see your eyes glazing over even behind the sun glasses. I lost you there, didn't I? You said there might be acting. What acting?"

His eyes had glazed over all right, because he was in shock. It was one thing to know in the abstract that the Polo Lounge was Junius Oakland's home away from home. It was quite another to see him walk into the Polo Lounge and sit himself at the pink table two feet away from them. Behind the glass partition that could easily be opened into the garden area. Ryder thought he had prepared himself mentally and physically for an eventual confrontation with Mr. Oakland. He found himself staggered by its immediate if half-expected reality. And further disconcerted by the man with Oakland. A Chinese. A handsome Chinese with the most marvelous teeth Ryder had ever seen. They were even, white, and always flashing as part of a glorious smile. The teeth of Li Ngor Sheung. The same set of teeth Ryder had seen only once before. In Singapore. At the Marco Polo Hotel where he had stumbled on Junius Oakland in earnest conversation with the smiling Oriental. A Junius Oakland who was supposed to be twelve thousand miles away in Washington. Dressed then, as now, in Savile Row pin-striped, vested splendor. The elegant lecher. The Princeton snob. The man who wanted to kill him. Because Junius Oakland knew, had come to know, thanks to Li Ngor, that Harry Ryder had seen him at the Marco Polo Hotel.

What had Terry asked? He searched back; remembered.

"If you turned the corners of your eyes upward a bit, and put on some appropriate makeup, you could pass for a Eurasian. Maybe even a native. Though you are a bit tall. But this might be useful. I don't know yet. It's just good to have options."

"Native what? Never mind. So there's danger for you and possibly for me. If I participate in the danger, would I be paid more?"

"Yes, but you won't have to participate. You are my cover. Because of you there should be no danger."

Li's badge read "Ralph Lee, Deputy Director, New China News Agency, Hong Kong." That would put him reporting directly to the State Council. Perhaps to his old intelligence boss, now foreign minister, Huang Nueh Yuet, one-time spy extraordinary. How nice to be part of the in-group.

"Yes, but if?"

"If I ask you to carry a gun, your pay will be twenty thousand. Does that do it?"

She laughed heartily again. Her whole torso shook. She wore no bra. Her torso did well. "I would have done it for ten thousand. I like danger, Mr. McClaren . . ."

"Peter."

"Peter, I like danger. I have lived dangerously most of my life. As you know. And I always carry a gun. I'm an expert shot. You don't think I'd fly alone into Baja California without a gun, do you?"

"So there you see, I did not know all about you. But you

will not carry a gun with me. The last thing in the world I want is gunsmanship. Brains, please. Brains, not bullets, Miss Jefferson."

"Terry."

"Terry."

"Peter, the gentleman's code is good enough for me. You can relax on the subject of sex. What's next?"

"Is your passport in order? Passport, airman and medical certificates?"

"Up to date."

"Can you get away in a week's time?"

"Nine days. I have some commitments."

"Nine days is fine. I can adjust for that in my timetable. You will receive half-pay before you leave. The other half will be waiting for you here in your name. A predated certified check. That's in case. You understand."

"Half of what?"

"You're really mercenary, aren't you?"

"Coming from a mercenary, that's funny."

"Half of twenty thousand. I'll come to your house the day before we leave and help you pack. I'm sure your wardrobe will be more than adequate."

"Your choice of the Brazilian pepper tree was perfect, Peter." She stood up. "I'll dash now. But one thing. When the three weeks are up, will you tell me your real name?"

18

He watched her walk away. So did Junius Oakland. He was leching. Junius Oakland was one of those men who would say, on seeing a seemly lady, "I think I'm in love." He was in love twenty times a day. Each time his forehead lit up, turned a pinkish enamel. His forehead beaconed now. At times like these Junius Oakland often turned subtle. His method was to walk up to his putative inamorata and say delicately, "My dear, will you fuck?" Sometimes he modified the question. He would say, "My dear, I'd love to engage in fornication with you. So. Will you fuck?" Princeton polish every time.

But Junius Oakland was also a trained Intelligence officer. He was trained to see. And what he saw, besides an extremely beautiful woman, was a distinctive stride. Terry Jefferson swung her legs from the hips. The swing was marvelous to watch, causing truly callipygian effects; but it was also unmistakable. At the end of a stride one leg was almost in front of the other. Jefferson could change her hair color and eye makeup a dozen times a day, but as long as she walked like a loose-limbed leopard she could be instantly recognizable.

Ryder paid the bill with cash. As he counted out the money, he was quite aware that Li Ngor Sheung was scrutinizing him. Did he penetrate through Peter McClaren to Harry Ryder? Or was he just amused by the December-May confrontation? Such a relationship is a most ancient Chinese pattern, and his smile suggested that Ryder hadn't come off too well. After all, he was only a white barbarian.

Ryder took great pains with his own stride. His shoulders drooped forward. His right shoulder was lower than his left. His right arm dragged at his side. His right knee betrayed the slightest of limps. Details, details, details. As he swung into the restaurant hallway he flashed a quick glance at the two men. Junius Oakland's eyes were following him thoughtfully. Li Ngor had swung around to see him out. His white teeth had exploded in a flashing smile. Jacob Holst was right. He did cut it too fine. Only it wouldn't be just a thumb he was in danger of losing, but leg and arm and neck, too.

There were three Chinese waiting for their car. He was

careful to ask the carhop to get his car only after they drove off. He eased down the driveway and watched carefully. No one seemed to be tailing him. He drove in the general direction of the post office. By the time he reached Temple and Main, he knew he was clear and clean. No car tailed him. No car paralleled him. No car preceded him. No helicopter pursued him. He claimed Emilio Lanante's large envelope from general delivery, drove back to the Kingsley Crown, changed into his Vandyke and bepillowed stomach disguise, drove to Pasadena by the Arroyo Grande Freeway, turned east on California Boulevard to the California Institute of Technology, went to a public phone booth and called Professor Mok Bing Goon.

"Doctor Mok, you don't know me by name or sight. However, I'm the man who worked with Arlo Thomasson to help you a few years back. My name is Harry Ryder. I'm calling you because the same man who caused you trouble then has surfaced once more. He's in Los Angeles. I don't think you are the object of his present activities. But I don't know what those activities might be. That's why I'm calling to ask if I can talk with you. I'm here at the campus. I want your advice as to what the Chinese think they want most now.

"You can call Mr. Thomasson to confirm my identity. Just tell him the twelve-three call worked out fine. Here are two numbers where he might be reached."

Professor Mok's voice had no accent at all. "I understand. Please come to my office in about an hour. I'll assume your credentials will check out and this will give me a chance to do a little thinking about your general question."

19

Professor Mok's door was open. He jumped up, sprang from behind his desk and thrust out his hand.

"You don't resemble Mr. Thomasson's description." He smiled. He was in his late forties, even-faced, alert, black-eyes, a small but obviously very athletic fellow. He wore jeans and a sports shirt. Papers and booklets lay jumbled on his desk. Two walls were filled with books. The third one displayed a large astronomical map and several small black-and-white photos of star clusters. "Ah, the maps. I'm doing a lot of work right now with JPL. Sorry, Jet Propulsion Lab. It's fun when one has millions to play with. Mr. Thomasson said you might be in disguise. I don't think you took great pains in putting on that remarkable Vandyke."

Ryder sat in the plain oaken chair. "A simple precaution. Not for you—for Li Ngor. He saw me today as I normally look—I don't dare have him see me that way with you. Li is not a believer in coincidences. But in any case, thank you for seeing me. I may be imagining things, but I don't think so. Patterns are patterns."

Professor Mok held up a delicate hand. "Before you go any further, Mr. Thomasson said he'd like to talk with you. He's home now and is awaiting your call."

"Arlo, how are you? The twelve-three call worked out fine. I drew the fish into the stream."

"Harry, you watch out your fish isn't a shark. He'll try to eat you. But anyway, thanks for calling. What I wanted to tell you was our mutual friend has taken a month's vacation. He's going to the Orient with his wife." This was Alison, Oakland's fourth wife. She was the first and only one who could care less about his sleeping habits. She had herself a Georgetown house, the best clubs, a handsome allowance, entree to the power society, a husband who some day might head the CIA. This was a fair trade-off from her point of view. Oakland had the wife he deserved. "Japan, Hong Kong, Singapore, the Philippines. *A la recherche du temps perdu.* A touching scene. Alison has been assured she hasn't seen a department store until she sees the Nihombashi branch of Mitsukoshi and she can't appreciate dress design until Celia Chien at the Peninsula whips up a gown for her. They'll spend eight days in Tokyo. Arrive in Hong Kong July eighth."

Ryder computed. He and Jefferson would reach Hong Kong on June thirtieth; and therefore must be out of Hong Kong on or before the seventh. He would have to phone Gutierrez to change all of the visa dates.

"Will this Orient frolic affect your plans?"

"Li Ngor Sheung and our friend had lunch together today."

"Dear me, dear me. I'll pretend I didn't hear that, Harry. If you weren't involved, though, I would have to act officially. Will you keep me informed?"

"If I can find out what this is all about, you'll be the first to know."

Bok Ming Goon lit a cigarette. "I've thought about your question. It made me recall Henry Adams. In 1903 he visited the Paris Exposition. Samuel Langley of the Smithsonian guided him through the scientific exhibits. This was the shock of Adams's life. He realized that he had totally missed the point of the nineteenth century. He had focused on a classical experience. The nineteenth century was focused on energy. Ever since his birth, production and energy and power had doubled every ten years. Langley, even then, pointed out to him that, with the energy latent in the atom, power production would continue to double every ten years. And it has. And it will continue. Are you a reader of science fiction? You should be. Science fiction starts with energy and builds on hope.

"Anyway. Here we have China. It wants to do the seemingly impossible. To catch up with the West's energy production. To bypass the long decades from 1800 until today, each one doubling its power production over the previous decade. A compounded doubling. And that's a staggering realization, even for us who deal with staggering experiences routinely. So what would you focus on if you spoke for the People's Republic of China, Mr. Ryder?"

"Energy."

"Exactly. Energy. And today energy means nuclear energy. And at present nuclear energy means fission; in the future, fusion. It means the engineering of fusion. And that means a knowledge of the state of the art in engineering's attempts to control fusion, including the use of laser technology.

"I've had my assistants assemble a bibliography for you on these subjects, Mr. Ryder. There are no secrets in the field. We are all in this together. It's all published. If there's a secret not published, that's because it was discovered only yesterday. Anything China wants, it can get by going to a technical library like Millikan—or by coming and talking to the men working in the field. They will be welcomed. If China can catch up with energy production, we want to help them do it."

"But there are secrets. For instance, they can't buy the most advanced IBM computers."

"That's not a secret. That's control of war material. They can't buy a cruise missile, either. But if they want to build their own computers, we'll help them. The Free World will help them. Ah, I see you're thinking of Jue Sik Kwan and Yung Song Hom. Cal Tech's best. They've made China a kind of satellite of our modest institute. But that was a long time ago when our country drove them back to China. The Chinese have more sophistication now. So do we. My case was, I believe, the last attempt you'll ever see to force a Chinese American scientist to find refuge in China."

"Perhaps. But what you're saying is that China wants increased energy production. There are no secrets about how to do this. And you—and your scientific colleagues—will help them."

"We'll help them. But remember, there's very little we can really do. The Manhattan Project cost two billion dollars. To produce an atom bomb, we had to create an enormous infrastructure of related and correlated technology. And a revision and refinement of that infrastructure is what the missing decades have supplied us with. For that original infrastructure's long since obsolete as we have built and rebuilt totally new ones. Only now it takes billions and billions of dollars, many billions—and the ineluctable passage of time. I don't think they can catch up, but we'll help. We'll help."

"I'm not sure I understand you, Doctor Mok. But thanks for the bibliography. I may need your help again. Will that meet with your approval?"

"Anytime. Here's my home phone number. I'll be happy to talk to Li Ngor Sheung or anyone he designates."

Before Ryder opened Lanante's envelope, he lay on his sagging bed and thought for an hour. What had Junius Oakland said to Li Ngor? And vice versa? Had Li entered the arena? Would they meet in Manila? In Hong Kong? Could he head Li off right here in Los Angeles? Was Oakland in such a panic that he was personally going to direct operations in the Philippines? Cruz, Calugas, Li, Oakland. Quite a garrison. With all the guns trained on Harry Peter McClaren Ryder. And perhaps on Terry Jefferson. He had not been entirely frank with Terry. But then, he hadn't thought through the implications of Li Ngor Sheung. Li was no Calugas. He added a different dimension. A competent dimension. Appointment in Manila indeed. Appointment in Grand Central Station.

And Lanante's envelope added to the throng. Four passports fell on to the bed.

> Dear Harry. Sorry about the way things are turning out. Manzano is bringing out two colleagues—Victor

Frega and Christopher Mori. They are on Cruz's hit list. Hence the two extra passports. I've marked who's who. We picked as close resemblances as we could find. Hope you don't blow your stack.

The phone number is set up—85-78-22. It will be attended at all hours. It is tapped. Nothing anyone can do about that. But all the Manzanos and Darangs—and there are thirty or forty of them in Manila alone—all have their phones tapped. So I think I'd better give you the regular number of Carmelita Pinson Manzano. It is 85-64-21. I'm not trying to call your shots, but you may find this useful. Ask for Mrs. Manzano on this number and talk to no one else. Identify yourself as Carlos Manzano. There are four Carlos Manzanos, so no one will be alarmed. Use the code you've set up. Speak in Visayan. The Carlos Manzanos all come from Leyte, Cebu, and Bohol. Mrs. Manzano can handle Visayan, though she is from Baguio. You'll like her.

Hope the biographies of José and Emerenciana are what you want. Best of luck. Let me know when you're off the starting block. I'm keeping the baying wolves at bay.

He examined the passports. Felicia Fortega for Emerenciana Darang, aged 35, with wide black eyes, long black hair, a sensitive face that would qualify as rare beauty anywhere else in the world. In the Philippines no one would look at her twice. Manuel Lagado, moustached, with a thin, almost emaciated face for José Manzano. Lee Colona, even-featured, heavy, bushy hair for Christopher Mori. And Alex Carpiso, very dark, possibly Negroid, for Victor Frega. He put the passports down and for five minutes enjoyed hearing himself swear. Two more refugees! When he started to repeat himself, he sighed and picked up the biographies of the brother and sister. Each one went on for fifteen double-spaced typewritten pages. The thrifty Lanante had put them in the form of obituaries. Thrifty—or prescient?

He read them through three times, then burned them. Jose Manzano came out as an honest politician. An honest politician in the Philippines starts off with three strikes against him. He was a gentle, intransigent soul, more a teacher than the fiery leader type. But he would not be silent. He just had to protest, vocally and in writing, at injustice and tyranny. Since there was no lack of these commodities, José Manzano had had a busy time for himself. And since he refused to muzzle his protests, the government had no choice but to clamp him in jail. There was no place else for him. How could he be exiled? He made it clear, honest man that he was, that if he went into exile he would devote all his time to organizing and leading a revolution in the Philippines; and if that revolution called for an armed invasion, he would be happy to supply that, too. But intransigent as he was, he was a lamb compared with his sister. She took to the streets as if they were her private salon. Every passer-by was a target for her sermons. And when a policeman joined the audience she would be apt to harangue him personally, urging him to throw down his arms and take off his uniform and join her in the fight for freedom. And her poetry only compounded the problem. Though the government had always tried to suppress her writing, her poems were smuggled from hand to hand, from province to province, island to island and even continent to continent. There were constant rumors she was being considered for a Nobel Prize. If she won one, it would be a shame the government wouldn't let her keep the prize money. For the Manzanos and Darangs certainly needed the money. The families were just a step above the poverty level. They owned nothing. Even their homes had been taken away from them. They worked as clerks and salespeople and lived in cheap apartments. The Manzanos' wealth had been split up among a dozen or so provincal henchmen. Twelve supporters in place of one enemy. Politics,

Filipino style. Lanante had added a postscript: "José uses Crest. His sister uses Budlet. That's made in the People's Republic of China. It has an orange flavor."

He laughed. It was time to go.

20

Gus Gutierrez took him past the thumping printing presses into a back office.

"How do they look?" His tone was anxious but his blue eyes were snapping with pride.

Ryder examined his new credentials line by line, perforation by perforation. They seemed entirely plausible. Even the driver's license looked authentic. "You do good work, Gus my friend. The way you handled the staples in the driver's license. High class forgery. And thanks for fixing the visa dates."

"You are going to the Philippines, Harry? Yes? Okay, I think you're going to the Philippines. Take this, will you?" He handed Ryder an envelope. "It's a thousand dollars. For my sister. She's living at the old home address in Baguio. She's not involved with my cousins. I don't want them knowing about this."

Ryder tapped the envelope thoughtfully. "If I happen to take a vacation in the Philippines—in July, mind you, always the best time for a Philippine vacation—and if I happen to have nothing better to do and find myself in Baguio walking up Benguet Street on the north side of the street, I may drop this off. That's a lot of ifs, my friend."

"Oh thank you, Harry. Thank you. I just wish I was going with you. We could work together again, like the time we put a grenade into that roomful of Japs. Hai, that was the life."

Ryder turned to go, paused, said idly, "Gus, from what you just said I gather Delfin Caumiran and Nolly Maglayan are still active?" Gutierrez swallowed, hunched his shoulders, spread his hands. When he spoke, his voice was cold, lifeless. "My cousins, Harry. My cousins. Yes, they are active." They should be. They probably were top dogs in the NPA by now. "Don't worry, Gus. They are not my mission. Just the opposite. They're something to keep clear of. For your sister's sake and mine, too."

He drove from Oxnard to Sycamore Street in the Hollywood hills and parked before a green apartment house almost completely enveloped in trees. It followed the hillside in a series of one story levels—now up, now down, now around. Eventually he found apartment 16. It seemed almost black in the heavy shade. His heart was thumping louder than Gutierrez's presses. Why should this lithe, leopardlike female disturb him so much? He was no Junius Oakland. "My dear, do you fuck?" She'd probably say, "Yes, how much can you pay?" Damn that bastard, Oakland. Damn him to hell, because ghastly as his approach was, it worked. "Look at it this way, Harry my boy. I'm just a salesman. All Americans are salesmen. I knock on doors. Will you be my agent and do a little spying for me? Ten people turn me down, the eleventh says yes. Girls are the same. Ten turn me down, the eleventh says, 'How soon and how often?' You just don't take these things personally. That's the secret." Well, he took them personally. And with Terry Gayle Elliott Jefferson he took them so personally he knew himself quite inadequate before he began. Inadequate? Say it bluntly, Harry. Impotent. All the erections in the world when it was safe. But faced with action, nothing but impotence. The gentleman's code—what a glorious refuge for impotence.

Bracing himself for the shock of her person, he knocked on the door. It swung open instantly and the shock passed all expectation.

"Good Lord, woman, what have you done?"

For Terry Jefferson did not stand before him. An exotic Eurasian confronted him. Eyes tilted up slightly, her natural long black hair flowing behind her shoulders over a green Chinese silk outfit, one of those affairs with a loose top over a slit skirt.

"You wanted acting. How do I look? Come, don't stand there like Tom Sawyer. You are a fifty-two-year-old, aren't you? Act your age."

His legs felt weak. He followed her in dumbly and collapsed on an overstuffed sofa. He said nothing, just looked at her. She put on an obstinate expression and said nothing right back.

"I knew a girl like that. A mestizo. Like the way you look now. In Leyte. She was from Tacloban. Teresa. Teresa Morgan. She was the only girl I've ever loved. The Japs gang-raped her and then put a forty-five slug into her. They made her huddle up. The bullet went in the back of her neck, through her chest, out her stomach, through her right thigh, out the back of the thigh, through her right leg, out the other side, and through her right foot. There were eight holes in her body from that one bullet. You reminded me of her. I've made a career of not letting myself be reminded of her."

There seemed nothing to say to that, so Terry sat quietly. The obstinate expression, though, did disappear. A radio sounded somewhere. A gentle jazz piano piece.

"I'm sorry for my reaction. You look great. But save your cheong sam outfit for later on. Here's your check. It's certified. For twenty thousand dollars. The whole amount. Don't laugh. Things have changed in the last week. I think there may be danger. I think? I know. A new element has entered the scene. The plot thickens. You can back out if you wish. I really didn't think you might have to share my troubles. But I'm afraid I've compromised my mission, I'm sorry. I am a fool."

"Where are we going?"

"Where? Oh, I see. Thank you. I know you said you like

danger. Well. We're going to Hong Kong on Pan Am. By way of San Francisco. Their nonstop flight. Here are your tickets—PSA and Pan Am."

"Is Hong Kong our final destination?"

"No. But I think it's better if we wait until we're finished in Hong Kong before I tell you. Hong Kong is the base of the element I mentioned. Out of the Bank of China. The mission may never get beyond Hong Kong."

"Bank of China?"

"Yes. That's the headquarters of the Chinese Secret Service. On the sixth, eighth, and thirteenth floors."

"We're not going into China?"

He couldn't help laughing. "Sorry, I wasn't laughing at you. Your question threw me off balance. I felt silly. No, we're not going into the People's Republic."

"I think I can guess where."

"Don't then. Come. Let's see your wardrobe. Bring the outfit you're wearing. And let me say, I've never seen anything more beautiful. That's all right, isn't it? You'll need light tropical clothes. And no guns. We can't take them on the plane. We'll get them in Hong Kong."

She clapped her hands. "All of a sudden it's guns for everybody! And a Cessna 310. Now I get it. We'll rent a plane and fly where we're going." Her face fell. "Oh, maybe my guess is wrong. Maybe it's going to be Vietnam. Or Cambodia. And a Cessna 310. God, not Cambodia! That's possible, isn't it?

"Okay. Be Mr. Mystery. Come along and I'll show you what I have. If it isn't right, I can still do some shopping." She stood up. "Chinese Secret Service. My, what has little Gayle Elliott from Chico, California, gotten herself into now? Ha, I see you do know about me. I've always known I couldn't bury my past. Not if it was important to anybody. It's a curious feeling. No outsider has ever known the professional Gayle Elliott. Only Gayle Elliott the student. You're the first. It makes me feel like a little girl."

She started toward the bedroom, turned back. "What

makes it worse, I don't know anything about you. You rattled off that sixth, eighth, and thirteenth floors as if it were the price of milk. What kind of a world do you move in?"

"Save this for tomorrow. We've got fourteen hours on the plane. I'll tell you whatever you want to know. There will be no secrets."

"And I thought I was secretive! Mr. McClaren, you're the most secretive man I've ever met. You'll talk for fourteen hours and you won't tell me a thing I really want to know."

This time he laughed in frank amusement. He didn't feel fifty-two.

Part Two

21

For ten hours on the plane Harry Ryder observed his mind with something approaching disgust and horror. When it should have been concentrating on his very real problems, when it should have been alert to Terry Jefferson's probing questions, all it kept thinking about was the sleeping arrangements at the Peninsula Hotel. Would he or wouldn't he be in the same bedroom with Terry Jefferson?

In despair he decided to distract his mind by telling her his worries about the dangers ahead. If he talked about them maybe he could divert his mind from contemplating a naked Terry Jefferson in his bed.

"Look, you've asked enough questions about my past. The past is past, it's the future I'm worried about. Let me talk in general terms about the future, about my . . . our . . . very real problems. I don't expect you to come up with instant solutions, but do think about them. Two minds."

He leaned near her so no one in the first-class compartment could overhear him. This way he smelled her faintly musky smell. Worse. Worse. What was he to do with the sleeping arrangements? He couldn't put her in a separate room. She was his cover. His fiancée. His mistress. His credentials as playboy.

"We're going to rescue two political prisoners. Now don't try to guess where. Every country out here has political prisoners. They come with the territory."

The plane was swinging down along the coast of Japan. The sky was mostly clear. Fujiyama lay somewhere behind a cloud screen that towered higher than they were flying—now there was a phallic symbol for you, Japan erect. They had been following the sun all day and at six o'clock it was still late afternoon. Terry turned to watch the coast.

"I'm listening. But I've never seen Japan before. Look at those fishing boats down there. And look, you can see the Izu Peninsula. That's got to be the Izu Peninsula. I've read *Shōgun,* you know. Japan is old stuff to you, but it's new to me. I'm not fifty-two years old and don't you forget it. Sorry. Fire away. I'll listen. And I'll think. Please."

"Our prisoners are in a military base. A large one. Right in the middle of a city. I know the base, of course. I've visited there several times. But not the prison compound. I don't know how it's set up. I don't know how difficult it will be getting our men off the base. Yes, I'm assuming we can get them out of the prison itself. I've already started the wheels in motion to accomplish that. But then what? Once out of jail they're still on the base, with checkpoints all over the place.

"Okay, that's the basic problem. Suppose we're lucky. Or good. And get them off the base. Then how do we get them out of the country? Fly them, of course. In our trusty 310. And we'll need the whole plane because two more are coming with us. Oh yes, another couple not at present in jail but scheduled to go there any minute. Four in all. Four plus us equals six equals the Cessna 310.

"Okay, so now we're on our way to the plane. Where at? The central airport? With the police hot on our tail, we pile into the airport, all six of us and we wave at the police —and by this time the Army, too—and take off. A pleasant sight, that, is it not?

"So we're in the air, with no military jets shooting us down and where do we take our four passengers? That's easy. Back to Hong Kong. And we put them on a commercial flight and ship them off to the U.S.

"Simple, isn't it? All we have to do is get by Immigration in Hong Kong—and in Japan, too—because I don't dare try to bring them home on an American carrier. It will have to be Japan Air Lines. With Hong Kong and Tokyo Immigration looking at the phony passports I have in my pocket and saying, 'My how your face has changed, Mr. Jones.'"

He paused and kneaded his moustache. The goddam thing itched worse than ever. "Those are the broad strokes. I don't know how to begin or how to finish. I don't know how to get my men off the base or past Immigration. Have you ever thought about Immigration officers? They are narrow, rigid, unsympathetic. There's no way an Immigration officer can suspend disbelief.

"So what do we need? We probably need a gun. A gun with a silencer probably. That's why we'll get one in Hong Kong. What about entry onto the military base? Do we need parachutes? Will I have to drop down like a deus ex machina? How much can I rely on local contacts? Our prisoners have enormous families. Not just their own, but their relatives. If they're all in this together, the police will have our timetable on a minute-by-minute basis. We'll be arrested when we set foot on the sacred soil.

"And to complicate these to-be-expected complications, we have my friend Junius Oakland and his friend Li Ngor Sheung. Let me tell you about them." If he couldn't have separate rooms or a double-bed arrangement in one room, what about the Peninsula's ineffable Marco Polo Suite? Too pretentious. A cover is one thing, but a five-hundred-dollar-a-night double-bedroom suite is not a cover, it's a rocket's red glare. That left double bedrooms, the poor man's Marco Polo Suite. What about a double bedroom? He could always lock and bolt his door. For, let's face it, Harry my American, it's neither "when" nor "if." How can a journeyman cocksman subject himself to a whore's critical analysis? Slam, bam, thank you ma'am, it's nice knowing you. No way. No way. "Back in sixty-two Junius Oakland helped Li Ngor Sheung kidnap a Cal Tech scientist, Yung Song Hom. Yung now heads up physics research in China."

Terry jerked her gaze from the fascinating Japanese fishing boats. "Kidnap? Why? Who is Junius Oakland? Why should he do a dreadful thing like that?"

"In 1962 it didn't seem so dreadful, not with a fleet of Russian freighters bringing atomic missiles to Cuba, not with the end of the world due at any minute. And while Kennedy and the rest tried to work out a resolution with Khruschev, the military establishment was hell-bent on making sure that, if we were to be annihilated, Russia would be wiped out not a nanosecond later. Except that we knew they had just installed some new missile bases in Siberia somewhere and we hadn't spotted them yet. We hadn't, the Chinese had. Junius Oakland had his thumb in the dyke. He flew to Singapore, met Li Ngor Sheung and worked out a trade. Yung Song Hom in exchange for a map of the missile bases. He was king of the roost. The Company roost." After six thousand miles, Terry knew what the "Company" was.

"Where do you come in?"

"I was on vacation in Malaysia. In the wilds; and I had just surfaced in Singapore. At the Marco Polo Hotel. It's a twin hotel to the Peninsula. That's where we're staying in Hong Kong. It's the greatest hotel in the world. The Peninsula, I mean. In my opinion. You'll see. Anyway, I had a dozen phone messages waiting for me—so far I didn't know a thing about the Cuban crisis—but I also spotted Junius Oakland with Li Ngor Sheung. In my territory. Or on the fringes anyway. I was puzzled to say the least. But when I answered my messages and got my assignment—I was ordered to Tokyo, by the way, but that's another story—I naturally became curious about my colleague. He was also my boss. At that time we couldn't be sure if the People's Republic wasn't working hand in glove with the Soviet Union. Had Oakland sold out to Russia through China? I tracked him to the airport, found out he was returning to Los Angeles, called a friend in Los Angeles, and had him tailed. It was a year or so before I pieced together the full story. By that time I found out Junius Oakland had done what all the computers and V-2's and satellites had failed to do. He could point our missiles squarely at their missiles in Siberia. He was a star. He was a living justification for the existence of the spy—the field man—in this age of the computer. Who noticed, in all this adulation, the disappearance of an obscure professor of physics from the California Institute of Technology? Obscure? Hell, he was a Chink."

"I gather your old boss never took credit for that disappearance. How did he find out you knew what he had done?"

"Li found out. Years later he got to know me. He's good. There's no one better in the whole world. He learned who I was and pulled a memory out of his head. He had seen me behind the proverbial potted palm in Singapore. He alerted Oakland and my time of troubles began."

"What do you mean?"

"Oakland took me away from station work and put me on special assignments. He had me play Uriah. He set me in the forefront of the hottest battle—only I managed to stay alive."

"I don't get it. So you were a peeping Tom in Singapore. What's that got to do with a Chinese professor and Siberian missiles?"

"I think Junius's agents in Los Angeles spotted my man tailing them. After all, it was a mad dash from Pasadena to a Chinese-manned freighter in Long Beach.

Everyone probably at first assumed my man was some Chinese Secret Service type, but when Li told them his people weren't anywhere around, that left only peeping Tom."

"Agents? Company agents?"

He thought of the Cadillac salesman, Tony Giambruno. "Hardly. Agents who are sometime-allies of the Company."

"And Li and Oakland were the men you spotted in the Polo Lounge? They're together again? They're up to something again?"

"When one hears a rattle, one assumes a snake."

"You . . . we . . . are the target this time?"

"Two secret service men of a foreign government have already tried to kill me. In my former physical appearance I hasten to add. I believe they were sent after me by Junius Oakland. That means he is betraying his country—or at least his country's interest—in order to eliminate me. The law of diminishing returns seems to apply to me."

"Foreign government? You mean Mr. Oakland, besides invoking the Chinese Secret Service to go after us in Hong Kong, has already tipped off the foreign government of the country we are about to enter and despoil of two—no, four—prisoner types. Mr. Oakland has already tipped them off that we are on the way?"

"We are rather in a glass house."

"You said 'our country's interest.' But you also told me you are not working for the Company or for the U.S."

"You are sharp. Too sharp after twelve hours in this flying bus. No, our government is not directly involved. But it did recommend me to the interested parties as an able consultant. I was hired. I hired you. But we do not represent anything more than some rather idealistic exiles who would like to come back to their country and turn the tables on the rascals who kicked them out. Believe me, if our side were on top, the prisons would be just as full. However, I assure you our side has the good guys. The ones we are against, the ones who will gladly kill us, are very definitely the bad guys. Very tough bad guys."

She thought a long time. Finally she looked at him with the abstracted, faintly obstinate expression he had become used to. "Something has obviously happened. You retired five years ago. You led a peaceful Rotarian life. Dominoes were the biggest excitement Contra Costa County could offer you. And suddenly people want to kill you. What has happened?"

"I don't know. All I know is my existence has become a threat to Junius Oakland. Why, I don't know. I intend to find out."

When she looked at him with this remote, obstinate expression, he felt he wouldn't have to lock the bedroom door. Maybe she wouldn't scoff at his technique, criticize his performance, shake her head at his staying powers—or lack thereof.

He maintained a fairly steady self-assurance until they were actually on the bouncy approach into Hong Kong, careening between apartment houses, skimming mountain tops and television antennas. Then she made the statement he had been dreading for the last two hours.

"You said 'a gun.' I told you in Los Angeles I wanted my own pistol. You said we would get guns for both of us. I don't care anything about silencers. I don't expect to be creeping over prison walls or behind guards' backs. But if anyone is going to start potting at me, I want to pot back. Two guns it is, my friend. Or no deal."

Now the obstinate look totally dominated her face. Holst was right. Terry Jefferson was a force.

22

"Where are you going? Immigration and Customs are that way. Look at the sign."

"Keep quiet. Please." He grabbed her left arm. This was the first time he had touched her. His body jerked as if undergoing electric shock. Her arm was thin but well muscled. "Just follow the crowd and look like a dumb tourist who always strays in the wrong direction."

For as they had crept into the aisle of the 747 he had heard the stewardess on the public address system: "Pan American Flight Five will continue on to Singapore in two hours and fifteen minutes. Singapore passengers may wait in the transit lounge until boarding time." The message was repeated in Cantonese, Japanese, French, and Spanish. And with each repetition his excitement grew. He whispered to Terry, "I think we've solved one of our problems. Look like a dope, please. No, not that way, smile like an idiot—and for God's sake, remember to walk like a marine."

He held back a moment to watch her critically. And she had improved. Her shoulders did not stoop as before, and her legs did not swing in front of each other leopard style. But she still whipped her legs from the hips, she still seemed a two-legged feline. No matter how many times he had made her walk up and down the aisle of the plane, he had not managed to teach her to bend her knees like a football player going through a rope walk. Cat she had been and cat she remained. Leopard.

A Chinese attendant looked at them. "Singapore?"

Harry nodded stupidly. Terry looked indignant, then stared at him sharply.

He nodded approvingly, "You've got it."

The transit lounge was a large room, brightly lit, with

rows of hard-backed chairs, a bar, and a snack counter. A gigantic black destination board faced the chairs.

"There's the entrance from the buses. Only a few planes dock at the terminal the way ours did. Most of them park out yonder and the passengers are bussed in. People in transit officially do not go through Immigration or Customs. They wait here. They are already out of here. In this room we are in Penang. Or Singapore. Or Palembang. Or Denpasar. Or Kaohsiung. Any of those places." He pointed to the destination board.

She laughed. "It's not Portland, Seattle, or Sacramento, is it? My God, I'm in the Orient at last." She sobered and nodded to the bus entrance. "Okay, so we park the 310 as close to the door as possible; our passengers scramble in here; at the appropriate time they head for the boarding area and someone meets them with their tickets and away they go to freedom and glory."

He led the way back to the Immigration clerks. "You see what this means. Either we get a third person to handle the tickets, or we split up. If we split up, you will come back here ahead of me on a regular flight while I shepherd my flock out of the hills. You'll arrange for the tickets and escort our friends to Tokyo and San Francisco or Los Angeles while I return the 310."

It took them almost an hour to get through Immigration, collect their bags, go through customs, and head for the hotel exit. This debouched into a cavernous tunnel filled with pullulating Mercedeses, Lincolns, Cadillacs—all squeezing into the curb, snuggling as near as possible to signs proclaiming the names of hotels: Mandarin, Hilton, Sheraton, Hyatt, Hong Kong, Ambassador, Merlin, Empress, Furama, Grand. Chinese porters danced around the cars, waving clipboards, calling out passengers' names, pushing bemused travelers toward this or that limousine, honking louder the slower it went.

Now Terry grabbed Harry's arm. "My God, what's this? They're all Chinese and they all shout and honk. Where is the silent mysterious East I've heard about?"

"Mysterious it is. Silent it is not." He held up a hand and a burnished brown Rolls Royce glided up to them. "The Peninsula Hotel, my dear. No Mercedes or Cadillac or Lincoln for us."

The Chinese porter and the Chinese driver were both clothed in immaculate dark uniforms with military style caps. Terry beamed. "I'm impressed. Chico rises again! How can I go back to my farm once I've seen Hong Kong?"

It was eleven-thirty when they pulled into the hotel. Chinese pages in white swarmed for the bags which were handed one inch to Chinese porters dressed in coolie garb. Harry passed out tips like the last big spender. A beautiful young British clerk in swallowtails escorted them to the registration desk and Terry hung back to gaze open-mouthed at the sheer posh grandeur of the Peninsula lobby. Harry came back to her and said nothing, just let her feast her eyes.

"It makes the Century Plaza look tawdry. Overdressed. Overstated. And believe me, I've always considered the Century Plaza the best we've got. Life isn't like this anymore. Those pillars, those incredibly awful gold faces, they're so bad they're magnificent. And look at all those tables." Even at midnight the dozens of tables were almost all occupied. "A glorified tearoom that comes across as a definition of elegance. Why hasn't someone done something like this in our country?"

"You've already said it. No one can think this way anymore. If anyone tried he'd be hooted out of court. No one writes like Shakespeare, either. Come along, you'll have to sign, too."

The Junior Suite reservation was in the name of Mr. Peter McClaren. No one batted an eye when he indicated he now wanted a double-bedroom suite. They went up to the fourth floor escorted by the young British gentleman, the only Caucasian face to be seen on the staff. Waiters, clerks, elevator operators, floor attendants, porters, cashiers, doormen, pages—all Chinese. The British gentleman opened the door and Terry shook her head in admiration. A gigantic living room with trim red sofas, a large central table and a smaller one to the side, desks, television, refrigerator; and to the right and left two oversized bedrooms with private baths. In the middle of the large table a beautiful flower arrangement; on the small one, a bowl of fruit. Someone must have done some fast scurrying around. Peninsula service. A white-jacketed attendant brought in a tea service; another one held up a tray of expensive soaps. With numb expression Terry picked a purple plastic box. The soap, she discovered later, was Marcel Rochas. Harry tipped the crew of four or five waiters, coolies, attendants, and clerks and shut the door behind them.

"Well," she said.

"I hope the arrangement is satisfactory."

"What does all this cost?"

"About two-fifty a night."

"Two-fifty! What are you, lined with gold?"

"The other choices were two separate single rooms; or a Junior Suite or one single, each of which has twin beds. There is the Marco Polo Suite, too, but that's for visiting royalty or General Motors. Two separate rooms do not substantiate our cover. Twin beds . . . well. . . ."

"Poor Peter. Well, so be it." She served him a cup of Jasmine tea for the weary traveler. "Now, what about my question?"

"Look, it's midnight. We've been going for twenty hours. We've had only one short nap. Let's talk about guns tomorrow. There are problems. And they are complicated and I'm too tired to maintain a coherent conversation. Certainly not an adversary one."

"I've never known anyone so bent on complications. All right, I'm reasonable. How long will we be here?"

"About a week."

"A week? What will we do here for a week?"

"What everyone does in Hong Kong. Go shopping or spying or both. Please save it all until tomorrow."

He did not bolt his door. He did shut it. She left hers open.

23

Harry was exhausted. And of course could not sleep. It was at least four in the morning before he collapsed into black slumber. For the first four hours of tossing and turning all he could think of was her open door.

What a mess he was. Other spies weren't like him. They seemed without conscience. He was like a scoutmaster with a group of nubile young Girl Scouts. Lookee, no touchee. Why couldn't he just get out of bed, open the door, walk across the living room and hop into bed with her? Why not? What a nincompoop he was. What a fool he had been to think up this particular cover story. At about two or three he even got up and stood by the door with his hand on the knob, only to creep back into bed. The worst thing of all was that he knew she was amused by him. What difference would a little sex make? Well, the very question showed the difference. Sex was never a little sex. Not for him it wasn't.

At eight in the morning he came brightly awake. He was astonished to see how alert he was. He listened hard. It was Terry's voice. He trotted to the door, put his ear against it, heard her ordering breakfast. It took him ten minutes to shave and put on his shorts and undershirt. He covered himself with the white terry cloth bathrobe provided by the hotel. It was too short, but he thought she would find it amusing. He opened the door, stared, and burst out laughing. Terry was also wearing the hotel's white terry cloth bathrobe. It was flung open carelessly so that he could see one breast clearly. It was a small, tight, fine breast. It had the very modicum of fatty glands necessary to qualify its breastiness. The nipple was also visible. A breast Gauguin could have painted.

"Damn," he said. "Cover yourself up. This is a business trip. A fifty-two-year-old and you. And now don't you forget it."

She shrugged. "You don't have to look." But she did cover herself up. "I've been reading the *South China Morning Post*. They pushed it under the door. What a marvelous paper. It makes the L.A. *Times* look like amateur night at the playhouse. I've also ordered two continental breakfasts. Okay?"

"Okay. Do you want to talk business before or after breakfast?"

"Why not now? I've thought out my questions. Ready? First, what do you mean, spying and shopping? Second, why must we do this for six whole days? Third, what are the complications about getting a gun? Why can't we just go into a store and buy a couple?"

"The spying is simple. In this case, it means mostly not being spied upon. You and I can't be seen together. We're compromised. Li Ngor Sheung has seen us together once. Twice will be too much of a coincidence for him. We've got to keep separate."

"Through? Then let's get something else clear. We're in this together. Whither thou goest, I will go."

"That's impossible."

"You begin to bore me. Either we're in this together or not at all. You can have your check back anytime you want."

"Don't blackmail me. I'm just trying to protect you. There is danger here. Real danger. I've told you about the two men in San Francisco. . . ."

"I've been thinking about that." She had pulled her

shoulders totally back so they were squared off. She looked almost Filipina in her erectness. Almost like Teresa Morgan. "You killed them, didn't you? You are a killer? I was right that day at the Polo Lounge."

"You're disgusting. Murder is nothing to salivate over."

She smiled happily. "I should have been a spy. I like this life. So it's agreed then? We'll be together? I can learn from the master spy?"

"Master spy! I can't tell you to act your age. You seem a thousand going on ten. Master spy! Good God above, if Oakland or Li could hear me called that. Me, the born expendable spy."

"Expendable?"

"Expendable spy. There are five kinds of spies. Sun Tzu defined them twenty-five hundred years ago. Native, inside, doubled, expendable, and living. Those are the five kinds of spies—what the hell am I saying? Listen, okay, okay, we're in this together as long as I don't have to teach you about spying. I'm the world's worst spy and getting worser by the minute. What's next? Oh yes, the shopping.

"Well, we've got to get wigs, my gun, a plane, some luggage, hair dyes, parachutes, a small shovel, and God knows what all."

She thought over the shopping list. "Some I understand. Why wigs?"

The doorbell sounded. Breakfast was brought in and served. Ravenous, he ate three slices of toast with cheese before he answered her. "I need a wig for myself and...."

"Wait a minute. You've already got a wig. I saw it in your suitcase. Along with a Vandyke beard."

He looked at her. She shrugged defensively. "I told you I'm a born spy. All right. A born snoop. What's the difference?"

"What else did you see?"

"Well, I confess. I know where we're going. While you were asleep last night—you are a heavy sleeper, aren't you? Is that good for a spy? I thought they slept with one eye open. Anyway, I came in and went through your pockets. I was looking for your real passport with your real name, but instead I found four Filipino passports. It's the Philippines, isn't it?"

He groaned and put his hands over his eyes. Both his own and the Roger Hiller passport were safely in the lining of his suitcase. With her that was no protection. He peeked through his fingers. "What time was this snooping?"

"Oh, about one o'clock. I couldn't sleep at all. I'm just too excited. I don't have nerves of steel like you. In fact, I have a slight fever this morning. Just nerves."

"This whole thing is a nightmare. I could swear I didn't get to sleep until dawn, and you find me already knocked out at one. How did I ever light on you? Okay, you know where we're going. I just hope when someone starts branding you with hot irons you don't find yourself spilling it out."

"Branding me with . . .? Oh no, Mr. McClaren. No branding for this kid. I'll tell anybody anything they want to know pronto pronto."

"They won't believe you. They'll brand you anyway. On general principles."

"I see. You don't mind my being tortured. You just don't want me to be able to spill the truth. A fine employer you are. Don't you dare leave. You haven't answered my questions."

"All right. I want another wig. A fall-back position. I have no definite use for it, but you never know. And I definitely want a wig for you. For right now. A brown matronly wig that will hide your black hair." He almost said beautiful black hair. "That hair, combined with your leopard stride would be recognized by Mr. Magoo himself, not to mention Li Ngor Sheung."

"Oh, and the hair dyes are for the same purpose, I suppose. You do like disguises, don't you? There's the real Peter McClaren, the Vandyke Peter McClaren, and the present David Niven Peter McClaren. Oh yes, don't look innocent and anonymous. You always go into a protective coloring of anonymity when you feel threatened. Only it doesn't work now. I suspect when you were round-cheeked, fat, and baby-faced your anonymous look worked pretty well. Who ever heard of a chubby spy? Hah, I got you there, didn't I? What about the luggage? We've got luggage. And I suppose the shovel is to bury the parachute. The plane I understand. Now, what does that leave?"

"You are sadistic." And was he not really masochistic? Were they not a better complement than he cared to admit? "All right, the gun. Let me explain this."

"Please do."

"Guns can be bought in Hong Kong. British citizens buy them as we do at home. There are at least two gun shops. And you and I can also buy them. With certain conditions. First we go to the ATU office of the Treasury. . . ."

"ATU?"

"I believe the full title is Bureau of Alcohol, Tobacco and Firearms. At first it was just the Alcohol Tax Unit—ATU to us ancients. They give us a Form Five to fill out. We could do that. Form Five—in Hong Kong—simply tells a gun store it's okay to ship a gun to a wholesaler in the U.S. A licensee. The wholesaler then can sell us the gun we've already bought."

"So in effect we can't buy a gun here."

"Exactly."

"Don't look pleased. You've already said we're going to buy a gun. Guns."

"The underground in Hong Kong is very ancient and respected. It began in the fourth century A.D. In 386 to be exact. In modern times we barbarians called them the Triads. Some of the tongs of California are probably affiliated with the Triads. We could get guns from them. And that would probably be best, except that the Triads are quite accustomed to working with the police if it's to their advantage. And since you and I have no standing with them, I don't know why they should oblige us."

"But?"

"But there is also an underground gun trade. It supplies Cambodian rebels, Burmese opium chieftains and rebels, Chinese opium runners, Indonesian Communists, NPA in the Philippines—the New People's Army—the Moros in Mindanao, and the Red Army in Japan. Every country, every city, town, and hamlet in the Orient. This is a big business. And also smart business. Handled by Mr. Chow Woon Chung. He will deal with a single person like myself providing I have the credentials."

"And you have the credentials?"

"I know the lingo."

"Good. Then buy two guns."

"It won't work. I'm going to negotiate for a gun with a silencer. This is a reasonable request. Guns with silencers are hard to come by. But if I also ask for a regular everyday pistol, that would not be reasonable. A man with my credentials should have a boxcar full of small arms. As it is, I know very well that the fat's in the fire when I surface to get my gun. Li Ngor Sheung will be on my tail the minute I walk out of the store. But if I ask for a regular pistol, I'll never even be allowed out of the store. Goodbye to dear old Peter McClaren."

"Li? What does Red China have to do with illicit gun smuggling?"

"Why, everything. The People's Republic controls the gun trade out here. And in much of Africa, too. Chow Woon Chung is an agent of the Chinese Secret Service. Li probably outranks him, but it doesn't matter."

For the first time a look of doubt and distress crossed her face. "Then how will we avoid being . . . being . . .?"

"Eliminated?"

"Yes, eliminated."

"That's why I have my Vandyke, my dear child. It's going to take some very fine last minute timing. That's where you will come in."

She ignored this diversion. "So I get no gun from you?" The obstinate look had once again hardened her face. "Then I'll get one by myself. You don't know everything Mr. Smartypants McClaren. I'm a natural-born spy myself. I'll show you. I'll get it today."

"Not today. Today we must start the wheels in motion to get our Cessna."

"Wheels in motion? Why not just go rent one?"

"Dear me, you are impetuous. Terry, there are no 310s in Hong Kong. This is not a small-plane market. Not with Cathay Pacific covering every nook and cranny of the Orient. The nearest 310 will be in Singapore or Tokyo. And it's going to take three or four days to work this out. Nothing is ever simple out here. Learn that. That's why it's a wheels-in-motion day."

"Okay. Then when that's settled, I'll get myself an automatic. And it won't be this cloak-and-dagger nonsense you're going through. It will be simple, I promise you."

She rose and went to her room. He called after her, "Dress as lightly as you can. It'll be in the nineties today. And take a salt tablet. We can't risk heat prostration." As she was shutting the door he raised his hand. "One more thing. If I had awakened last night while you were frisking my pockets, what would you have done?"

"Why stupid, I'd have said I was there to seduce you."

24

The Bank of America in Hong Kong could have been the Bank of America in Bakersfield. Except for the Chinese. As always, each of the four floors was wall-to-wall Chinese.

"I'm beginning to get the idea," Terry whispered as

they rode up the elevator. "We're interlopers here. We're just a pimple on the body of China."

Her face was glowing. The matronly wig helped a little, but the joy and excitement in her face only made her seem more beautiful than ever. She had been awestruck by the Star Ferry. She insisted they ride over and back and over again. She had leaned over the rail and simply gaped at the junks and sampans and freighters and U.S. warships and ferries and tugs and excursion boats. Ryder heard the Chinese comment on her beauty and naiveté. One of these, a well-dressed young business type, even said, "That grey-haired old man better watch out. She'll be kidnapped from right under his nose. And I'll do the kidnapping."

His pals guffawed with him. Harry had to restrain himself from showing his irritation. Especially since he was sure these lecherous brats were quite capable of a little white slave trade on the side. "Peter, you get all this for thirty cents Hong Kong. What's that, seven cents?" And she had grabbed his arm unaffectedly and beamed at the throng and it had beamed back.

Mr. Bailey was ready to see them. He was the only Caucasian on the executive floor. He had a British accent that almost concealed his Oklahoma bleat.

"How do you like Hong Kong, Miss Jefferson?" She threw her hands behind her head. This made her braless breasts thrust out. Mr. Bailey had thick lips. They became thicker. "I love it, Mr. Bailey. I had no idea the mountains were so high. Or so beautiful. And the buildings, my goodness, you have more skyscrapers in a few blocks than we have in all Los Angeles. And the lights at night. And the explosion of signs all the way across streets. Incredible. I've read about Hong Kong, but no one told me how beautiful it is. Really."

Ryder had had enough of this paean to the Hong Kong Tourist Association. He pointed to the certified check in Bailey's hand. Mr. Bailey gulped and brought his eyes away from Terry's nipples. He fingered the check with sensuous pleasure. Clearly he was imagining himself fingering Terry's breasts. (The disgusting bitch. She couldn't help doing this to men.) He tilted the check. He laid it on his polished, paper-free desk and studied it thoughtfully. (His lips were thinner now. Somewhere in Mr. Bailey lurked a potential thin-lipped banker.) He hawked, swallowed, said daintily, "Fifty thousand dollars. Drawn on Los Angeles Main. Yes, yes, yes. And you wish to deposit it with us. Hong Kong Main."

Since this was where the conversation had begun, Ryder said nothing. He got out a cigar, an Optimo Corona, about the most harmless cigar he had yet discovered, unpeeled it, crimped the end to enlarge the hole, and looked questioningly at Mr. Bailey.

"Go right ahead, oh yes, yes, yes. Go right ahead. The fifty thousand—do you plan to conduct business with it? Buying and selling? Buying and selling? There are certain —you understand?"

"I understand." In Los Angeles Ryder had laundered the remaining seventy-seven one thousand dollar bills through Security Pacific Bank. There had been no raising of eyebrows or furtive phone calls. The heat had not extended to Los Angeles. Junius Oakland was, then, not omnipotent. Ryder had deposited the seven hundred and seventy-one hundred dollar bills in the Los Angeles Main Branch of Bank of America. "I do not intend to conduct business here. Miss Jefferson and I do intend to rent a plane. That will require more than our open, honest faces."

"Of course, of course. A deposit. A deposit. I understand. We'll be happy to confirm the transaction."

Terry's mouth had fallen open. Ryder was afraid she might start chortling. This was no time to display her superior sense of humor. "We intend to rent from David Thompson. Of British Empire Aviation. We'll call on him tomorrow, so we'd very much appreciate it if you would confirm the deposit before then. My contact at Los Angeles Main is Mr. Arthur Barnett. He expects your cable."

"David Thompson, David Thompson. Yes, we know David Thompson." Mr. Bailey looked thoughtfully at Ryder. Mr. Bailey's eyes were a good deal sharper than his tongue. They said—or Ryder thought they were saying—"So you are renting from an agent of the British Secret Service. From the man who covers all private plane needs of British Intelligence from Borneo to Taiwan. I wonder who you really are, Mr. Peter McClaren? Well, that's Hong Kong for you. No one's ever said Hong Kong is Tulsa, Oklahoma." Mr. Bailey finally nodded. "Just have Mr. Thompson call me. There'll be no problem."

Terry Jefferson stopped him as they came out on Ice House Street. "What was that all about? David Thompson, David Thompson, yes we know David Thompson."

She didn't seem the least bit troubled by the heat. He felt numb and faint. "You have too much curiosity. I've told you, this is an involuted, convoluted world out here. It took me ten years to get a glimmering of how it works. You can't just jump in and expect to swim that easily."

That obstinate look settled on her face.

"All right, all right, don't pout. We'll go across the street to the Mandarin and have a beer in the Captain's Bar. I can't take this heat. Or are you hungry? No, it's too hot to eat. I'll tell you all about David Thompson."

He waited until the San Miguel beer was poured. "I've never known anyone like you. But then I know very little about women. My secretary thinks I'm the perfect Rotarian type. She's always trying to get me to join."

"I understand. Rotarians tend to submerge their unconscious feminine nature. They tend to be sensation thinkers. Block builders. Or perhaps thinking types. But not intuitive or feeling types. That's where your secretary is wrong. You'd never be a Rotarian. I'm sure you're an intuitive. You try to hide it with pedantry, but I've caught that about you."

He spluttered over his beer. "You're playing my game. That's what I do when I meet people. My God, pistoleer, actress, pilot, ah, woman of the world, and now Jungian analyst. The Renaissance woman, that's what she is. All things to all men. Sorry, I didn't mean—well, sorry." He chewed peanuts, drank some more beer. "David Thompson runs an aircraft school and charter service here in Hong Kong."

"That won't wash. I tell you I'm also an intuitive. That phony American-British banker was trying to impress you. Why?"

He ordered another beer. He sighed. "You always throw me off. I had you pegged as a sensation type. You think everything through so carefully and slowly. How could I be so wrong?"

"Don't change the subject. But to correct you: I don't think slowly. I just think slowly over what I've thought. That, by the way, is another reason I'd make a good spy. I'm no blabber-tongue. Now, what about David Thompson?"

"Well, he also works for the Hong Kong station of the British Secret Service. Maybe by now he is the station."

"Good. Then I'll find out who you really are. When we meet Mr. Thompson tomorrow."

"I'm afraid not. Thompson knew the previous me. Not Peter McClaren."

He stood up and looked at his wristwatch. "I'm going out to the airport and watch planes come in. JAL and other lines. You're welcome to come. But the observation deck is an open air affair and you stand in the sun all the time and there is no shade. Just you and an oval window and Chinese relatives waving good-bye. And the sun."

"No thanks. I'm going shopping. I'll start with Lane Crawford and work my way back along Queen's Road and then up Des Voeux. Aren't you impressed?"

"Only if you don't try your pistol stunt without me."

"Don't worry. We'll do that together after we finish

with Thompson tomorrow. I need a handsome, mature male escort for my little scene."

"You notice I don't pout because you won't tell me what you're up to. Okay, be a good girl and I'll take you to Gaddi's for dinner tonight. A man can do no more."

He thought she raised her eyebrows as if to question that. Damn, what a language English is for unintended double entendres.

25

When they left David Thompson's office on the twelfth floor of the P.& O. building, Ryder said, "You handled yourself beautifully in there. Thompson was mightily impressed."

"Impressed! That scum propositioned me. Where was my gentleman killer then? Weren't you the least bit annoyed?"

"Annoyed? What did you want me to do, challenge him to a duel? Actually, I was delighted. The more he looked at you the less he looked at me."

"Looked at me? He got me up against the back wall and rubbed up against me and he was prepared to rape me right then and there while you sat fat, happy, and dumb in the front room. Ugh, I need a bath."

Thompson had ushered them into an office placarded with photos of David Thompson in or about all kinds of planes—not the least being a Hawkesly Sidderly Buccaneer with Lieutenant Thompson waving the RAF victory salute. At that time he had been a slim, red-headed, toothy macho type; today he was a bulky, red-headed toothy macho type. Incredibly, he wore a heavy tweed jacket and wool flannel trousers; but fat-faced as he was, there was not a drop of sweat showing. His fat seemed a compacted plaster. He had glanced at Ryder, beamed all his teeth and fillings at Terry Jefferson.

"What can I do for you? Do you want to take a trip over the islands? Learn to fly? Just name it, I'll take you on myself. This is a privilege, an honor. We poor Asia hands don't get a chance like this often."

There was no doubt what kind of chance he had in mind. Screwing beautiful Chinese whores, his leer said, was never the same as screwing a beautiful American. (After an early dinner at Gaddi's last night, Ryder had taken Terry to a topless joint in the Wanchai district. He had done it deliberately, maliciously. He wanted to show Terry her sisters under the skin. The East and West are twain for all that. She had infuriated him. "I'll take that round-eyed Chinese girl. The one with the turned-up tits. You can have all the rest. She's the only real pro here." And he had been shocked. Probably he was a Rotarian after all. Reading about deviate sex in *Penthouse* was not quite the same thing as coping with it in Terry Jefferson's flesh. But she had taught him a lesson. He would not try to upstage her again.) Terry threw her shoulders back so her breasts thrust out at Thompson and the nipples actually projected a half inch—and said her piece.

"No, Mr. Thompson. I want to rent a plane. My friend here wants to explore the East. See off-beat places. Taiwan, Okinawa, Luzon, Palawan, Leyte, Mindanao, Sabah, whatever. I think we'll want a Cessna 310."

"You? You're a pilot!"

She opened her ample straw purse, pulled out the papers. Thompson studied them carefully. "Over six hundred hours of air-time. Twin-engine license." He whistled. Somehow he seemed disapproving. Beautiful girls are made to spread their legs, not their wings.

"You don't need a 310 for that. A 180 will do all you want. You'll be island hopping anyway and it's a better deal. A hell of a lot less expensive."

She gave him that look which told him he was being quite crude. "I said the same thing to Peter. I tried to explain two engines are not necessarily safer than one. In fact, they can be much more risky. But he just can't forget all that water."

"And the parachutes," Ryder murmured. He somehow seemed owlish, almost stupid. His cigar even dangled unlit from his lips. Thompson now studied him. How did an oaf, a grey-haired dunce like Ryder get himself a girl like Jefferson? And when Thompson had worked this out, he sighed distastefully. It was all right to buy one's pound of flesh, but to attempt to hoard it was ghoulish.

"Oh yes," Terry nodded. (And now she seemed to be saying, "You're right, David. You're the man here. This fuddy-duddy can be gotten around. Britain and America can unite again." Ryder felt a tinge of jealousy even as he swelled with admiration. The girl could act. If it was an act.) "Water. Parachutes. You understand."

Thompson's face said he didn't understand a word, but he nodded. "Parachutes. Okay. How long do you want the plane?"

"Oh, two weeks. Maybe sixteen or seventeen days. We should be able to cover the mysterious East in that time."

"Myster . . . Wait a minute. You're not going near the People's Republic. I hope you understand that. That's a no-no."

Terry's expression was beatific. "Red China, oh dear me, no. Not even Vietnam. Peter here feels very uneasy about all those Commies in the world. Now. We understand this will be—Peter, if you please."

She held out her hand. Ryder handed her a check and she passed it on to Thompson. (Now her expression was bolder. Her eyes were saying, "Yes, you're right; it's just a question of money. But money is not a man. I know a man when I see one.") Thompson stared at Terry as if he were about to spring at her before he glanced at the check.

"Ten thousand U.S. dollars. . . ."

"Yes. You can confirm it with Mr. Bailey at the Bank of America in the St. George Building. He's expecting your call. Will that be adequate as a deposit?"

Thompson nodded. "Adequate enough." He called Mr. Bailey and listened intently. When his face wasn't heated with lust, it had a hard, thoroughly competent expression. There was little doubt as to his priorities between business and pleasure. "All right," he said to Terry, "that's in order. When do you want to start?"

"As soon as you can get the plane here."

He nodded. "I can bring one up from Djakarta. Some oil men have just turned it in. We'll get it here in two days. Then we'll want to check it out. I'll go up with you and we'll see how it spins. Come with me, if you will, and I'll show you the stats."

"And that," Terry said with disgust, "was when he started feeling me. No man—no man, ever—has done that to me."

"What did you say to him?"

"I said there's nothing I'd like better than a roll in the hay with him. What did you expect me to say? By that time I had squeezed out from under, so I could do it up brown. I said, 'Just wait until we get back. Right now, that old fuddy-duddy out there keeps a tight leash on me, but when I bring the plane back he'll be so exhausted he won't care what I do!"

Ryder shook his head in admiration. "You are something else. Where are you going?"

"To get a car. A little beauty. A 911SC."

"What's a 911SC and why did you buy a car, of all things?"

"Not buy, silly. Rent. While you were off chasing planes, I changed my mind about Lane Crawford and went to four rental agencies before I found what I wanted. A pretty little yellow Porsche. It's just one step away from the racing Porsches. Come on, the agency is out in North

Point. On Watson Street. We need a cab. And anyway, we can go right from there out King's Road and eventually over Tai Tam and out Stanley Gap to Repulse Bay."

"You are something else. Or did I say that before? Where are we going in Repulse Bay?"

"To the Royal Hong Kong Gun Club."

"What in God's name for? I want to go back to the airport and watch the planes again. I've found a flight that qualifies. JAL Flight Two leaves for Tokyo and San Francisco at thirteen-fifty. And it was right on time yesterday. Mussolini would have been proud of JAL. Now I've got to study all incoming flights from all the airlines to see which ones land somewhere around thirteen-fifty. Thirteen-fifty is about right. That means if we leave the Philippines around six A.M. we'll make it handily. Even six-thirty is okay."

"Good for you. You've got four days to do all that. We've got to get me my gun."

"From a gun club? You're out of your mind."

26

The manager of the Royal Hong Kong Gun Club came out himself to greet Miss Jefferson. And her guest, Mr. McClaren. Maybe he had watched her sweep that animate little Porsche up the shrub-lined drive as if she were crowding it close at Le Mans.

Certainly Ryder was impressed. This was a different Terry he saw. Terry the driver. She spurted up and around the narrow Tai Tam mountain road with total concentration on gears, revolutions, driving conditions. The unnatural left-lane driving fazed her not at all. She whipped around the buses and vans like a chipmunk darting between crevices. It was a work of beauty. She was a work of beauty—even with her matronly hairdo.

"Yes, Miss Jefferson," said the manager, one Osbert Trefethen. "We've been expecting you. We're delighted you want to use our facilities. Our members have certainly used your Southern California Club." He was a tall, ruddy, bemoustached Briton. Even though the temperature outside was well over ninety, and the humidity higher—and inside, even with air conditioning, it didn't seem much cooler—he wore a grey wool pin-striped suit with a vest. "If you will just follow me."

He led the way through a cool, dark oaken passageway covered by a two-inch-thick Persian runner. As they passed little rooms, members looked up from their *Morning Post* and watched Terry. With admiration, of course. Terry was wearing a simple blue blouse, a grey skirt, and her flats. But they were also smirking in anticipation. Terry was, as always, oblivious. But Ryder could see her coming was indeed expected; and as they passed through the enormous dining room that looked out over the shooting ranges, he saw members put down their papers and drift after them. They were going to have an audience. Suddenly he halted. "You go with Mr. Trefethen, dear. I'll watch from here. All that noise, you know."

If they were going to smirk from the dining room bay windows he was going to cramp their style. Trefethen nodded. "Miss Jefferson, I've assumed you want to go your basic National Match Course—but it's no trouble doing the full aggregate round if you prefer."

"Then let's have a go at the full round. How about a thirty-eight for the centerfire?"

Trefethen raised his eyebrows, looked at a Chinese attendant who promptly vanished. Ryder now realized that over half the twenty or so members sifting into the room with him were Chinese. "Of course. Please, this way."

Terry wasn't the only marksman out there, but the others—five in all—stopped to watch. Of course. They had probably never seen a woman in their club before. Terry took her position beside the stand and in a moment the attendant trotted up carrying a thirty-eight and a forty-five. The twenty-two was already there. Terry put on the earmuffs, set the timer, and began to shoot with the twenty-two. Ten rounds at timed fire—five bursts in eight seconds and then five more in nine. A rotund Chinese beside Ryder sucked his breath and with a gentle smile handed Ryder his binoculars.

"Why, thank you." He looked at the target. Nine holes formed a cluster around the bull's-eye. One was off to the lower left.

"She is good," the Chinese said. "Very good. Certainly an expert. Maybe even a master." Ryder handed him back the glasses, said—foolhardily perhaps, but he was bursting with pride—in Cantonese, "She is a continual surprise to me. A woman of infinite capacities. Pardon me, a person."

The fleetest flicker of astonishment around the Chinese's eyes. He accepted his binoculars but looked at an attendant and another pair was instantly procured for Ryder. Apparently words were not necessary at the Royal Hong Kong Gun Club. "No, woman is correct. Perhaps in the People's Republic one takes these revolutions for granted. Maybe even in your country. But not in Hong Kong. She has made us all ashamed. I am sorry. I apologize. I will go, if you please."

"No, please stay and watch with me. All of you." This also in Cantonese. None of the Caucasians had lost any face. They were doing the jolly-good-show bit and that seemed to justify their presence. "I am the one who is ashamed. I had less faith in her than any of us. That's why I stopped in here. If you will be so kind."

Terry shot three courses. After two of them, Mr. Trefethen came up beside Ryder and the Chinese who had introduced himself as Sam Them Nai. "Though around here I am known as Charlie." "Mr. McClaren," Trefethen said, "I hope you and Miss Jefferson will stay for lunch. Will you join us, Sir Charles?"

"Thank you," Ryder said. He looked reproachfully at Sam Them Nai. Known as Charlie, indeed. "Miss Jefferson will be delighted. Perhaps you can help at lunch. She is a modest target-pistol collector, and perhaps you can help her find something along that line."

"Sir Spencer Smith!" Trefethen and Sam spoke together. Trefethen pointed to a man in his late sixties. He was at a window with his binoculars steadily on Terry even when she was not shooting. There was no escaping the expression on his face. Ryder groaned silently. Another one, God how awful it must be to be a beautiful woman. Stupid thought, that. But probably quite true with one emendation: a poor beautiful woman. For such a one there could be no protection. Still stupid. Terry had been a poor beautiful woman. He picked up Trefethen's words.

"Sir Spencer has quite a distinguished collection of military small arms, but he's getting along and he's gradually disposing of it. But only to qualified recipients. Money is not the object, you understand. He loves his guns and he wants them to be loved in the future. Come, I'll introduce you."

Sir Spencer's face and body were both monuments to dissipation. His stomach started at his belt and protruded below it a foot or more. It made him look like Humpty-Dumpty, except that his pendulous lips and alcoholic veins bespoke the archetypal satyr. When Terry returned he bowed and kissed her hand like a caricature of an ancient regime roué. "You were marvelous, my dear. Just marvelous. You'd place in any competition from Singapore to Tokyo. God, I'd like to see you in the Queen's Best. That'd shake 'em up, wouldn't it, Charlie? The Queen's Best with the best of princesses."

It was disgusting. The lunch was disgusting. Terry let Sir Spencer lean over her and obviously fondle her between her legs. What was all that crap? "No man has ever done that to me." Well, certainly Harry Ryder hadn't done it. For which there was no one to blame but Harry Ryder and he had better get off the subject. If he had wanted to go to her, he could have done so last night. She had left the door open and, as she undressed for bed, she had looked at him—how? Quizzically? Enticingly? Approvingly? Anyway, she had given him that look and in reply he had shut his own door again. And, even if his face didn't have an obstinate pout, his heart did; for, as he had shut his door, he suddenly knew what this was all about. Terry Jefferson expected to be asked. Men always asked her. Well, he wasn't the asking type. If he passed through her door, it would be only because she had openly, plainly, unequivocally said, "I want you."

None of which, obstinate heart and all, made it any less painful to watch her operate on Sir Spencer Smith.

"My dear," his grotesque puffy lips were saying, "I'm sure I have something or other that will suit you. You must come out to my house. I live near here. At Stanley Fort. On the Fort grounds, yes. A kind of grandfather clause, I think you would call it."

Sam Them Nai whispered to Ryder, "Sir Spencer's great-grandfather was a mighty opium runner. He gave the government his land. That gave the government Stanley Fort, himself a knighthood, and his ships the green light. Great-grandfather was good to Sir Spencer."

Ryder nodded glumly. He was quite aware of the amused expression on Sam Them Nai's face. The Chinese knew that Ryder was prepared to throttle Sir Spencer but lacked the guts to make a move.

Terry turned to him. "Darling," (oh, the malice in that word) "I'll go with Sir Spencer to look at his collection." At least it wasn't his etchings. "I know how boring this would be for you, so if you'll drive the Porsche back to the Peninsula, Sir Spencer will see that his chauffeur gets me back to the hotel. Won't that be good of him?"

27

Four days later David Thompson called as Terry and Ryder silently ate their continental breakfast.

"Your 310 is here, Miss Jefferson. We've checked her over and you can take off any time. Why don't we meet at Kai Tak and we'll give it a spin?"

Terry looked at Ryder and he mouthed the words, "We'll leave tomorrow." She nodded. "Kai Tak is fine, Mr. Thompson. How about eleven? We'll be leaving tomorrow."

She put the phone down, looked at Ryder. "I'll let him take me up, but I'll die before I go up alone with him. He'll put the plane on automatic and rape me. I know him. I want you with me."

For four days the rage had been festering in him. Now it poured out, a vile bile. "What is the difference between David Thompson and Sir Spencer Smith?" And the second the words were out he regretted them. They were appalling. He was henceforth totally at her mercy.

To his surprise she showed no emotion, just looked at him calmly. "I've been expecting that. I could say a lot of things, but why should I stoop just because you crawl? Let me show you something."

She went into the bedroom while he hunched over and wept unseen tears of self-pity. The last four days had been unmitigated pain. He had had nothing to say to her. He had gone through his necessary preparations for departure day, making a reservation at the Mandarin for Arthur Twilling and one at the Luk Kwok for Roger Hiller. He had checked out the arriving flights for around two in the afternoon and found that both Cathay Pacific and Singapore Air Lines would have passengers using the transit lounge. He had cased Chow Woon Chung's stereo store and found that it closed at six P.M. He had bought a JAL ticket to Tokyo in the name of Roger Hiller. He had even gone once with Terry for a drive through the New Territories. He had taken her to Lok Ma Chau and they had climbed the hill to look at Red China. He had shown her Kam Tin and Tang Tai Uk walled villages. He had taken her to lunch at the Shaker Heights Hotel and pointed out the Amah Rock, shaped like a woman with a baby on her back. And though they had discussed the sights and the tropical scenery with its unending green, there had been no communication between them, only a frosty wall. What had he read once? "The eight inches between man and woman can be the greatest distance in the universe."

Terry came back carrying her gigantic straw purse. She fumbled around in it and pulled out an automatic pistol. "Isn't this a beauty? A Browning High Power."

He knew the gun of course; he concealed the fact routinely. Never tell all you know, because all you know is mighty little. "So?"

Terry hefted the pistol. "About two pounds, I'd say." It was actually one and nine-tenths pounds empty, just over two and a quarter pounds loaded. "Uses nine-millimeter Parabellum cartridges. Thirteen of 'em. I've never had one of these. I was brought up on forty-fives. Anyway, this particular gun was manufactured by Fabrique Nationale in Belgium and belonged to General Albert Duquesne. It has quite a history, so Sir Spencer told me, but more to the point, it's a fine handgun and I have it without incriminating documents. A month from now Sir Spencer will record the sale, do all the necessary paperwork, and claim that he shipped it to a responsible licensee in Los Angeles.

"Now this was all done simply, with a minimum of fuss. I've heard you making your reservations. Arthur Twilling. Roger Hiller. Ticket to Tokyo. Your way may be the master-spy way to get yourself a silencer. But it's complicated and risky and probably just dumb. Someone is going to be shooting at you, I can feel it. There was no risk my way.

Sir Spencer has no venereal diseases. I take the pill. I have me a beautiful handgun. And it didn't cost one penny."

"No risk! Suppose he had had a heart attack."

"You are astonishing. You astonish me. What torment you must have put yourself through. Heart attack. There are ways to help control that. Would you like me to describe how I avoid that risk?"

He pictured for the thousandth time Sir Spencer Smith's enormous belly flattening Terry beneath it and he shuddered. "No. I've said enough stupid things. There is no use apologizing, but I do apologize. I should know better. I have no claim on you. And I have to admit, your way is best. I should have had you get me a silenced weapon from Sir Spencer. I didn't think of it."

"Well, I did. And he doesn't have one. He would have none of the bloody things in the house. Well. So much for that. Now will you talk to me again? I want to hear more about the Philippines and your stories about spying. You haven't really clarified that East German bit for me."

"West German. It started in the East but it finished in Frankfurt."

"All right, West German. Will you do it? Good. I want to hear your stories, but again more to the point, I want to know why you're going through all these complicated deceptions. It's the future that counts, you taught me that. Foresight and foreknowledge, the essence of espionage. I've got to know what this is all about. Tell me about your disguises as we drive out to the airport to meet the macho David Thompson. The future is our future together, Okay?"

28

"You have a reservation for Arthur Twilling. For one night."

The clock behind the Mandarin's registration desk showed eleven. The clerk pulled out the forms, nodded. "Room eight-seventeen, if that's satisfactory."

"My bag is over there by the captain's stand." Ryder pointed to a small suitcase. "I'll pay in advance, if that's agreeable. There'll be no other charges. Just in and out, you know."

Many people think the Mandarin is the finest hotel in Hong Kong. But he knew that Junius Oakland was not one of them. If he didn't stay in the Company wing of the United States Consulate, he would be found a block away at the Hilton. There, no one questioned the girl for breakfast, the girl for lunch, or the girl for dinner. (Sometimes there was another for after dinner. Junius had made no bones about it. "I've tried 'em all over the world, Harry, my boy. Even once in an Arabian harem, so help me. But there's absolutely nothing like Suzie Wong. She's born knowing all forty-seven positions and she wants to demonstrate her knowledge. I'm the world's best student.") Of course, traveling with his charming Alison would cramp Oakland's style. Or would it? All he would have to do would be to put a credit card in her purse and sic her after Hong Kong's gaudy baubles. Wouldn't it be interesting, though, if Alison returned unexpectedly from her greedy shopping and found her husband entangled with Suzie Wong like a modern Laocoön.

Ryder tipped the bellhop, double-locked the door, and pulled the drapes. (Thereby shutting out the view of the harbor. Terry would have liked this view; he could see from Sheung Wa to North Point and on this clear smog-free day he could actually distinguish the cols and crevices of the New Territories' mountains looming behind Kowloon.) He unpacked his suitcase, took off his cotton trousers and light blue jacket, and worked carefully for the next hour to recreate Roger Hiller. He couldn't be careless this time. The man he was going to see was no Professor Mok. When he had finished, he studied himself carefully in the mirror. Vandyke. Slicked-back black hair. Dark glasses. Plump cheeks. Goodly belly, fat even, since the pillow he had purchased was a bit larger than he would have liked. Loose-fitting but still good-looking safari suit. He was the same Roger Hiller who had revealed himself on Hollywood Boulevard. He was the Roger Hiller they were looking for in Hong Kong, the Roger Hiller he wanted them to be seeking in Manila.

"I don't expect this to fool Junius Oakland," he had explained to Terry as they cruised to the airport. "He knows very well I'm a face-changer. But he can't afford not to alert his allies to be on the lookout for one Roger Hiller. I appeared in this disguise in Los Angeles. I reappeared in Hong Kong. Maybe I'll pop up again in Manila. Sun Tzu said, 'The enemy must never know where I intend to give battle. For if he doesn't know that, then he must prepare in all directions. In many places. And when he prepares in many places, he leaves only a few men to face me when I do attack.' "

And Terry had replied, "Sun Tzu also said, 'All warfare is based on deception.' Which is what Chairman Mao also said twenty-four hundred years later. 'It is also possible by adopting all kinds of measures of deception to drive the enemy into foolish defensive measures.' Sun Tzu said the enemy is deceived by creating shapes, Mao said, by creating illusions."

"Sun Tzu? Mao? What's this all about?"

And she had pointed to her purse and he obediently reached in, fumbled past the pistol, and pulled out two books. *The Selected Works of Mao* and Sun Tzu's *Art of*

War. "There's a marvelous bookstore two blocks from the hotel. Swindon's. While you have been sulking these last four days, I've been reading. The owner of the store is a most considerate Chinese gentleman. He told me if I was interested in Sun Tzu, then I should read his greatest and most influential pupil, Mao-Tse Tung, especially his *Guerrilla Warfare* and *On the Protracted War.* I know now what an expendable spy is. You're not the expendable type; your bosses don't supply you with fabricated information and have you feed it to the enemy. Like the British did to deceive the Germans about Normandy. You don't qualify. You're Sun Tzu's exemplar of the living spy. A living spy is a man who is intelligent but appears stupid, who seems dull but is strong at heart, agile, vigorous, hardy, and brave. That's my master spy."

And as he looked at Roger Hiller's face in the mirror, he felt touched all over again. She was the peacemaker, the adult guiding her sulking child. If they pulled this mission off, it would be because of her grace. She showed up better and better with each passing day, while he acted more and more like a spoiled brat. He told himself solemnly, "I seem dull because I am dull. She can't transform me by magic. Her personal magic. I know myself better than that."

Bracing his shoulders, he inched the door open. He couldn't let anyone see Roger Hiller emerge from Arthur Twilling's room. From this moment on he was in danger. He had no doubt Li Ngor Sheung had his people on the lookout for Roger Hiller. And in a short while he would be facing one of Li's colleagues. Chow Woon Chung might be briefed on Roger Hiller, but he doubted it. Chow had a full-time job running arms to many if not all of the revolutionary groups in the world; he could hardly be expected to be an immigration cop also.

The coast was clear. He scurried to the concrete stairway, hidden behind paneled walls, and walked down six flights. At the second floor he took the overpass to the arcade in Prince's Building, bought a suitcase in the Prince Luggage Shop, went next door to the Harris Bookstore, filled the suitcase with thirty paperback books, walked down to Des Voeux, and took a cab to the Luk Kwok on Gloucester Road in the Wanchai district.

Without appearing to see anything except the registration desk, he itemized and scrutinized every furnishing, every person in the lobby. And this wasn't any great feat, since the Luk Kwok lobby would have fit in the travel agency office at the Peninsula. To the left, the registration desk—a plain rectangular hole in the wall. Elevators straight ahead. Dim sum restaurant to the right. Only three patrons, even though the clock said one thirty-five, peak lunch time for the Chinese.

"I'm Roger Hiller. You have a reservation for me for tonight. I'll pay in advance if you don't mind. Just in and out, you know. That's my bag over there."

The fourth floor room cost seventy dollars Hong Kong —about fifteen dollars U.S. A far cry from the Peninsula or Mandarin. But fifteen dollars buys fifteen dollars, and two hundred and fifty buys two hundred and fifty. Basic lesson of life. At least the twin beds looked comfortable and inviting. He had four hours to kill. (A bad choice of verb, that; four hours to pass through. Better.) He could nap or he could eat. And incidentally get out of this trap. For so long as he stayed at the Luk Kwok he was vulnerable. Perhaps the Chinese clerk had already phoned to report the arrival of the much-wanted Roger Hiller. Perhaps Li Ngor Sheung had already dispatched a team to appropriate him. Perhaps he was even now phoning Junius Oakland in Tokyo.

"Don't wait until tomorrow to get here. Catch the seven-thirty flight and get here tonight. Because I've got your man trapped. Just as you described him to me in the Polo Lounge. And using the same name. Roger Hiller. Hurry."

Perhaps. Perhaps. Perhaps. What had Oakland promised Li this time? What could Li—the People's Republic—want so badly they would let themselves wash Oakland's dirty linen? Professor Mok thought it might be energy-related. Maybe. But the more he had thought about this possibility, the more disenchanted he had become. Li—the Chinese—were hardly fools. With the overthrow of the Gang of Four, the Chinese no longer regarded themselves as outcasts. They were hell-bent for leather on joining the Western—anyway, the modern—world. They no longer had to steal men or knowledge. They could buy or borrow both—and the Western powers and Japan would scramble for the privilege of supplying them with all the energy production China could possibly absorb. Energy maybe. But if he knew his Li—as type, not as man; he knew little more about Li than that he had the best teeth and happiest smile in the world—the Chinese secret agent would want secret information. Of what? Even God might have to guess. With China now encroaching on first, second-, and third-world powers in every continent, Li and his superiors might focus their demands for secret information on any country from Afghanistan to Zaire. Zaire? Zaire by any name would always spell Russia. Li—the Chinese—were obsessed by Russia. They didn't like Russians as a people. (They liked Americans, but this flattering acceptance was a bit tainted in that they also liked Germans. What possible similarity could the Chinese see in Germans and Americans?) They didn't like Russians as a government. And they were beyond paranoia in their dislike of Russians as a military. Genghis Khan and Batu Khan and Berke Khan and the whole Golden Horde had the right idea. The only good Russian soldier was a dead Russian soldier.

Carrying a briefcase, once again Ryder carefully walked down the back stairs. He could just picture the scenario if he were to use the elevator. He would ride it down, the doors would open on the lobby, and six burly Chinese thugs would surround him and hustle him to a waiting black car. Funeral car. No, he needed a preliminary peek at the lobby.

And he slid open the lobby door and as far as he could see nothing had changed. No burly thugs. No unusual activity at the registration desk. Only two customers left in the restaurant. Briskly he swung the door wide, walked the fifteen steps across the lobby, went out into the blazing heat of Gloucester Road, and walked quietly one block to the Swiss Inn. If anyone followed him, he was unaware of it.

The tiny bar was immediately to the left of the entrance, the dining room to the right—and both in authentic mountain Swiss decor. He sat at the bar, ordered a San Miguel beer, and sweated even in the refrigerated air. This was the naked moment. He was unarmed. Helpless. Terry had proffered her Browning High Power, but he had declined. "Chow Woon Chung is no Tony Giambruno. There is no way I will be allowed in his presence with a pistol at my belt. I must go into this as helpless as a newborn babe."

The front door was jerked open and he jumped. But it was only three tall, blond, blue-eyed Aryan German Swiss. They whooped as they saw the waiter and addressed him in idiomatic Swiss. Ryder could make out every fourth word, but the young Chinese replied as if he had been born in Altdorf, Uri, itself.

He finished the beer as slowly as possible, ordered a second, finished that even more slowly, went into the dining room and lingered over a garoupa and tea until it was three-thirty. More relaxed now, almost prepared to believe he had not been blown as yet, he went outside, walked down Gloucester to the corner of Fenwick and waited until a cab deigned to pause and pick up a street passenger. He could see the doubt in the driver's eyes. Where did he want to go, up in the hills, maybe, far away from any possible return pick-up?

He settled the matter as soon as they were launched

down the one-way feeder street into Harcourt. He said a few words in English, saw the incomprehension and switched to Cantonese. He didn't want to, but otherwise there could be no possible way of communicating what he had to say. This was a British Crown Colony. In theory all the Chinese had a mastery of rudimentary English. But this was theory. This driver—most drivers—knew enough English to understand destination words and prices and that was it. He said, "Mr. Gong," (the driver's card read Gong San Lim) "I would like your services until six-thirty tonight. That's three hours. In three hours you could possibly expect to make one hundred, possibly even one hundred and twenty-five dollars." This would come to about twenty to twenty-five U.S. dollars. "That's if everything went perfectly and you got good tips. You can estimate better than I your chances for accomplishing this." In truth, if Mr. Gong did fifty dollars he could have cause to celebrate. "Here is my proposal. Because I want you to wait for me for perhaps an hour while I talk to some people, and I want a cab available the minute I have finished my meeting, I will pay you five hundred dollars. If this proposal is agreeable, I will tear this five hundred dollar bill in half and give you half now. I will supply the remaining half when I see you after my meeting and you take me to my destination on the island."

The Chinese did not labor long on that one. He grinned and said, "If I told my wife what you just said, she would want to know exactly what you are up to, and she would also want me to hand over the five hundred dollars. She is saving up for a color TV." He reached his hand back. "A man can do other things with five hundred dollars. Wives never understand the need for this, not even after four thousand years of Chinese history, custom, and experience. And they never know not to pry into matters that are none of their concern. Not even Chairman Mao was able to stop them."

"In that case, let's enjoy ourselves. I haven't done a

sightseeing tour here in many years. Let's go back out Queensway to Yee Wo, up Tai Hang to the Tiger Balm Gardens. Why not? It's been so many years since I first saw them. Who knows when I'll be able to see them again? We won't stop, though. It's too hot. And then let's go over Wong Nei Chung Gap Road to Aberdeen and back by way of Tai Tam to Shau Kei Wan. That's our eventual goal. I'll want you to park on Nam Hong Street while I make my visit. If you could plan the trip so that we get there about four forty-five, this will make a perfect afternoon."

The round-faced Cantonese—for Kwantung was where he was obviously from, probably San-Shui village by the sound of his dipthongs—nodded. "One of the great sightseeing tours of the world, I'm told. This will be the first time I'll be able to enjoy it like a tourist. And with a foreigner who speaks my language as if he were almost a native of Tai-shan." So it wasn't San-shui. A timely reminder not to let himself get smug. "But if I may ask, why didn't you learn Mandarin? There are so many of them, but so few of us."

He replied in Mandarin, "But then how could I talk to a waiter in San Francisco?"

The driver laughed. "A witty white devil. They are the worst. May I ask two questions? Will you be in one piece when you come back after your visit?"

"Yes. Else I'll not be coming back at all."

"Ha! My poor five hundred dollars. The next question: will we be followed?"

"Most certainly. And I'll hand you over your half the minute I get in the cab. But I do not foresee any trouble for you."

The driver nodded. "You won't have to. I'll do the foreseeing for myself. Four forty-five it is, then. I'll get you there on time."

And he did.

29

Harry Ryder walked down Nam Hong and turned left on Shau Kei Wan. He walked leisurely. He was the boulevardier American tourist window-shopping as American tourists have ever done.

His destination was one block down Shau Kei Wan. Across the street. A standard stereo shop no different from hundreds of its kind in Hong Kong or Kowloon. Terry had been awed by the endless succession of antique shops, curio shops, stereo, clothing, camera, perfume, leather goods, gift, fur, diamond, china, glassware, men's tailor, women's tailor, shirt, shoe, pearl, watch, general jewelry, furniture, lamp, cloth, silver, handicraft, art, rug, drug, dress and jade shops, not to mention restaurants and department stores. "My first couple of days I thought it was just around Nathan Street in Kowloon, and in central Hong Kong on the island. But it's every street. In all directions. An incredible supermarket of goods. Who can possibly buy all this stuff?"

The sign read "Chow Woon Chung, Stereos." But the window held an enormous ivory tusk carved into an incredibly intricate landscape bridge. Temple, gardens, people strolling, waterfalls, soldiers. A teeming medieval scene. With a discreet price tag. H.K. dollars: a hundred twenty thousand. Twenty-six thousand U.S. Terry was right. Who could buy it? He looked past the ivory and jade. A typical deep narrow room with stereo equipment piled high along the walls, behind the counters. Not a single customer present, but eight clerks standing patiently, three women and five men. Whoever was buying was not buying from Chow Woon Chung. He wandered in the door and smiled idiotically at a Buddha-like, most imposing giant of a man sitting behind the counter just to

133

the right. All the Chinese watched Ryder. All could see that he was quite intimidated by Mr. Buddha. They blinked their eyes when he stopped before a petite and unusually pretty girl. (Terry had pointed out that most of the Cantonese women were not naturally pretty. But they often had an eerie serenity that lent a radiance to their faces. As a result they could be even more beautiful than if they were naturally beautiful. He had professed to understand her.) He peered down at the counter before the girl. It held trays of diamond rings, jade ornaments, and Omega watches.

He spoke to the girl. Almost a whisper. "Is Mr. Chow in?"

Her eyes flickered to the giant Buddha and she pointed. Harry glanced at his watch. Exactly five. By now Terry was sitting in the Cessna 310 and was going through the check-off. "At three o'clock," he had told her, "I want you to sign out of the Peninsula. Here's cash. It should cover everything. About eight thousand Hong Kong I should guess. Also, please turn in your Porsche. Take a cab to the airport. Don't take the hotel Rolls. Then file a flight plan for Kaohsiung. That won't fool anybody who really wants to track us. But if David Thompson or anybody else checks on our first destination, he'll see it's Taiwan and be at peace. We'll stay overnight in Kaohsiung at the Holiday Inn and go on to Taipei first thing tomorrow morning. Here are our passports; I've gotten the Taiwan visas all set. Be sitting in the plane and have it ready to take off from five-thirty on. We may have to move fast.

"Be sure to keep away from Mr. David Thompson." (Thompson had been highly annoyed to have Ryder present on the trial run. As soon as he had seen that Terry knew all about the intricacies of a 310, he had sat glowering in a back seat. Terry had been quite right. Thompson had other plans for this excursion.) "I don't want you raped at this juncture."

"I'm sorry," he said to the pretty girl. "I meant Mr. Chow Woon Chung."

The girl's face snapped shut, a blank wall. No one could do this sort of thing better than the Chinese. Ryder refrained from looking toward the rear of the store. There sat a nondescript skinny little fellow of about fifty-five or sixty. He was wearing shorts, a sports shirt with short sleeves. His face had a subservient, idiotic expression on it. His back was against a small door. Ryder knew this door led to a gigantic block-long warehouse that fronted on Shau Kei Wan Harbor. Ammunition was taken from the warehouse to Chow Woon Chung's own fleet of shabby ocean-going tramp steamers, all registered in Panama or Liberia under perfectly anonymous corporate names. No one—but no one—could ever trace their ownership. Ryder had once spent three months trying to unravel the corporate maze and given up. Mr. Chow Woon Chung looked the idiot. He was as good in his cover as Ryder was in his. Terry Jefferson could have been proud of both of them. Living spies both.

The Buddha unraveled himself from his stool, waddled to Ryder like a bear. "I am Chow Chan Sang. May I help you?"

"Certainly, sir." A family enterprise, this. The Chows came originally from Chung-shan in Kwangtung. Every person in the shop and the warehouse, all the freighter captains, and a goodly part of the crews were Chows. "I wish to speak to you about some specialized merchandise."

Ryder gestured feebly. He was a modest man who preferred to speak in privacy, away from busy ears.

"Specialized merchandise?" The Buddha's placid eyes looked from one end of the store to the other, took in the Pioneer stereos, the jade, the watches, the rings, the ivory. He even threw out his hands in a classic gesture of bewilderment. He made it official, since Ryder's flaccid face showed total incomprehension. "I do not understand."

"Please," Ryder said. He leaned closer as if he wanted to whisper to Mr. Chow Chan Sang. He did whisper. But the skinny idiot at the rear had no trouble picking up his words. "I am told by Delfin Caumiran and Nolly Maglayo that you would be able to help me."

Now the silence in the store was absolute. Suddenly the street noises seemed a gushing torrent of sound. The silence in the room continued. The giant kept staring directly at Ryder, then shrugged. Obviously he had picked up a message. His peripheral vision must have been phenomenal. "Follow me."

Ryder turned after him, went through the large door at the rear. The skinny man had disappeared through his small door. He now sat behind a messy desk in a large office. Books and papers were piled everywhere—on the floor, on chairs, on shelves. Mr. Chow Woon Chung was not the model clean desk executive. He looked deferential and idiotic as ever, except that his piercing eyes could not maintain the front. He tried to keep shifting them around, but they kept coming back to meet Ryder's eyes.

"I am Chow Woon Chung. Who are you?"

"My name is Hiller, Mr. Chow. Roger Hiller."

The two Chows pondered this and came up with nothing. So Li Ngor Sheung had not briefed them. If he had, Harry Ryder's career as master spy would have ended right then and there.

"You mentioned two names."

"Yes, Delfin Caumiran and Nolly Maglayo."

"Who are they?"

He would have liked to refresh Chow Woon Chung's memory. It was 1945. In the terraces above Bantoc in Mountain Province of Luzon. General Tomoyuko Yamashita was holed up below Bantoc. The Americans were making no effort to go after him. The war was coming to an end. Time and the hangman's noose would take care of Yamashita. And one night late in June, Harry the

American sat with a group of Filipino guerrillas around a fire and for the first time heard the name Hukbalahap and learned that his wonderful wartime allies were not quite the saints he had come to love and admire. Sitting cross-legged on the outskirts, another outlander, a skinny young Chinese, also listened intently to the conversation. His eyes had glistened as the Filipinos—the Huks—told of the landlords they had marked for murder. He had only spoken once. "Right now you have plenty of guns. But they will not last or be enough. Not in the future. I will see that you are supplied." And the men he addressed were Caumiran and Maglayo, cousins of Gus Gutierrez, who had sat off to the side looking faintly troubled. Gus, the printer, was never as bloodthirsty as his cousins. Yes, he would have liked to prod Mr. Chow's memory.

"They are my friends. They live at present in Baguio."
"How do you know them?"
"I have done them a few favors. Not in the mountains. But the New People's Army has occasionally needed a helping hand in Manila and Washington. I have been glad to oblige."

The Chows considered this. They considered him. They took in his good-looking clothes, his fat body, his dull, vacuous expression. (Ryder was sure he controlled his eyes better than Chow Woon Chung did his. He had worked hard on this art over the years. The trick was to keep his eyes out of focus.) They assessed the words *Manila* and *Washington*. The skinny Chow suddenly nodded.

"We hear many stories in Hong Kong, Mr. Hiller. We believe a part of all of them. Mostly they do not concern us, so we ignore them. What should concern us in your story?"

"Mr. Chow, my affairs have taken an unexpected turn. I am not a man of action, you understand. But sometimes even a sloth like me must bestir himself. I find myself with enemies who do not work in my metier, which is words and contracts and contacts. They deal in violence. I foresee that I must respond in kind. But I do not wish to make a noise about this, if you follow me. I need a silenced weapon."

Neither Chow moved a muscle. Chow Woon Chung said, "Where are you staying, Mr. Hiller?"

"At the Luk Kwok."

Chow Chan Sang picked up the telephone. He spoke in Cantonese and when he said Chow Woon Chung wanted the information, he plainly met no objection. He said, "You are there for only one night."

Ryder reached in his pocket and passed him a plane ticket. "I am booked on JAL for Tokyo at nine forty-five tomorrow morning. At the moment I must move faster than I like."

They examined the ticket carefully. Chow Woon Chung said, "May I see your passport, Mr. Hiller?"

The same scrutiny took place. They studied Gus Gutierrez's handsomely forged visa marks in the Roger Hiller passport: Japan, Taiwan, Philippines, Indonesia. They read the entry date into Hong Kong. "You arrived this morning, the sixth, and you are leaving tomorrow the seventh." Junius Oakland was arriving the eighth, but he did not point this out. "That does not give us much time for our discussion." Chow Woon Chung had been speaking softly and slowly. Suddenly his voice took on a hard rasp. He shot out the words. "How did you know my cousin was not me? Where have we met?"

"We have never met, Mr. Chow." This was the truth and would have registered as the truth on a polygraph. That night above Bantoc no one had introduced him to the Chinese. "You were described to me. Your cousin seemed somewhat different from the description I had."

A glint of amusement crossed Chow's face. He handed back the passport. He spoke to his cousin. In Cantonese. "Tell Chow Bik to be ready to follow this fellow." As he spoke, his eyes bored into Ryder. This was rather a trying moment. It is very difficult not to betray understanding. He looked back steadily at Chow Woon Chung and kept his eyes so unfocused he did not even see Chow's face. This, he knew made him look excessively dull and vacuous. But ever such is the living spy. Chow continued, "Set up the usual routine. I want to know what this fellow is really up to. He may be a professional assassin. Fair enough, but we may not want his target assassinated. Tell Chow Bik if he does anything the least bit suspicious, bring him back." He did not say dead or alive. The Buddha nodded and left the room to contact Chow Bik. Chow Woon Chung switched to English. "Please follow me, Mr. Hiller."

Ryder felt an absurd impulse to protest. "I am not a professional assassin. There is no one in the world more peace-loving than I." But he stood up and followed the skinny man through a concealed door into Chow's real office. It was paper free. And as he stepped through the door a buzzer sounded. Two men sitting in the beautifully furnished room sprang to their feet. He was reminded of Tony Giambruno's office. Both Chow and Giambruno were lovers of art and objects of beauty, only Chow's taste was entirely Chinese. The scrolls and prints and vases and rugs and chairs in that room were, he suspected, beyond price. The room temperature, he noticed, was considerably cooler than the outer office. Probably set to seventy-two, like a museum, to protect these priceless antiques from the Han, Ming, Sui, Ching, and God-knows-what dynasties. The buzzing sound continued and Chow looked reproachfully at Ryder.

"My God, an airport electronic scanner. Sorry." He reached into his pocket and pulled out a handful of heavy coins. "Let's try it without these." Uttering a prayer of thanks for not having the Browning High Power with him, he went back through the scanner and the machine voiced no protest. "Your Hong Kong coins are still substantially built. Inflation has not reached here yet."

Chow Chan Sang returned and nodded. The surveillance team was set up. It would consist of four men on foot and one or two large cars. If he took off in his own car, they would all pile in and follow him. The driver would know his trade.

"Mr. Hiller," Chow Woon Chung said, "silenced weapons are very difficult things to come by. The authorities are unusually squeamish about guns that kill silently. Arms, from pistols to tanks, can be supplied by the boatload to revolutionaries and the authorities say boys will be boys. But a silencer? A silencer is the tool of a criminal mentality."

He was enjoying himself, so Ryder nodded his comprehension. "True enough. But today even the military—some militaries—have taken a lesson from the criminal mentality. Differences blur."

Chow Woon Chung nodded. He was dealing with a professional. "Yes, the military. The military bent. Without it, and its gift for waste, people like me would be jobless. I do not invent my merchandise, Mr. Hiller. I simply scrounge up the leavings from the military feasts."

And use those leavings to supply the revolutionaries in Angola, Rhodesia, Libya, Lebanon, Italy, Germany, France, Indonesia, the Philippines, Cambodia, Laos, all the countries in South America, and any and all groups, parties, armies, criminals, terrorists, and just plain citizens who might want to kill someone. There are an awful lot of such people on the face of this earth. Ryder nodded his understanding and waited patiently.

"Such handguns are also quite expensive, Mr. Hiller."

Ryder shrugged.

"Good. Then let me see what I can scrounge up from my leavings."

This time he did not speak to his men. He pulled out a piece of paper and drew a series of ideographs. The man —he could have been a brother of Ryder's round-faced cab driver—took the paper and returned carrying one gun in a plastic bag. Chow waved for it to be given to Hiller.

He pulled it out and looked at it distastefully. It was an unusually ugly-looking weapon. The silencer was a thick ugly unevenly machined tube that sat above the barrel and extended back above the trigger. Like bugs copulating. Not your usual-looking silencer at all.

He shook his head. "This is an assassination weapon, Mr. Chow. The Type 64. Put out by the People's Republic oddly enough, even though assassination is not the PRC's usual modus operandi. It's quite large, over thirteen inches, and it weighs over three pounds. That's just too much. Manually operated it is quite silent. But as a self-loader, it's not really up to snuff, is it?"

The Chows sighed ever so slightly. Roger Hiller was not an assassin. The man went out and brought back another handgun. He took one look and his face showed even greater disappointment. No Chinese trader would ever have any trouble following Roger Hiller's likes and dislikes. It was the Szech Model 61—the Skorpion.

"This is really a submachine gun, Mr. Chow. Quite fine for a Valentine's Day massacre. But its cyclic rate of fire is just too fast. It simply can't function silently. Not as silently as I would like, anyway. I'm sorry."

Chow Woon Chung nodded. "Nevertheless, I appreciate your professionalism, Mr. Hiller. You'd be surprised at how rare that is. Pardon me, of course you wouldn't be surprised. Ah, the gulf between amateur and professional. I do have a Sleeve Gun." Ryder repressed a start. The Sleeve Gun is an antique, but in its prime, many OSS men behind many lines owed their lives to its silent effectiveness. "But it's really somewhat beaten up. It was actually found ten years after the war beside a mountain trail in Burma. Well. I seem to be running short of ideas. I do have some other silenced submachine guns. The Sterling Mark 5, for instance. But as you say, it is just a submachine gun. Perhaps you have some ideas?"

Ryder could not repress a laugh. "You have me, don't you? Well, beggars can't be bargainers. Yes, I think you know what I want. A Hush-Puppy."

He did not try to conceal his enthusiasm. In the first place, no American could outbargain a Chinese. He could smell a buyer's passion or lack of it. And in the second place, if he tried to conceal everything, he would conceal nothing. He had to keep his mind on his cover, not on buying protocol. Mr. Chow nodded. He seemed almost sorry for Hiller, like a man squashing a spider. Spiders are good things but they must be squashed.

"I think we may have one."

In a moment the assistant came back with another plastic bag. Reverently Ryder took out the automatic and the unattached silencer. Their combined weight was under three pounds, the length under thirteen inches. This was the Smith and Wesson Model 39, the finest military handgun he had ever seen. With the silencer it became the Hush-Puppy, since it had been used to hush puppies—nasty war dogs they were, really—in the Vietnam War. From time to time they had also been used to hush nasty two-legged puppies.

He unscrewed the silencer and examined the silencer insert carefully. The insert for the Hush-Puppy is good for about thirty rounds of subsonic cartridges—but it would last only six or seven shots of standard, full-strength bullets. As far as he could see, the silencer insert was brand new. He sighed and looked up at the politely attentive Chinese.

"How much?"

A flicker of disappointment on Chow's face. The American was taking the fun out of the game. There would not be the leisurely civilized haggle. Just a price.

"Twenty thousand dollars. U.S."

Ryder's astonishment was unfeigned. In fact, it bordered on the thunderstruck. "Twenty thousand. . . . I'm sorry. I do want a silenced weapon. I want this silenced weapon very badly. It's perfect for my purpose. But even if I do value my life at more then twenty thousand dollars, I don't have that kind of money."

New, a Smith and Wesson Model 39 might cost somewhere around three hundred dollars. With an illegal silencer, it's value would be several thousand dollars. He had expected to pay around five thousand U.S.

He stood up and bowed to each of the Chows. "Thank you, gentlemen. I'm afraid I shall have to defend myself noisily. Well, maybe I can set the scene in a soundproofed room. A silenced room I can afford."

The Chows made no move. Chow Woon Chung said, "Mr. Hiller, the Hush-Puppy is in extremely scarce supply. It's even scarcer than the High Standard HDM Military the CIA likes to use. That's the gun the Russians found on Gary Powers when they shot him down."

"I know the gun. It uses a twenty-two long rifle cartridge. I prefer the Hush-Puppy's nine-millimeter Parabellum. I'm not that good a marksman to be comfortable with a Twenty-two."

"And being scarce, the Hush-Puppy simply must command a high price, one that might even be called exorbitant." Chow's face had a glow to it. He was delighted with the turn of the conversation. The American was bargaining. He might not know he was bargaining, but bargaining he was. The spider would be squashed delicately. "I'm sure you knew this when you came in here. We did not ask you here. You asked yourself. Surely you didn't plan on wasting our time like this?"

It was five-forty. Terry would surely be sitting at the controls, the flight plan filed. He laughed, and in spite of himself it was an infectious, merry laugh. "Gentlemen, I was prepared for what I thought was an expensive purchase. Not for a Kohinor diamond. I thought I would be paying around five thousand dollars. I expected you to set an opening price of about seventy-five hundred. I would counter with twenty-five. And like civilized human beings we would settle on five thousand. We would both be happy. The essence of the fair contract, two satisfied participants."

Chow Woon Chung shook his head. He was quite sad. "I see. Well, frankly I don't see. You are a professional. At least, you talk like a professional. You know guns. Surely, you must know prices better than that. Five thousand dollars? Out of the question. The lowest price my cousin and I have ever considered was seventy-five hundred dollars. And that would only have been to a close colleague."

Ryder nodded. He reached in his safari jacket and pulled out a calendar case. From it he extracted seven bills. He showed that the case was now empty. "Mr. Chow, here is my capital. Seven thousand dollars. Oh, I have some Hong Kong dollars in my pocket. Walking-around money to get me out of the city tomorrow morning. Now, here are seven one thousand dollar bills. This is money in hand. It is not idle capital, an idle gun, sitting in a safe. It can earn interest. In one year it will be worth much more than seventy-five hundred dollars. And, though I am not your close colleague, I am a close colleague of colleagues of yours. The seven thousand dollars are yours, gentlemen. For the gun."

He set them on the magnificent Ming table. The Chows could have taken them and dumped him in Shau Kei Wan Harbor. He could see them considering this. But he was, after all, a colleague of a colleague. Chow nodded. "Yes, I must remember Nolly and Delfin. They are indeed my good friends. For them I will do that which is against all my principles. You may have the Hush-Puppy, Mr. Hiller. . . ."

Ryder raised his hand but Chow continued. "And we will even throw in the Accessory Kit, the MK26. Complete with twenty-four rounds of subsonic cartridges. There is also an extra silencer insert. We do have a contract. Maybe when the interest mounts up on the seven thousand dollars I will be prepared to agree it is a fair contract."

Ryder wanted to ask them bluntly, "What was your lowest price, you slimy bastards? Just how much did you take me for?" Instead, he placed the pistol, silencer, and accessory kit in his briefcase, bowed, and said, "Gentlemen, thank you for your courtesy." He turned. "Will this thing buzz at me as I go through?"

"It has been turned off, Mr. Hiller. A pleasant voyage to Tokyo."

He walked through the messy office into the narrow store. There were still no customers. It was six o'clock. Outside the door the surveillance team was waiting for him. Maybe its mission included the retrieval of the Hush-Puppy.

He smiled at the pretty girl. "Thank you, miss. You have wonderful specialized merchandise in your store."

30

Six o'clock on Shau Kei Wan Road was prime shopping time. Throngs paraded up and down the sidewalks. Somewhere amidst them four men were watching him. A car was standing by, motor idling, ready to take off. The men he could never spot, not in this mob scene. The car was easy. It was a gigantic Mercedes. One of those enormous extra-length jobs used by ambassadors. And gangsters.

He walked to the corner, turned up Nam Hong and seemed about to jaywalk. He paused in the street, watching the traffic. His back was to Gong, the cab driver.

"Start your motor, Mr. Gong. Do it quietly, gently. In a moment I will get into your cab. Go down Shau Kei Wan with the light. Toward Wanchai. I'll get in as soon as you say you're ready to pull out."

The motor started. Gong said, "Now."

Moving without undue haste, he turned and eased himself into the rear. The cab swung nicely into Shau Kei Wan. With a clear stretch in front of him for two blocks, Gong shot up to thirty-five. Ryder leaned forward and adjusted the rear-view mirror so he could see the Mercedes. It swung out from its parking place. Of necessity it moved so fast it could not stop to pick up four men who had leaped into the street. "You may go more slowly now, Mr. Gong." He handed him the missing half of the five hundred dollar bill. "We are being followed two blocks back by a large Mercedes. Do not try to escape it."

As far as he could make out from the mirror, the Mercedes had only two riders in the front seat. Ryder opened his briefcase and took out his purchase and assembled the silencer to pistol. Gong turned to watch him from time to time.

"So you called on Chow Woon Chung. I wondered if that was your destination. Please keep the gun under your briefcase. People can see into the cab from second-story windows and from buses. They may not identify you, but they can certainly identify me."

"Very wise, Mr. Gong. Please continue down King's Road and Causeway to Des Voeux. I would like you to leave me off at Prince's Building. Just slow down and I'll hop out."

"What are you looking at that bullet so closely for? Pardon my curiosity, but you expose me to a world I have of course heard about—after all, this is Hong Kong—but I have never ever been involved in."

"I'm making sure I got what I bought. Can you see the green tip on the bullet? That's a distinctive mark. This bullet has less powder in it, so it comes out at subsonic speed. This is essential for a truly silenced effect."

"Very interesting. In view of all this, I have changed my

mind about what I will do with the five hundred dollars. I will give them to my wife after all. She deserves to hear this story. I daresay all Hong Kong will know about it from her in a few days, but I imagine you will not be staying long in our beautiful city. However, I will not tell her until the day after tomorrow."

"Thank you, Mr. Gong." The mirror revealed a glint in the front seat of the Mercedes. Were they going to shoot at the cab? He started to alert Mr. Gong, then subsided. One of the men was holding a telephone to his ear. Reinforcements were being summoned, directions given. "Please time your approach to Prince's Building so the Mercedes is at least a block back. They have a telephone and are calling for help."

"Gladly, sir. With one proviso. I must make sure they see you get out. I don't want them pursuing me through the Central District. I want them pursuing you. You understand?"

"Very wise again, Mr. Gong. I will be happy to accommodate you."

And, so, serenely they paraded down Causeway, Yen Wo, Hennessey, Queensway, and Des Voeux. At the corner of Ice House Street Ryder patted Gong on the shoulder, said his thanks again, and sprang out. Now there was no delay. He sprinted into the building. As he disappeared, he saw the Mercedes shoot forward and a door open. From now on, the timing would be close. He trotted to the elevator bank, pushed his way through a door that was just closing, got off on the Arcade floor and half-strode, half-trotted across Chater Road overpass to the Mandarin Hotel. Here he had to wait fifteen seconds for an elevator to come. As the door closed, he saw a thin, tiny, Chinese sprint around the corner. For a moment their eyes met. The Chinese was in a state of towering rage. And anxiety. Mr. Chow Woon Chung did not pay his help to fail at their jobs. Ryder sighed. This episode was not over.

He took the elevator to the tenth floor. The elevators formed a central bank. Corridors were at either end of the bank. He walked to the right corridor, stood at the corner so that his body was half-exposed. He took out the loaded, assembled Hush-Puppy from the briefcase, set the briefcase on the thick carpet, held the Hush-Puppy by his right leg. Terry had been right. His way was too complicated. Someone would be shooting at him. He hoped he would be able to shoot back. Hoped because a sudden thought sent his body into a paroxysm of panic. Was Chow Woon Chung's gift of the bullets an Oriental fraud? Would the goddamned things work or were they actually powderless?

He started to raise the gun to fire one round into the beautiful carpet when the elevator door opened and the tiny Chinese sprang out. He saw Ryder instantly. A look of horrible joy crossed his features. He waited until the elevator disappeared and whipped out a pistol.

"You should not have run," he said. "We were told if you did anything suspicious we should bring you back."

"Dead or alive, I suppose."

"Ced or alive." He waved the pistol. "Please step out. We will walk down the stairs."

Ryder replied in Cantonese, "Sun Tzu said, 'To a surrounded enemy you must always leave a way of escape.'"

And while the Chinese's eyes grew wide with astonishment, he whipped the Hush-Puppy forward and pulled the trigger and, joy of joys, the Hush-Puppy gave a phut and the Chinese crumbled onto the floor. He grabbed his left thigh with both hands. His pistol tumbled four feet away. Ryder picked up his briefcase and walked forward.

"I am a very bad shot." He still spoke in Cantonese. "I aimed for your heart. But, after all, you left me no way of escape. I had no choice." He leaned forward and whacked the recumbent moaner on the head. The moans stopped. He picked up the gangster's pistol. Two for the price of one. Still probably a bad bargain. He walked down the stairs to the eighth floor and went to room eight-seventeen.

Twenty minutes later Arthur Twilling Aka Peter McClaren—thin, hollow-cheeked, bespectacled, bemoustached—came out of the room. The silencer was in his left pocket, the newly acquired pistol—a Heckler and Kock 7.65 millimeter it was—in his right, and the Smith and Wesson Model 39 Hush-Puppy at his belt in the rear. He felt like a walking fort. The Roger Hiller disguise was left behind, carefully packed and locked in the suitcase. A note was attached to the handle: "Have been invited to the New Territories for three weeks. Please hold my suitcase until I return to pick it up. Thank you. Arthur Twilling." Not brilliant, but it should do the job.

He took the elevator to the mezzanine and walked out into the mezzanine bar and restaurant, the Mandarin's counter to the great expanse of the Peninsula's lobby bar and restaurant. He swung around to the right, followed the tables to the end of the room and came to the stairs leading down to the lobby. A muted mob scene confronted him. An ambulance crew was wheeling a gurney from the service elevator. The Chinese gunman lay on it. He was still in a rage, but he could not take his eyes off the great Buddha standing by the registration desk. His eyes were frightened as they followed Mr. Chow Chan Sang, who was talking earnestly to the clerk and the clerk was denying everything. He obviously did not like denying whatever he was denying, but Ryder knew the poor man had no choice. He had never seen a Roger Hiller.

Ryder turned to the right toward the front door and, as he did so, he sensed rather than saw a pair of flashing, smiling white teeth partially hidden behind Mr. Chow Chan Sang. Li Ngor Sheung's teeth. Why not? The Bank of China building, Li's headquarters, was two blocks from the Mandarin. Li could have been called by Chow Woon Chung, or the bank of electronic telephone-sensing devices could have monitored the telephone calls from the

Mercedes to Chow Woon Chung. In any case, however, Li Ngor Sheung now knew that Roger Hiller had surfaced in Hong Kong. Armed and dangerous. Mr. Li would have a lot to tell Junius Oakland tomorrow.

The passenger-loading area was cluttered and impassable, what with a Mercedes, an ambulance, three police cars, and two trapped cabs. The two Chinese assistants from Chow's back office were standing to the right and left of the door and examining all patrons leaving the hotel. Out of the corner of his eye he saw one suddenly leap forward toward a stoutish gentleman who was escorting his wife out the door. Ryder did not look at them. He walked to the Star Ferry underpass, rode the next ferry to Kowloon and took a taxi at the ferry stand to the flying school at Kai Tak airport. He walked out into the parking area, and there was the Cessna 310, a beautiful sight in itself, but more so—understandably more so—with Terry at the controls and waving to him. As he trotted up, she nodded and started the left engine and the lovely 260-horsepower Continental 10 470-US-6 engine sang its lovely song.

He climbed up the wing, swung in beside her, and nodded. "I'm a walking Springfield Armory. I'll tell you about it later. Any problems? Good. Let's get going. The warm-up is over. The ball game begins."

31

He prided himself on being an early riser, but five A.M. was ridiculous. That's what happens when a man goes celibate for a week or so. Time to put a stop to that nonsense. What was his agenda for the day? Wasn't there something on it about the Queen of the Baguio Festival of Flowers?

General Maximus Cruz, Minister of the Interior for all the Philippine Islands—all seven thousand of them, regardless of what the Moros or the NPA or the CIA might think—sprang from his bed, put on his bathrobe and went next door to his office in the Baguio Summer Palace. It was already light. He could see the agenda open on his Philippine mahogany desk. And next to it lay the daily report from his own private intelligence service. Maybe this report was why he hadn't slept well last night. "Apparently as ordered, Ernesto Zamora spent the evening with Congressman Richard Milwhite and two call girls. Price for the pair, $1,500. Reliable sources indicate Milwhite gave careful consideration to the offer of a condominium on Maui. It is not known if he accepted. But the next day Milwhite voted in Committee against revising the lease terms for Subic Bay and Clark Field."

Congressman Milwhite. When would those idiots in Washington learn that just because a man likes to bandy words and actions with a $750 a night bawd, he was not necessarily susceptible to the blandishments of a two hundred and fifty thousand dollar condominium. Bribery was not the way. Why hadn't they gotten the usual incriminating photos of Congressman Milwhite and his lady for the night? Blackmail was always better than bribery. What a shame the powers that be hadn't given him the assignment of corrupting Congressman Milwhite. If he had stage-managed this business, they'd not only have Milwhite's vote but the votes of two of the colleagues Milwhite dominated.

General Cruz ran his eye over the agenda. He was having lunch with Ambassador Johnson and the President. What an idiot, Johnson. He had lost his bid for Governor of California, so they gave him the Philippines. He knew as much about the Philippines as Cruz did about Sacramento. For the millionth time he asked himself how long America could continue as a significant force in the world. God must love that country. His paradise of folly.

Doctors Penniman and Schaustein, representing the American Medical Association, at nine. Colonel Calixto Calugas at ten. What did he want?

Golf at two with the President and an advertising representative from *Newsweek*. Ah, here it was. Crowning of the Beauty Queen and her attendants at five.

That would be emended. He would have a clear shot at the Beauty Queen. The President was taking his wife to dinner at the home of the mayor of Baguio. Great timing. Cruz's bed would not be lonely tonight. And pray God she wasn't one of those emancipated women like that terrible Valentina Moreno. Committing suicide just because a worthy general wanted to screw her. What was this one's name? Mhila Maralan. What a lovely name. What a lovely day this was going to be.

He shaved and bathed and dressed himself and came back to his office and stood by the window. It was raining. It always rained in Baguio. What a beautiful scene. The pines, the swooping vistas, the incredible flowers and the lovely, cooling rain. What a shame all Filipinos couldn't spend a month in Baguio. Wouldn't that be something, to transport every denizen of the Tondo to Baguio for one month. They would emerge from one of the world's worst slums and descend on one of its most beautiful cities. And he laughed aloud. If anyone ever knew the kind of daydreams their tough, cruel, ruthless minister indulged in, how long would he last? The emperor has no clothes on. And he was still chuckling when he heard a knock on the door. Three knocks, then three more knocks. Calugas. At this hour. Six-fifteen. Even before he had breakfast.

He looked at his square-jawed colonel. Now there was a genuinely tough, cruel, ruthless face.

"Yes?"

"He's here. Or on his way. Harry Ryder."

"How do you know?"

"He bought a gun from Chow Woon Chung in Hong Kong. A silenced weapon. A Hush-Puppy. He shot one of Chow's men with the gun he had just bought. And disappeared."

"How do you know all this?"

"I have my sources."

Calugas's eyes were on the intelligence report on the desk. The son-of-a-bitch could read upside down as readily as right side up. Cruz moved back to his desk and picked up the report. Wouldn't his precious Director of the National Security Intelligence Agency be shocked to hear of Cruz's own private intelligence service? The report also told of Calugas's sex life. The miserable bastard had a sixteen-year-old boy holed up in his bedroom. Practically a prisoner. Calugas apparently let the boy whip him each night. Well, each man to his own jollies. "I insist on knowing who your source is. In this one instance, my friend. I don't mind your little secrets. For instance I know you know who heads up the NPA and where the Moro headquarters really are. . . ." Cruz relished the look of astonishment on Calugas's face. ". . . and I couldn't care less. Without the NPA and the Moros, how long would you and I last? But this is different. Who are your sources?"

"A CIA man."

That put a different light on this matter. Was the United States government behind this attempted escape? Did that pathetic Maricar Macasieb in San Francisco have this kind of influence—or was the U.S. president simply trying to get insurance on his treaties? With José Manzano in the United States, the CIA could be setting up another Bay of Pigs. Only this time Luzon would be the target.

"Who?"

"Junius Oakland. He's in Hong Kong. He wants to come here. He's trying to head off Ryder."

"The CIA is not behind the venture? Did I misunderstand something? It's only Macasieb?"

He walked to the window and admired the bougainvillea and orchids growing along the palace wall. He kept his back to Calugas. Someday Calugas would take such an opportunity to stab him. But not today.

"I don't know for sure." Calugas spoke reluctantly. He was still shook up that his boss, the man he considered a depraved nincompoop, should know about the NPA and the Moros. "I think the CIA is in this somehow, somewhere. But I get the impression Oakland is after Ryder."

"Well, so are we. What are you doing to stop him?"

"I have a photograph here of the way Ryder looks now. Oakland sent it to me after Ryder surfaced in Los Angeles."

"You've had it all this time and haven't shown it to me!"

"I didn't trust it. I remember Ryder too well. I was with him on Leyte. He loved to disguise himself. Hell, once he even put on a Japanese uniform and walked into the village and killed eight Japs before they knew what was killing them."

"Disguised as a Jap? How could he get away with it?" Cruz was too intrigued to keep his back turned. He could see Calugas was surprised again at his minister's curiosity. How could such an insensitive man have any concept of what Intelligence work was all about? "Well?"

"He could speak enough Japanese to get away with it."

"A boy of nineteen or twenty? Impossible. No, sorry, tell me about it."

"Ryder enlisted in the Army the day after Pearl Harbor. He lied about his age. But the Army wasn't fooled. They put his baby face with the troops guarding the Jap compound on Molokai. Lepers and Japs. Since he had nothing really to do, he spent his time learning Japanese. Then one day the Army discovered he could speak Visayan and so they shipped him to Leyte with Colonel Kohleon. He's got a talent for languages. He learned Visayan from the Filipinos around Watsonville in California. Now he knows Tagalog and Spanish and Cantonese and God knows how many other languages."

Cruz took the print and examined the portrait with its round face and Vandyke beard.

"Well, I recall him as round-faced. That much agrees. I saw him once in Mountain Province. You didn't trust the picture before. What's changed your mind?"

"That's also the way he looked yesterday in Hong Kong. He stayed at the Luk Kwok Hotel. Under the same name. Roger Hiller."

"And?"

"And so I'm distributing the print to the P.C. and police. Everywhere. I don't know where he'll surface. Of course I'm checking every plane and ship that comes in. But I think he'll slip off some fishing boat and swim to shore. Probably Leyte. Where he's at home."

Cruz started to remonstrate "What idiocy!" Instead he said, "Good. And you'll start the plan with José and his sister?"

"The TV monitors will be turned off today. The front door will become accessible, the guards lax. José and Emerenciana will see they can practically walk out of the place."

"Excellent. And what are your plans if Ryder succeeds? What will you do if they do manage to escape?"

"Manage to escape? Manage to—why that's impossible."

"I know it is. But suppose they get out? After all, we're dealing with Harry the American. The man of many disguises. Where would they go?"

"I don't know. They'd have to hole up someplace. Until the heat cooled down somewhat."

"And where would that be?"

"Why I suppose with the obvious people. Chrisostomo.

Father Armas. Fermi. Garrabato. Mori. Frega. . . ."

"Mori? Frega? I thought you would have them in jail by now."

"Since the papers weren't to be signed until after the American Medical Convention, you know very well they're not in jail yet."

"You're right. I've pictured myself giving you the original papers so often I feel it's already been done. Well, don't put them away yet. Please do this. Let the American community know that José and Emerenciana are plotting an escape. Do it with a wink. That way, if they do get away, we can take credit for it. We got them out of the Philippines because of our great humanitarian heart. Our love of human rights. And at the same time, have men tail each suspected ally on your list. Frega and Mori and all the rest. I want twenty-four-hour surveillance. But don't let them know they are being watched. I don't want José and Emerenciana being scared into sanctuaries we don't know about."

"I tell you, this is not necessary. Fort Malolos is impregnable, and it's escape proof. All right don't look at me like that. I'll do what you say. Though, if you're concerned, why this charade about killing them as they try to escape? I still think we should prop them up against a wall and shoot them down. . . . No? Well, it's a thought."

And that, Cruz mused, was about all it was. Colonel Calixto Calugas was becoming a bore.

Part Three

32

"While I do what control says, that'll give you a chance to photograph Fort Malolos. It's that big park ahead right in the middle of Manila. Quezon City actually. Philippine Army headquarters—where José Manzano and Emerenciana Darang and God knows how many more government opponents are imprisoned. The President and Cruz want to be loved. And the only way they can be sure the people will love them is to keep every recalcitrant locked up."

He slowed the 310 to just above the minimum speed, made a wide turn, and Terry Jefferson shot as fast as she could click the Nikon. "That's your last able-bodied chore. From now on you are what you look. The all-American playgirl."

For Terry was wearing what he called her Jean Harlow wig. Her face was framed like a Botticelli angel—a divinity even the devil would lust for. She laughed, then pointed. "Look at the soldiers. They're standing by each plane."

"Not soldiers. P.C. Philippine Constabulary. Police. I've been watching them. I haven't seen any go inside a plane. They're giving each arriving passenger the once-over, but that's all. If they come inside here, we've got problems."

The pistols and four Filipino passports had been hidden behind the inside cover to the door. This cover could be removed with a quick turn of a screwdriver; and it wouldn't take a suspicious policeman long to go through the fore and aft baggage compartments and start in on the secondary hiding places.

Ryder came in thirty seconds behind a Cathay Pacific 707 and swung to the right as directed. A P.C. guided them to their slot and then waited by the wing. He held a clipboard in his left hand. His right rested on his holster pistol—until he saw Terry. Then his jaw fell open and he scrambled forward to assist her off the wing. For a second Ryder could see the paper on the clipboard. It was a photograph of Roger Hiller. The Polaroid shot taken by Tony Giambruno's henchman. The P.C. gave one glance at Ryder, then turned and yelled for a porter.

"Welcome to Manila," he said. He was lean, thin-shouldered, quite good-looking. "You're a Charlie's Angel, aren't you? I can tell. Welcome, welcome. The boy will be here in a few minutes. We have your picture at home. I wish we could get your autograph."

Terry smiled at him and her even white teeth, set off by tanned cheeks, and both of them framed by her blond hair, made a composition a bit on the glorious side. Ryder was delighted. His cover story was sound after all. No one had ever known Harry Ryder as a womanizer. He felt himself a kind of Pygmalion-type genius—except, of course, that Terry Jefferson was no Galatea. More the Atalanta type. She whispered to Ryder, "Not Farrah Fawcett-Majors. Just a Charlie's Angel. Which one, I wonder?"

Customs was a snap and even the sour-faced Immigration official couldn't do more than glance at Ryder once he set eyes on Terry. He even became chatty.

"Where are you staying? Do you have a hotel picked out?"

Ryder hesitated the briefest of seconds. He didn't like this. The P.C. had followed them in so he could keep up his adoration of his angel. "We'll be at the Bayview Plaza."

The two Filipinos looked astonished. They expected something like the Mandarin or Intercontinental or Philippine Plaza or Peninsula or Hilton. Not a second-class hotel. "I was told it has one of the best views of Manila Bay. And it's right across from the American embassy."

The view part left them cold. Who wanted to look at Manila Bay? Manila Bay was Manila Bay but the embassy part struck a chord. They nodded sagely. "You're right," the Immigration man said. "Except Ambassador Johnson is up in Baguio now with the President."

"Of course. And we'll be going to Baguio. Driving, not flying. We won't use the plane again for a week or so, then we'll go to Tacloban."

Now the Filipinos looked carefully at Ryder, estimated his age, nodded gravely. "Ah, a sentimental journey."

There was no other conceivable reason for an American tourist—with or without his beautiful girlfriend—to go to Leyte. He nodded with equal gravity. "Yes. A sentimental journey. I've always wanted to come back."

In the cab, Terry said, "What was that all about? After the Peninsula and the Grand, are you losing your touch? I know you're not running out of money."

She had been awestruck by the Grand Hotel in Taipei. They had spent two days amidst its Oriental splendor. The flaming reds and the marvelous grounds had actually set her to skipping and dancing like a child or ballerina. After the first day she had accused him, "You said the Peninsula was the best in the world. It's a convent beside this place. God, I like the Chinese. I wish I could create a Chinese world in Los Angeles."

"Call it a whim, but I do like Manila Bay. You'll see. It's an incredible kaleidoscope. The clouds and sun and rain and ships and boats form ever-changing patterns. I used to stay at the Filipinas just to watch the bay, but the Filipinas burned down. There's nothing wrong with the Bayview Plaza. It's echt Filipino. And it also happens to be one block from Rizal Park. That's where we'll meet our friend. I'll call as soon as we've registered."

The adjoining rooms were thoroughly ordinary. "Not even a TV set," Terry complained. "And did you see the look those bellhops gave you? Why a separate bedroom for me? You could get away with this at the Peninsula and the Grand. That had suites with two bedrooms—but even then I saw the Chinese examining our two beds to try to figure out just how we made out. You're blowing your cover, my friend. It ain't natural—it's worse, it's highly suspicious."

He grunted and sat by the phone. "In the Orient, impotent rich men with luscious females are a commonplace. The Chinese, I'm sure, thought I owned you. You're my slave, did you know that? The Filipinos—well, they'll try to make you. Different cultures, different patterns. Now please keep quiet. The next language you're about to hear will be Visayan."

But Terry interrupted him. "My God, look at that traffic. It's a three-lane thoroughfare and the cars are five abreast on it. Not cars, but silver horses and silver dragons and silver horns stuck all over those gaudy silver concoctions on wheels. Greens and yellows and silvers and reds. What are they? How can anyone drive a car in this chaos?"

"Please. They're jeepneys. Each one driven by a Formula One driver. Please, let me make my call."

"On an open line? I thought spies always used pay phones?"

"My dear child, I am not James Bond. I'm not putting hairs on doors or powder in bureaus. I'm not checking for bugs. I will not use a pay phone, even if I could find one that works. If we are blown—God, you've got me doing it. I'm going to forget English if I stay around you. Okay, if we're blown, the next stop is Fort Malolos prison for you and me. Clap clap. Just like that. And anyway, no spy has ever stayed in the Bayview Plaza Hotel. It's against union rules. Now let me make my call, please."

At the third ring the phone was picked up. A child answered. Of course. It was Sunday, July tenth. Ryder said in Visayan, "Is your mother there? Mrs. Manzano? Tell her it's Carlos."

Ryder could hear the tap click on. The child breathed heavily. A tape job—so there would be no possible traceback. Hell, the child . . . he . . . her . . . it . . . couldn't understand Visayan. She finally spoke. In English. "I'll get my mother. Just a minute, please."

A pleasant voice came on. Also using English. "Please, this is Carmelita Pinson Manzano. May I help you?"

Harry persisted in Visayan. "It's good to hear your voice, Carmelita. This is Carlos. I thought I'd report back before I went home. I went out to the Balintawak district and looked for the antique shop, but I almost cried because I couldn't find it."

She was sharp. The hesitation was only momentary. She switched to accented Visayan. "Too bad. Well, I was sure I saw it. The Liga Filipina banner. Maybe I'll go out there myself sometime. Thanks for trying."

"Give my regards to your family."

Terry was watching him with something like respect in her eyes. He took off his glasses, rubbed his itching moustache. "It's on. We meet tomorrow. At noon in Rizal Park. A block away. Under the dapdap tree. Let's have lunch and then go out to Makati and see if we can talk Hertz into renting us a car without a driver. As you now understand, Filipinos know no American tourist can drive in this chaos. Manila has the worst traffic jams—and accidents—in the world. That's why Hertz insists on drivers for their cars. We'll just out-insist them."

Terry's eyes were wide. "Under the dapdap tree? You've got to be kidding."

It was not until that night, as he was almost asleep, that

he suddenly remembered Terry's "it ain't natural." What was that? A proposition? Well, she would have to do better than that.

33

They left the hotel at eleven-fifteen and strolled up Roxas to the park.

"I want to be there early. The old antennae at work."

"What's that copy of *Shōgun* for? All of a sudden the man blossoms out as a bookworm."

"You know very well what it's for. Aren't you the apprentice master spy? We'll exchange copies on the bench. His will have in it, I hope, a detailed map of the prison compound and the grounds. And information about our friends' schedules."

A couple of children—pre-teenagers—came up. "Hi, MacArthur," the younger said. The older whistled and cried out in Tagalog. "What are you doing with the old man. You need a real man."

Ryder laughed. The children laughed and he translated for Terry. "I got the same message from kids in Hong Kong." Impulsively she took his arm. "No, it's different here. In twenty-four hours I've heard children call you Uncle Sam, G.I. Joe, and now MacArthur. You love this place, don't you? I can feel a change in you. Not so hard, not so suspicious, more open. Last night at the Aristocrat you sat there beaming like a happy drunk. The beam is not the hawk-nosed, sardonic Peter McClaren I've been enduring these past ten days."

They walked up T. M. Kalaw to the park entrance and entered a grove of lofty swaying trees.

"These are narra trees. The Philippine national tree.

Our dapdap tree is over yonder—beyond the Rizal monument, over there by the children's swings." He stopped to stare up through the narras and breathed deeply.

"Well?"

"Yes. I love it. This is my spiritual home. Not California."

They walked out of the shade into the blazing sun. "Or rather, it's all mixed up. I grew up on a country road outside Watsonville. Down by the creek a group of Filipinos lived. They sang all the time. Filipino songs and the most haunting guitar music I've ever heard. After school, almost every afternoon and weekends, from the time I was seven or eight, I went down to their camp and listened and fished with them and did chores for them. After about a year of this they started teaching me the songs. I couldn't carry a tune, but I did learn the words. They spoke Visayan. They were from Leyte. Sad, pathetic, courageous little people. And very kind to a lonely little boy. And so I learned Visayan—to me it was just Filipino—and I became part Filipino." He paused, laughed. "The British have their mad desert lovers, their Doughtys and their Lawrences. Californians have their mad Asia hands. They're all over the Orient. All over the Philippines, too. Not the ones who live huddled together in Forbes Park—but you go up into the mountains of Mindanao, into the rice terraces of Banaue, anywhere, even in Palawan or Balabac, and you'll find Filipino-struck Californians. I am one of them."

She was thoughtful the rest of the way to their destination, a cement bench that surrounded the dapdap tree, with its coarse leaves and gnarled trunk and thick limbs, not unlike the limbs of a live oak. They sat on the bench, quite alone. In this heat the park was deserted. It was eleven forty-five. No one was approaching them or even in sight. "How did you reconcile your love with your duties as a CIA man? You hinted last night that a lot of things stuck in your craw. No? Yes?"

Now he could see a girl crossing Taft Avenue and heading leisurely, unconcernedly, in their direction. She was carrying something under her arm, he couldn't tell what.

"In the last five years I've had a lot of time to think. Oh, I don't just mean about how I interfered in Filipino politics. And not everything was bad. No way. I helped position Magsaysay. Ramon Magsaysay. He was a great president. If he hadn't died in a plane crash, the Philipines today would be the world's foremost Third World power. I was proud of that." The girl was definitely heading their way. She was young. Possibly a teenager. "But other things I did were just terrible. The pressure I helped put on President Garcia. The way I bought Magsaysay's boys —Pineda and the others. Most of the time I supported the wrong people. Most of the time the CIA supports the wrong people everywhere.

"The CIA—or the U.S., to put this in proper perspective —faces the same choice today that the Roman Catholic Church faced from the twelfth to fifteenth centuries. The Church could defend and support its parishioners. The poor and humble and meek. Or it could ally itself with the barons. With the kings, emperors, princes, counts, dukes, earls, viscounts, marquises, baronets, knights, chevaliers, ritters, caballeros, and plain everyday nobles who scourged and oppressed and lived off the people. The Church chose the barons. It has never quite recovered from that choice."

The girl was a hundred yards away. "Well, we have the same choice. Either we live up to our heritage and support the poor and the humble of this world, or we ally ourselves with the barons. With the tyrannies that bedevil almost every country in South America, Africa, Asia, and Eastern Europe. So far we have chosen the tyrants. But it is not too late. This I firmly believe. We started out as the world's great hope for freedom. We can still live up to our promise. And this child who is going to sit on the bench must be our emissary. Anyway, she's got her *Shōgun* with her."

Terry gulped and started. She had been totally engrossed in Ryder's peroration. With that kind of concentration, he'd better warn her she'd never make her master-spy rating. She gave a quick glance at the girl and whispered, "My God she's as beautiful as all the rest of them."

For at the vast open-sided Aristocrat restaurant where he had taken her last night, she had exclaimed over and over at the beauty of the Filipina girls. He had been his sententious best. "The most beautiful women in the world. Some have a Eurasian—mestizo—quality, but they are no more beautiful than the pure-bloods. And the curious thing is they don't think of themselves as pretty. They think American girls are the pretty ones. Every Filipina girl in the place tonight is looking at you and admiring you —not envying, they don't do that—and sorrowing that she cannot be truly beautiful like you."

The Filipina was wearing a white blouse, beige skirt, and sandals. She was older than she looked—probably twenty-one or twenty-two. Her shoulders were typically erect and square. Terry had also exclaimed over that quality last night. "Their posture! I have never seen women —not even professional models—with such beautiful posture. And it's not stiff, either. They stand absolutely erect and square-shouldered, but they're relaxed doing it. They could be meditating in the lotus position. No wonder you fell in love with a Filipino girl. I'm sorry, Filipina. I could become a full-fledged lesbian myself. My, wouldn't that be something. In bed with one of them—and don't look so shocked."

The girl suddenly seemed to become aware of them and smiled sweetly and apologetically—and stumbled over a gardener's hose so that her book fell from her arms. Ryder was on his knees almost as soon as her copy of

Shōgun hit the ground. He picked it up and handed it back to her. She smiled with that radiant, gentle grace of the Filipina and said, "Thank you." She went to the bench about ten feet away and looked placidly at the children's swings. A dollar bill now projected from Ryder's book. He pulled it out so Terry could see it was torn in half. He faced Terry, but spoke so that his voice reached the Filipina.

"Thank you for doing this. Meet us again four days from now. On Friday, July fifteenth, at three o'clock. We'll meet at the restaurant over there run by the deaf and dumb. By three we should be the only customers. I'll sit with my back to the help. They'll be at this end. You face us at the next table. In this way I can talk to you. You won't be able to say anything yourself, of course, but if there's anything you want to add we can probably exchange books again. Once I've studied this material I'll work out a plan and give it to you on Friday. I expect to set up the rescue for the night of July twenty-first. That's Thursday night, July twenty-first. As soon after lights-out as possible. I should guess that will be after eleven. Between eleven and twelve. But the exact timing will have to wait until I've studied this material. I just want you to be able to alert your people as to the overall timetable. D-Day is ten days from now, the night of Thursday, July twenty-first. And we'll meet again four days from now on Friday, July fifteenth, at three o'clock."

Without a glance at the girl, he helped Terry to her feet and handed her the book. "You'd better carry it in that suitcase of yours." He wore a short-sleeved yellow sports shirt. She was wearing a barong tagalog she had bought yesterday afternoon at the Shoe Store in Makati. It was lovely on her. "Girls don't wear barongs," he had told her. "Barongs are for men." But she was right again. Her barong, with its intricate design, made her seem almost Filipina herself, in spite of her blond hair. And he noticed that she was attempting to square off her shoulders. That she couldn't handle.

She took the book and dropped it into her bag. "I didn't see you make the switch and I was only five feet away. You are fast. Where are we going now?"

"First back to the Bayview Plaza to buy the tickets for our friends. You won't have to go back to Hong Kong to get them. Dumb of me. The Japan Airlines ticket office is right there in the hotel lobby. Then we'll go to a rental darkroom. I want to develop the photos of Fort Malolos. The Yellow Pages list a rental darkroom off Claro Recto. . . . Hell, everything is off Claro M. Recto. And there, by the way, was a man I could never handle. Neither buy, sway, nor intimidate. Senator Claro M. Recto."

34

Emerenciana Manzano Darang came out into the exercise yard. She was carrying a calico dress.

"I just finished it. Do you like it?"

She handed it proudly to her brother and he took it but kept his eyes on her. What a woman. He knew why everyone loved her. Every man, woman and child in the Philippines. Well, almost everyone. The police hadn't been obvious with their approval. But the police, hard as it might be to comprehend, were Filipinos too. When a policeman went home at night and lay down on his bed and tried to forget the cries and anguish of the prisoners he had tortured, what did he think of Emerenciana? Did he say to himself: "When the revolution comes, I know she'll forgive me"?

"It's lovely, Emmy. Just lovely. A poem worthy of you."

They began to do their setting-up exercises. He said: "You noticed? The same pattern?"

"Same pattern."

They did a few push-ups together. What was there to say? The guards barely seemed to notice them. They didn't even stand around the exercise yard any more. The TV monitors had gone kaput. Their doors were as often unlocked as they were locked.

"It's Tuesday. Carmelita comes today. In an hour. I want a rubdown after all this. I'll tell her."

Emerenciana nodded. She was a widow. Her children had been sent to relatives on the island of Negros. She could have had a gaggle of lovers but not once over the years had she summoned any of them. She would not be free with herself until the Philippines were free of its tyrants. She stood up. "You do that. But tell her to be cautious. I feel I'm more closely watched now than when the monitor gaped at me."

35

"Shit." Ryder hesitated a moment, then propelled Terry to sit opposite him. "What the Christ is she up to?"

For their young Filipina contact had disobeyed orders. She was already sitting in the open-air deaf-and-dumb restaurant. And her back was to the entrance, not facing it as he had instructed. And beside her sat another Filipina girl—even younger, and naturally as pretty or prettier. They were carrying on an animated conversation in Tagalog and they barely glanced at the two Americans.

Terry laughed at his expression. "Don't you get it? She wants to talk to you. And so she brought her friend.

You were right. Sir Francis Drake it is."

He managed a smile. On the ride to Baguio she had wondered about the girl's extreme youth. He had shrugged. "Sir Francis Drake was captain of a ship at twenty-two. This girl's at least twenty-one. And they trust her, so we have no choice."

"Be careful," he said to Terry. "The attendants can probably read lips."

"They are certainly talkative. Well, that's not the right word, I know." There was a youth and two girls to wait on tables and no other customers. Their fingers were flicking and flashing and they smiled at each other fondly. "Here comes our waitress."

The girl smiled shyly at them. She had the usual beauty. Keeping her eyes on Terry, she put menus in front of them and placed an order blank with a pencil in front of Ryder. He wrote out adobo and beer for both of them and the girl nodded. At this hour it would take a few minutes to warm up the adobo. The two placid Filipinas sat one table to Ryder's right. He waited until the San Miguel beer came and then raised his glass to Terry.

"What do I call you?" he said, as if to Terry.

"My name is Pilar. Pilar Manzano. This is Maria Manzano." She accepted his lead and used English. "I am José Manzano's niece. Maria is my sister. She told the school she's sick today. We've been shopping along Mabini Avenue."

"Terry, you say something every so often. Now."

"I would like to tell Pilar and Maria that they are exquisite people. All the Filipinos I have seen are exquisite people—even the people in the Tondo you showed me, poor and starved as so many of them are."

On the way out of Manila to Baguio, Ryder had driven Terry through the rusty corrugated shacks and slime and mud and stink and horror of the Tondo. And her only comment had been, "It's ghastly enough. But notice the people. They have self-respect. Their shoulders are as

171

erect and square as those of the upper-class folk out in Makati."

"Pilar," he said, "I've studied the map. It's pretty obvious what must be done. The only way out is through the windows overlooking the exercise yard. The tools should have been delivered to cut the bars and screen. At eleven o'clock your aunt and uncle will go through the yard and the garden until they reach the garden fence. Turn right and follow the garden fence until they meet the cross-fence. This part is tricky. There are searchlights here. But also a ditch along the cross-fence. Tell them to cut their way through the garden fence and crawl along the cross-fence until they reach the outside wire fence of the compound.

"Once outside the compound, they have to go about a kilometer through cogon grass until they reach one of the main base roads. Your map ends there, but there's no way we can use that road. It's too heavily traveled and I can't park there to meet your friends. Yes, I'll be the one to meet them. Terry, you say something."

"The rain in Spain it raineth every day. It also raineth every day in Baguio. What a beautiful place. Thank you for taking me there. I'm almost as much in love with the Philippines as you are."

He started to speak but Pilar interrupted him. "Sir, I must tell you something. My aunt and uncle report that surveillance has become extremely sloppy. It's almost not even a prison any more. The TV monitors are off. The doors frequently unlocked. When they go by the front door, they can't see any guards there. So they wonder—would that be the way to go out? Through the front door?"

The waitress brought them their order and smiled timidly at them. Terry picked up her tablespoon in her right hand and shoveled rice into it with her fork in the left hand. "See, I'm becoming a Filipina, too."

The Filipina girls giggled and he started to censure

them, then realized their amusement was, under the circumstances, legitimate.

"When," he asked, "did this sloppiness begin?"

"Begin? Why, let's see. . . . This week, I think. No, last Saturday it was. Last Saturday."

Saturday was the day following the Chow Woon Chung episode. "Pilar, this is a trap. They know I'm here. Don't be alarmed. They can't recognize me. We're playing the perfect tourists. Baguio so far. Manila for a couple of days. Then Tacloban. And then back here for the night of the twenty-first. Next Thursday. Tell your aunt and uncle not to make any moves out that front door. Obviously Cruz wants them to try to make a break. So that means they'll be shot down. Cruz wants an excuse to kill them. Tell your uncle that Harry the American will meet them on that night. He knows that name. I'll explain where we'll meet in a moment. Terry."

"Harry the American." Terry laughed. "Well, well, well. I like Peter much better. Harry is really Rotarian. Peter is more my style."

In spite of himself he laughed. "We're not laughing at you, Pilar and Maria. My friend is laughing at me. Her name is Terry. She sees me as a comic figure. I probably am, but not when it comes to escaping from a maximum security prison.

"Okay. Your map stops at the base road. However, we took aerial photographs of the base. And about two kilometers beyond the road on your map there's another road. Still in Fort Malolos. A secondary dirt road. It leads to an exit. In all, that's three kilometers of tall cogon grass. It may take them two or three hours to go all the distance —but I'll wait. And it's rough going, I know. Our friends will be pretty well cut up by the cogon, but I'll have Band-Aids and towels ready. When your aunt and uncle reach me, I'll put them in the trunk and take off." Their Mitsubishi had a small trunk but two normal-sized Filipinos could just squeeze in. "Now comes the tricky part. I'll need a girl with me in the car. I need a reason for parking there. In case some guards come by . . . and also to justify my being there so late and to explain why I'm pulling out at two or three in the morning. She'll have to be . . . well . . . she has to be a . . ."

"A whore!" Terry snarled the words. Her rage was quite honest. "You! A whore! What do you think you're doing! You want a whore. You've got a whore. You'll take me."

"Pay no attention to her, Pilar. She doesn't understand. But I'm sure you do. I need a Filipina girl. This has to be authentic . . . and my friend just doesn't look like a proper prostitute. Can you do this? Can you have her meet me in the Bayview Plaza lobby at nine P.M. next Thursday? By the bar?"

Pilar and Maria looked solemnly at each other. He interrupted. "I know, I know. I could bring my own. There are two or three girls who parade through our hotel every day. But I need someone I can trust. Someone you can trust."

Terry shut her eyes and put on her unpleasant obstinate expression. Pilar was embarrassed but nodded her head slowly. "Yes. It can be done. . . . We have . . . we have . . . in our family . . . since the Manzanos lost everything. . . . You understand . . ."

"I understand. I'll see no harm comes to her. And . . . and she'll be . . . well . . . she'll be well reimbursed. Just for sitting with me. You understand?"

"I understand."

"Good. Now the last thing. Victor Frega and Christopher Mori are to come with us. We'll want two cars, Pilar. In case one breaks down. Where do we meet?"

"They live in the same apartment building. In Urdaneta Village in Makati. On San Vicente. Number fifty-five. They'll be together in Mr. Frega's apartment. Just ring three times and they'll come right down. Everybody is ready."

"Terry, be nice and say something witty. Speak softly so

I can hear Pilar. Pilar, please repeat to me the arrangements for next Thursday night."

"I am not witty. I am not amused. Every time you plan something it's so goddamn complicated somebody gets shot. Well, this time, Mr. Harry the American, I hope it's you."

Pilar played back the arrangements. She was letter-perfect. Her eyes were both puzzled and frightened as she contemplated the rage on Terry Jefferson's face.

36

"This is Leyte. This is Tacloban. This is home."

He spoke to the tower, then swung the 310 far out over Leyte Gulf. "That's Samar under us. There's Homonhon Island straight ahead. Mariquitdaquit Island is just below you to the right. And altogether it's Leyte Gulf. Where MacArthur returned. And where was I? I happened to be south of Dulag about to hop a banca down the coast to Abayog and I look out and I see the whole goddamn Navy piling up opposite Dulag. I try to signal the ships, but my flashlight registered about like a beggar on a millionaire. So I figured the coast was no place to be the next morning, so my buddy and I—that was Emilio Lanante, he's now a fat professor of International Law at Cal Berkeley, but he was skinny as a bamboo shoot then—so we headed for the hills and watched the bombardment and invasion from a bird's-eye view."

He pointed to the coastline. "Isn't that a marvel?"

"I see a blue sea and blue sky. I see a coastline with coconut palms almost to the water's edge. I see brown sandy beaches and fishing huts on stilts. I see banana trees and bamboo trees and rice fields and corn fields and narra

175

and mango trees. I see carabao tethered to the trees. I see flowers everywhere. I see a lot of mountains. Except that it seems drier and dustier, Leyte looks remarkably like Luzon. What happened?"

"What do you—oh, the next morning. Well, the landings started at ten and by three in the afternoon I thought it was time to rejoin the Army, so I did."

"And?"

"Well, I got Emilio and me behind some thick palm trees and I hollered out to the guys and they shot up the trees pretty good until they decided we weren't Tokyo Rose. When the first soldier saw us, he called back, 'Fuck, Lieutenant, it's a fucking Tarzan and his trained ape. Shall I shoot the bastards?' But the lieutenant . . . I've never forgotten his name. I still see him from time to time in San Francisco. Dan Robinson. A very nice man. He didn't shoot us because he said the general would probably want to see us."

"General?"

"General Krueger. He saw me and Emilio the next day. He actually had some of my radio dispatches with him. That was my chief job, you know. Sending dispatches to Australia. Mostly about Jap ship movements. I did it for eighteen months. I never thought anyone paid any attention."

"That's what this is all about, isn't it? You took on this assignment just so you could get back to the Philippines. You were homesick."

"Well, partly that. *Queque ipse miserrima vidi, quorum pars magna fui.* I don't know Latin. I read that in Morison's naval history. He translates it as 'Those most lamentable events I witnessed, and a great part of them I was.' Virgil knew what he was talking about. I spent eighteen months here. I lived every second of 'em. I think I remember every second."

"And Teresa Morgan?"

"You should have been a Grand Inquisitor. She lived

near Dulag. That's Dulag below us. That's where the landings I'm talking about took place. We'll turn north now. We'll go past Red Beach and White Beach on the approach to the airport. I'll show them to you tomorrow."

"You planned this tourist cover, this sentimental journey as the Filipinos call it, just so you could have an excuse to come back to Leyte. Two people are sitting in a maximum security prison stewing about a mad escape plan that depends on a childlike Filipina girl and a romantic knight of the skies, while you dream about your lost youth. And I'm trapped in your dream, your nightmare."

The airport was in sight. He shook his head. "No, it's all essential. Colonel Calixto Calugas knows I'm somewhere about. Believe me, he's taking a good look at every American in the Philippines. I'm sure he has had a report on everything we've done."

"Even the Baguio caper?"

On the second day at the Pines Hotel in Baguio, at dusk, he had had Terry drive with him down Session Road into central Baguio. He had her dressed as nearly like a Filipina girl as possible. Blouse, skirt, sandals, natural hair kept above the shoulders. He had driven up a hillside just off Governor Pack Road until they reached Benguet Street. She held an envelope in her hand containing seventy-five hundred pesos. She had walked into an apartment building (it had a shoe repair shop and barbershop on the street floor), knocked on a door, handed the envelope to a chubby lady, and said, "From your brother in California. From Gus Gutierrez." And she had fled back to the car and sat there shivering and sweating at once. The would-be master spy.

"No. We got away with it. Else we wouldn't be here now."

"I want you to take me there."

"Where?"

"Where Teresa Morgan lived."

The airport was a mile away. "It's not a good part of my

memories. I don't mean just her death. But I made a terrible mistake."

He was silent while they landed. As they taxied to the terminal, a small one-story affair that could have doubled for a small airport terminal anywhere in California, he shrugged. "All right. After they killed her, I went in and killed eight of them. Up beyond Burauen. Where the Japs later tried their only parachute landings. That's where she really lived. Near Burauen."

"Why was it a mistake?"

"Because the Japs rounded up three hundred Filipinos and machine-gunned them and then incinerated them."

"Death does seem to follow you."

"That was the last Jap I killed, at least until just before the invasion. We got orders straight from Australia. No more killing of Japanese occupation troops." He waved and smiled to the airport personnel coming out to greet them. There were no police among them. "Smile at them. Don't look so sad." She flashed her teeth. "The worst part was, not one Filipino reproached me for what I had done. Neither reproached me nor betrayed me nor any other American. Not one betrayal from Luzon to Palawan."

One of the red-shirted porters sprang onto the wing and guided them down. His name was stenciled on his back: ANDRES. "Welcome to Tacloban." His smile lit up his broad face. "Come, follow me, I'll get a cab for you. Is this all you have? Two bags? Follow me."

The cab was as red as his shirt. A tiny Filipino stood beside it. His name was stenciled on the cab: HERMIE. "This is my uncle," Andres said. "He'll take care of you. Where do you want to go?"

"Why, to the Grand Hotel."

Andres and Hermie shook their heads. "It's the best hotel in Tacloban," Andres said. "But it's totally full. There's a marketing convention here. Tacloban is becoming a convention center. You know. Adoring. The President's wife."

"Ah," Ryder nodded. He turned to Terry. "Adoring Raymundo comes from Leyte. Okay, where do you suggest?"

"The Primrose?" Andres and Hermie looked unhappy saying it.

"The Primrose it is."

Hermie's cab was an ancient Toyota, at least fifteen years old. He backed it out and Terry said, "Oh, wait a moment. I forgot my cosmetic case. I'll go back and get it. You wait here. I'll be right back. Give me the key, Peter. You stay here."

He looked at her sharply. Her face was guileless. He cursed silently. The bitch was going back to get the Hush-Puppy. She had protested unsuccessfully when they went to Baguio. "You never know when a gun'll come in handy." "You idiot," he had said. "We can't go back to the plane at Domestic, and anyway, suppose we have a pistol and we shoot somebody, then what?" "Then that person won't be able to tattle on us, will he?" This time she wasn't going to be unsuccessful and he couldn't stop her.

When she returned she was flushed and triumphant. "Sorry, I took so long. But I decided I'd better bring another blouse. I had to open two suitcases. It's hotter here than in Manila, don't you think?"

He ignored her, concentrated on taking in every sight and sound on the twenty-minute ride to Tacloban. His heart beat fast and his soul soared. It was true. Terry was right. He had been homesick. This was his Leyte.

"Hermie, where can I rent a car for tomorrow and the next day? I know there are no rental services here.... But I'll pay five hundred pesos a day. A thousand pesos for two days."

Hermie was not a fast thinker. To make it easier on himself, he slowed the car from its maximum speed of thirty-five down to twenty. "I can't rent you the cab. The insurance. But I could drive for you."

"No, Hermie, we want to bum around. Ah, that is, wander where our fancy takes us."

"Yes, bum around. I understand." He thought for another two miles. "I have a pick-up. A 1960 Chevrolet. But it runs. It's all mine and I could let you have it."

"Fine. Bring it to the hotel tomorrow at nine in the morning."

"You will pay for the gas?"

Ryder almost choked but he managed to gasp an assent. The Primrose was a block from the wharf. It consisted of an open front door, a narrow concrete hallway, a desk with two Filipinas behind it, and a sofa beyond the desk. A concrete stairway was beyond the sofa. The younger of the two women took his registration. "Ah, three days. That will be forty-five pesos a night. Six dollars. We can put you in number five." She rang a bell and a skinny, middle-aged Filipino in an undershirt came down the stairs, picked up the suitcase and led them past the mezzanine to the second floor. He unlocked the door and Terry and Ryder stopped as if they had bumped into an invisible wall.

"My God," Terry breathed. "From the Peninsula to this."

The room was a concrete box with a very high stucco ceiling. The concrete floor was clean, but the concrete and stucco on the ceilings and walls and floor were chipped and cracked. One bare feeble light bulb was in the center of the ceiling. "See," the porter cried enthusiastically, "your own private shower."

They looked. The shower and bathroom weren't just chipped, they seemed battered. Ryder tried the taps in the shower. Only the cold-water tap worked. It was probably warm enough to be bearable. The porter turned on the window air-conditioning unit. It harrumphed and sputtered and then settled into a steady roar. Ryder tipped the porter and they watched him skirt the worn, torn sofa and go out the door. He had dropped the key on the bed. It was a double bed. A double bed built for Filipinos. Ryder and Terry looked at the bed and they looked at each other.

37

Terry's laughter at his head-flip seemed to come to a gurgling halt. It was her first laugh of a very grim morning. He wanted to say, "Thank you for laughing again. It was funny last night. I'm sorry, but it was. I was noble beyond belief to keep from laughing at you. And myself." But he followed her eyes as she said, "We've got company."

Indeed they did. Two P.C. with drawn and pointed pistols were approaching them across the rice field. This had been one of the three airfields around Burauen during the war. After driving her past Teresa Morgan's house he had followed the potholed dirt road another two miles to the isolated field. "This was supposed to be an airfield, but in November 1944 it simply never dried out. It was unusable. The Japs didn't know that. They thought we were going to use the field. They tried a parachute drop here. I believe it was their only use of parachute troops during the Philippine invasion. They bombed the hell out of Tacloban and sent four transports here. Three of them never got close. They were destroyed further on, down by Dulag. The fourth was shot to hell as it approached the field. It was nighttime and I was standing right here trying to figure what all the shooting was about—hell, the nearest Japs were ten miles to the west in the high hills—and I looked up and here's this Jap parachutist coming down and he was pointing his rifle right at me. So I did a head-flip. He was so surprised he didn't shoot. I did." And he had felt his body take wing and he had performed his head-flip just like thirty-three years ago and she had laughed and here they were.

He moved to Terry's shoulder and watched the two men approach. One was small, but the other was taller than Ryder. The small one held a clipboard in his left hand. They came up and the tall one said, "Well, well, well. Peter McClaren of the 96th Infantry Division. Everyone in Tacloban knows you've arrived. A sentimental journey. How touching."

He took the clipboard and examined it critically. He showed the photograph to them. "You don't look like this man, this Roger Hiller, do you, Mr. Peter McClaren. Or should I say, Sergeant Harry Ryder? Harry the American? How could Harry the American look like either this photo or like Peter McClaren?" He stepped forward, grabbed Ryder's moustache and tried to jerk it off. It didn't jerk. For a moment a flicker of doubt crossed his eyes. "It's real. Well, it may be; but you're not, you're Harry the American. And you know who I am. You know me."

Ryder's eyes were flat and dull. Terry was watching him closely. He said calmly, firmly, "I've never seen you before in my life. I'm Peter McClaren. This is my fiancée, Miss Terry Jefferson."

Each of these statements was a lie, although the fiancée part might not be. Not after last night, ridiculous a fiasco as it had been. For from the moment they stood over that miserably small double bed, they knew the barriers had fallen. The defenses known as Terry Jefferson, the defenses known as Peter McClaren, simply melted. They were, at that moment, one. And nothing—no word, gesture, touch—would ever bring them closer. They had floated from the room to go sightseeing, riding backwards on a putputting tricycle all around Tacloban, walking in the twilight through the city's noisy, thumping fish factories, dining at the Chinese White Dragon restaurant, laughing as the regular evening blackout came, stumbling back to the hotel, undressing solemnly and shyly in the dark, and lying side by side, her head on his right arm. There was no hurry, no movement on either part. Movement, motion, would be change, irrevocable and committed. Then suddenly she screamed and jumped up, crying, "I'm being bitten!" And the lights came back on at that moment and she was pressed back against the headboard, her knees up to her chin, and she was staring with horror at the foot of the bed. She was quite right. She was being bitten by fat bedbugs that were trundling across the lower part of the bed. He squashed them and blood splattered on the sheet and Terry sprang from the bed to stand shaking and quivering by the shower. He jumped up an instant later, wrenched up the mattress and proceeded to squash each of the bedbugs. They made quite a mess. There was no thought of sex—on her part—for the rest of the night. Terry sat up all night against the headboard, legs drawn up, her eyes fixed on the bloodied sheet until she finally dozed off. It was as sad as it was funny, but he had the wisdom not to laugh. In the morning he brought the porter up and showed him his massacre, and the porter blanched and swore they would have a new bug-free mattress forthwith.

"I am Gemi Mandares and you know it," the tall policeman said. "You killed my brother Raoul."

Gemi's twin brother, though he had had the same giant build, high cheek bones, slanted eyes, did not have Gemi's courage. Raoul had been killed because he had turned tail and run as a Japanese patrol passed beneath them. The Japs had killed Raoul and then hurried away without attempting to challenge the others. Maybe that was because, by that time, they often seemed to patrol with haunted, furtive looks as if every step they took told them the soil, the very earth, did not want them. Ryder was tempted to tell Gemi the truth about Raoul, but he repressed this stupidity. Gemi already knew all there was to know about his brother.

"I killed many people in October, November, and December around here. And later my RCT was transferred from the 96th to the 32nd Division in Luzon and I killed many people there. At Salacsac Pass. But they were all Japs."

Mandares sneered. "You are wondering how I recognized you, aren't you?"

This was not true. Ryder knew exactly what had betrayed him.

"You don't think it was this stupid picture, do you?" Mandares handed the clipboard back to his colleague, who was keeping his finger on the trigger of his pistol. An S and W Police Positive. It had a sensitive trigger. "Those idiots in Manila. I could have told them Harry the American would not look like that. I know you too well. No, I recognized the head-flip. Hah! Are you surprised?"

"I am surprised by everything you're telling me. This is like a nightmare."

"We saw someone driving Hermie's pick-up, so we followed." He pointed to the road. The dull red P.C. car was barely visible around the bend. "Then when we saw it was just two Americans, Mr. Peter McClaren and his beautiful Charlie's Angel, we started to go away and then you jumped through the air. And I remembered. I didn't see you that night when the parachutists came. But I heard the story. Everyone heard it." He switched to Visayan. "And I was sorry you weren't shot down like the traitor you are."

"Pardon me?"

"Pardon you." In English again. "Never. No pardon for an enforcer hired by those cowardly overseas Filipinos to assassinate our president. Pardon? Hah! I could shoot you down right now and I would be a hero." He grabbed the clipboard back. "See, it says dead or alive, preferably alive. Preferably alive, well, that's what's going to save you." He waved his pistol. "Come along. I'll take you to Tacloban. This will make me a lieutenant and I can retire. I'm sixty-two, and now I have a chance to retire with a comfortable pension, thanks to Harry the American. Thank you. Raoul will be avenged. Come along."

"What about Miss Jefferson?"

The two policemen looked at her thoughtfully. They got that far-away look in their eyes he had become so used to. Mandares nodded. "She is not wanted. Not yet. She can drive Hermie's pick-up. You drive in front of us, lady, and we'll follow you. That way, there won't be any tricks, huh, Miss Angel?"

Ryder looked around the field. It was totally deserted. Rain clouds had formed and drops were coming down. He looked at Terry. "Do you understand?"

"I understand."

She led the way. She had forgotten all her lessons on how to walk like a marine. She had reverted to her natural leopard stride, one foot in front of the other. The Filipinos observed the incredible callypigian effect and sighed. Mandares pushed him and he followed Terry. She got in the pick-up while he was marched to the patrol car. They searched him and handcuffed both hands to the bar at the right front window. Terry started the pick-up and began to pull slowly toward them. The small man put his pistol in its holster and climbed into the rear seat. Mandares put his pistol away, slid in behind the steering wheel and reached for the car radio. Terry pulled up besides them on the driver's side. The small man started to shout, there was a phut sound and Mandares, mouth gaping in astonishment, turned to face Terry. Ryder watched her point the Hush-Puppy squarely at Mandares forehead. The hole in the silencer seemed like a cannon. The phut sound was heard again and Mendares was hurled against Ryder's shoulder. First Raoul, now Gemi. The hole in his forehead was surprisingly small. It always is.

"Sam Them Nai—Sir Charles—would give you a gold medal for that. Come on, get the keys and get me out of here."

But Terry sat there, eyes enormous, mouth drooping open, Hush-Puppy sagging. She was in shock. "Terry! Terry! Hear me. You've got to move. Fast. Please."

And she stumbled from the pick-up, pistol still in hand, silencer bumping against the steering wheel, and could only find the keys after she dropped the pistol into the cogon grass.

Ryder ran around to the driver's seat, started the patrol car and swung it fifty yards away and buried it amidst a thick cluster of bagawak trees. He vanished and, after a moment of vacant staring, Terry trotted over to see what had happened to him. She found him fumbling in the trunk.

"It's got to be—ah, here it is." He held up a can of paint. "They use it for repairing highway signs." He found the brush, opened the can and walked to the side of the car. She followed him, watched him think a moment, then print a message on the door. It read *"I kamatayan ni Raymundo at sa lahat ng kayan al agad—ng NPA."*

Her hand went to her hair and she nibbled at a strand. The words suddenly seemed to register. "What's that?"

"'Death to Raymundo and his running dog capitalist thugs—NPA.' It can't but help. The NPA are Communists. They don't operate in Leyte but there's plenty of them in Samar. Leyte will give Cruz and Calugas something to think about. Come on, let's get out of here."

After restoring the paint and brush, he took her arm and found her totally unresponsive. However, she did accept his guidance. He led her gently into the pick-up, retrieved the Hush-Puppy, put it back in her bag, and drove carefully back down to Dulag and fifteen miles up to Red Beach. He made her get out and examine the enormous monument, a replica of the famous picture of MacArthur, Osmena, Romulo, Sutherland, and Kenny wading ashore. He read MacArthur's speech aloud to her. "People of the Philippines, I have returned. By the grace of Almighty God our forces stand again on Philippine soil. At my side is your President, Sergio Osmena, worthy successor of that good patriot, Manuel Quezon, with members of his Cabinet. Rally to me. Let the indomitable spirit of Bataan and Corregidor lead on. As the lines of battle roll forward to bring you within the zone of operations, rise and strike! For future generations of your sons and daughters, strike! In the name of your sacred dead, strike! Let no heart be faint. Let every arm be steeled. The guidance of divine God points the way. Follow in His name to the Holy Grail of righteous victory!"

They were the only tourists, but some Filipinos working on the sea wall stopped to listen. They nodded solemnly. Ryder waved to them and drove back to the Primrose Hotel. He slowly and carefully undressed Terry. The sight was magnificent. She lay there with eyes shut. The bed was no longer an issue. They had watched the porter bring in a pristine pure mattress. He undressed and mounted her and came off after barely two strokes. The orgasm was only a faint tinge of sensation on his part. She did not move the whole time, felt nothing. The act was more a benediction, an affirmation, rather than a sexual experience.

He lay beside her and, while she slept, listened to the torrential rain pound the window and admired her breasts and stomach and thighs and hips and pubic mound. For the first time he realized what a beautiful neck she had, pure Modigliani. An hour later she opened her eyes, looked at him and flung herself against him. Four hours later they emerged from a semi-catatonic state and she looked at him and said, "I love you, Harry my American. I have never said that to a man before." And that was good for two more hours.

Why had he ever been afraid of this woman?

38

"This is Lake Taal. A volcanic lake. Ten miles across. I'll circle the perimeter. It's expected of tourists."

"It's magnificent. But what's that hill in the middle? It looks like a volcano in the middle of the lake."

"Exactly. A volcano within a volcano. Now look off toward two o'clock. That field on the outskirts of Tagaytay. The field is over three hundred yards long. That gives you about a hundred yards to play with. The building on the west end is the constabulary barracks. Yes. Our friends the P.C. The building on the east beyond the soccer field is a school. The wind is from the west, of course, so you'll come in over the school top, land, and taxi back to the school. We'll be in that row of bushes over there. When you've finished your turn and are facing west again, we'll hustle out for the plane. All five of us. Manzano, Darang, Frega, Mori, and me. And that's all there is to it."

He turned west to Nasugbu Airport. Terry said, "That's all, providing the P.C. don't machine-gun us as we go over them. And then there's radar and the interceptors."

"Yes. There's that."

"And of course you'll have had no problems squiring José Manzano and his sister out of Fort Malolos."

"No more than we had in Tacloban." They had stayed one more day in Tacloban. After three hours in bed in the morning, they had driven Hermie's pick-up over to Ormoc on the west coast. He had recreated the battles for her. "Every time you see a P.C. and feel your heart constrict, that's the way we felt every time we poked our head from behind a coconut palm trunk."

Nasugbu was only twenty minutes from Tagaytay. As he began the descent, Terry said, "I don't like being a spy.

I've had enough. I'm not a killer, Harry. You understand?"

"I understand." He didn't tell her one is never a killer. "And I approve. It's a dreadful life."

"I recognize that unctuous tone. My Sunday school teacher in Chico talked to us like that. He was the first male, boy or man, to try to feel me. I liked the idea. I didn't like him. Keep up that tone and I'll change my mind back again about killing." They landed. Without a bump. "I've been thinking about the Nasugbu Restaurant and Lodging House. We'll register there all right. But I'm worried about tomorrow morning. You'll be off in Manila and I'll be downtown in Nasugbu and suppose I can't get to the airport by five-thirty tomorrow morning? Suppose those two bodies are found in Leyte? Suppose the P.C. tie us in? Suppose they come for the plane. For me?"

"Suppose, suppose, suppose."

"You're the one who's preached forethought to me. Well, this business has put me beyond forethought into paranoia. I can't help it. So tonight I'm going to slip back out to the airport and sleep in the plane. With one eye open. If someone comes near the plane I'll gun it out of there, d'you hear?"

"I hear."

"And one more thing. You remember your gentleman's code, don't you? The gentleman's code? Well, don't you touch that whore tonight. I'm the only whore you're allowed to touch."

39

It was eight in the evening and the colonel was still at his desk. Any moment now he expected the direct line to ring. Goddamn it, this time he would let it ring. Minister or no Minister. Enough is enough.

"Colonel?"

Calixto Calugas looked up from the chaos on his desk. Porforio Montanez was at the door. He was visibly shaking with fear. Good. Before the night was over he would have everyone in the whole goddamn palace shaking with fear. Including himself.

"Yes?" "Mr. Oakland is here. Your appointment for eight. Mr. Junius Oakland. You said . . ."

"Goddamn it, man, I know what I said. Well, what are you waiting for? Send him in. He's here. It's eight o'clock. I'm here. Well?"

What timing. He looked at the report headings again. "NPA bombed a truckload of P.C. at Dumingay, Zamboanga Del Sur. Two men killed, six wounded." What in hell was a truckload of them doing up eight thousand feet in the mountains? The bastards. They had gone hunting or mountain climbing. Goofing off somehow. They deserved to get killed. "Moros bombed a bridge at Lupon, Davao Oriental." A bridge. What in hell for? And now this. Just ten minutes ago. *"Katayan ni Raymundo at sa lahat ng kayang al agad."* The NPA in Leyte. Impossible. Just impossible. Four good men dead. What were Caumiran and Maglayo up to? Mindanao okay. The Luzon mountains, Western Samar, okay. But Leyte? Impossible. Unfair. This was war. If he lasted out the next twenty-four hours, it was war. Bringing Leyte into it. Wait until Cruz got this news. Wait until the phone rang again. And Cruz would know. Tsismis? The whisper that sweeps from one end of the Philippines to the other any time Cruz farted? No way. Tsismis his ass. Somebody in the palace was betraying him, was tipping off Cruz. If he had any sense he would call General Cruz right now and tell him before the General's manic scream came at him over the direct line from Baguio. Tell him now! And he grabbed the phone and Junius Oakland came in.

The elegant visitor made little concession to the heat. He wore a jacket and vest. He actually had on a striped tie to accompany the pin-striped suit. His lean, handsome face had no sign of sweat. Junius Oakland should have been a mad Englishman. He wasn't. He was a mad American. And a perceptive one.

"Colonel, I caught you at a bad time."

And the sympathy was too much. "Never worse. Four good men killed, six wounded. And worst of all, outside the limits. Leyte is off bounds because of the President's wife. But they killed two men in Leyte near Dulag. They've been dead two days. A passerby smelled the bodies. And I haven't told Cruz yet. Yes, you can say you caught me at a bad time."

"I'll go. If it's at all convenient tomorrow, I'll come back then."

"No, old friend, stay. Your worries are my worries. Here, please sit down."

"Thank you. You're right. I am worried. I left my wife in Hong Kong. She was sympathetic. Even she knew I was troubled." And he shook his head at the surprise of it. Alison had brought up the subject at breakfast. "Darling, something's bothering you. Please, I can tell. Not just today. This whole trip. Don't you think I know why you brought me? I'm your cover, aren't I? Don't you think I know you haven't even looked at a woman on the whole trip, much less had one? Oh, please, Junius. . . . I'm not critical. Now or ever. I just want to help." And he had shown his astonishment, he knew that. And after staring at her a moment, he had told her. "My whole career is in jeopardy, Alison. There's a man in the Philippines who can destroy me. I thought he'd be dead by now. I thought my friends in the Philippines would have killed him, but nothing's happened. He vanished a week ago. That's why I couldn't take it in Washington. I had to get out here. But now that I'm here, I don't know what to do." "Silly, go to the Philippines this minute. You're not accomplishing anything at a fashion salon in Hong Kong. Go to the Philippines and do what you have to do." "Alison, you astonish me. When we get back to Washington, we'll. . . ." "Now, Junius, don't make any rash promises. I like you just the way you are. I like me just the way I am. When we get back to Washington, we'll be Mr. and Mrs. Junius Oakland. As always."

Calugas nodded. "Ryder. He bothers me, too. Even with all this."

"What's been happening, Calixto? Where's Ryder? Why hasn't he surfaced?"

"You know him better than I do, Junius. The anonymous man. The man of many disguises."

"What are you saying?"

"Harry the American could be Juan the Filipino right now. How do I know? He speaks perfect Visayan, perfect Tagalog. Not many Filipinos can do that. He's a bit tall, but many Filipinos are taller. For all I know he's gotten a job as a janitor in Fort Malolos. Your government did well in selecting him, Junius."

"My government? My government had nothing to do with it. Maricar Macasieb asked for help and I suggested Harry Ryder. He's acting entirely on his own. My government has nothing to do with this."

"You? You suggested Ryder? Why? Why did you do this to me?"

"Because I wanted Harry Ryder dead. Because I thought you'd be better off knowing who was working for Macasieb. And because I knew you could kill him. 'Better the devil ye know than the devil ye know not.'"

"You had no right, no cause, to mix a personal vendetta into purely Filipino problems." Calugas frowned. "Well, spilt milk. Let me work this out. If your government is not behind this. . . . And let's spell it out. I don't want ambiguity. . . . If your own CIA is not behind this, who's paying Ryder's expenses?"

"Why, Macasieb, of course."

"Macasieb? He's living on welfare in San Francisco. An unemployed theologian."

Junius Oakland sucked in his breath and leaned back. "The people around Macasieb? What's this cost?"

"Ryder was your man. What does he cost? How much does he value his life?"

Oakland shut his eyes, shook his head. "No. It's the Filipino exiles. It has to be."

Calugas said nothing. Oakland shut his eyes again, thought some more. And knew he faced disaster. The Company was paying for this to-do and had not told him. They had, in fact, assured him this was a purely Filipino exile operation. They had set him up, knew he would pursue Ryder, expected Ryder to kill him. Neat. Very neat. But why this Byzantine approach? If they knew about him, why not simply boot him out just as they had already fired many others? Why not? Because they had no real proof. Because they could not risk a stink. Because (and why not take the optimistic position?) because they wouldn't mind if he succeeded in his attempts to dispose of H. Ryder. They wanted him to win out. And if they did mind, if his optimism was foolish, that was just too bad. They had no hold on him. No proof. And once he finished with Ryder, there would be no proof ever. And he opened his eyes and lied calmly.

"Calixto, I know Macasieb has no funds. But the exiles have access to all kinds of money. Of course they asked us to finance them at first, but we rejected the idea out-of-hand. We can't get involved in internal politics. Not any more we can't. This is a Filipino operation, pure and simple. And all we did was point the exile to a freelancer. But since I seem to have thrown in a monkey wrench by recommending the particular freelancer, why, let me see if I can help. I recommended Ryder because I loathe the man. And he knows things about me I don't want told. So I started this; let me see if I can help finish it."

Calugas shrugged. "As you say, you have a problem. And since your problem is also mine, I would like to help you. But what do I do now? I've done all the obvious things. Every foreigner who's come into the Philippines has been thoroughly scrutinized and checked out. And I mean every foreigner. Even the Japanese and Chinese. Ryder speaks both Japanese and Chinese—Cantonese and Mandarin. The search included every airline, every private plane, every ship—and I've even checked out the crews. No Harry Ryder. I think he slipped off a China Sea junk and came ashore somewhere looking like a Filipino. I told Cruz it was Leyte. . . . Leyte!"

Calugas grabbed the three-page report from Tacloban and studied it line by line. "The men killed were Gemi Mandares and Paul Lechoco. Mandares was a guerilla in Leyte during the war. . . . Do you suppose . . . ?"

Oakland nodded. "That's possible. And should be checked out. But what about Roger Hiller? The photo I sent you? Remember, Hiller/Ryder was in Hong Kong only thirteen days ago."

"Hiller/Ryder. Cruz/Calugas. I tell you, Ryder likes disguises."

"You say in disguise from a China Sea junk. What about in disguise from a private aircraft?"

"What do you mean?"

"Ryder is a pilot. He could fly a plane in here."

Calugas shook his head in wonderment. "My friend, why didn't you tell me? What have you done? No one here knew Ryder was—is—a pilot. That's a talent he must have picked up later. Sure, we've checked out all arrivals, but we haven't watched them subsequently. We had no reason to. God, how many private planes have come in here since July seventh? Well, we'll find out." And he grabbed the phone and fired off instructions in rapid Tagalog. "We'll know by morning, Junius. I demanded a complete rundown by seven A.M. tomorrow morning. I don't care if they work all night. It's nine now. Private plane!"

The direct-line phone buzzed and he reached forward. "Stay. You hear this. It's Cruz. And I'm going to tell him it's not the NPA, it's Harry the American. I wish I could see his face. And do you know the beauty of it? He can never prove me wrong. Not even if my men were executed by direct order of NPA headquarters itself. Listen."

40

At eight forty-five in the evening Ryder came down to the Bayview Plaza lobby. He seated himself at one of the round tables near the tiny bar at the south end of the lobby. He could see all the front doors and also the entrance from the coffee shop. He ordered a San Miguel beer and looked around for his lady of the evening. And saw no one who remotely qualified.

At nine he started to order another beer, when Pilar Manzano came through the front door. She was wearing Levis and a print blouse. It fitted so tightly it framed her round little bra-less breasts. They jiggled only slightly as she walked through the lobby, shoulders square, head erect. The house detective started to come after her from his cubicle. She looked the part. He knew a whore when he saw one. But when he saw that she was heading for the coffee shop, he stopped and watched her quizzically. Whores have a right to eat.

Ryder signed his tab and went into the coffee shop. Pilar had gone straight through it and was standing on United Nations Avenue. He followed her. He was very aware of the astonished look on the house detective's face. But then they had been astonished all day, ever since he showed up at four P.M. without Terry. Well, let 'em smirk. Hotel personnel were paid to see everything, think anything they want, and keep their mouths shut. He took Pilar by the arm and steered her toward his Mitsubishi parked in front of the hotel. He didn't say a word until they were going up Burgos on their way toward Aurora Avenue. Then he managed a censorious "Well?"

Her gentle, placid face came as near a frown as it could manage. "Please, do not be angry. But my family talked it over and we think this is best. I already know you. And, well, I am best qualified."

He couldn't think of anything to say to that, so he said nothing. She pressed on. "And please, if there is any danger, we couldn't ask someone not as close to my uncle and aunt as I am. Please, do you understand?"

If there is any danger. Terry was right. He made things too complicated. He should have figured out a way to bring Terry with him. Now Pilar reached over to touch his arm. "Or do you object to my appearance? Don't I look right?"

"For a whore, you mean. Yes, you pass muster. You've got the proper uniform." He turned up Epifanio de Los Santos, cut left into Fort Malolos, saluted the guards at the gate and headed past the commissaries out toward the cogon fields. What a waste of space. They should be growing beans and corn and tomatoes and what-all here. "Have you eaten? Good. But I've got some sandwiches and beer in the rear seat with the towels and Band-Aids. It's going to be a long night."

He switched off the lights and drove in the darkness. "This is the way they drive in the People's Republic. And in Turkey, too, and Lord knows how many other countries. Lights out for safety's sake. We're going to stop by a row of narra trees, if I can find them in this blackness." He inched along for over a mile and, by poking his head out the window, managed to guide the tiny car under the narra trees. Or at least under some kind of trees. "I think we're far enough off the road so we won't be picked up in anyone's lights. I hope."

He switched off the motor and the night noises enveloped them. Soughing wind and then, faint at first until the ear became attuned, the cicadas' hum which swelled into a shrilling wail.

"Nine forty-five. They won't be making their move much before eleven. Then it will take two or three hours to get here. We should expect them from one o'clock on."

Pilar nodded and, to his incredulity, he found himself thinking of her as a woman. A damned attractive woman. Terry had done this to him. For him. In place of a semi-comatose moribundity she had given him life. New life, new horizons, new expectations, new values.

"We're about in line with the escape route of your aunt and uncle," he said. "If they follow instructions, they should come out about here. But if they get lost or mixed up and crawl around in that cogon, they're liable to get totally confused; then they might come out anywhere from a mile in either direction. I think at one o'clock we should split. Keep the car as our base and each of us go a couple of hundred yards or so east and west along the road. That will extend our range. What do you think?"

They talked generalities. Families. Politics. Life in the Philippines under a martial law dictatorship. For instance, Mori and Frega, the men they were going to pick up after the rescue, were scheduled to go to jail. Everyone knew that. The government wanted their businesses. It was very difficult for the former great families, but endurable for the masses, who had never had much of an occasion to experience freedom and democracy. The old exchange: peace and food for slavery. Well, not too much food. Millions of Filipinos were close to starvation. And as one o'clock approached, she asked, "How will you get them out of the country?"

"The first step is to put your aunt and uncle in the trunk. We go out the Bagumbayan gate. Past the guards. That may be a problem. I have a little helper." And he reached under the seat and pulled out the Hush-Puppy. In the confined front seat it seemed like a machine gun. Pilar winced and pulled back. "I hope I won't have to use it. Once through the gate, we go to Makati and pick up Victor Frega and Christopher Mori. I have passports for all of them and plane tickets on Japan Air Lines, Flight Two to Tokyo and San Francisco from Hong Kong."

"Hong Kong? How do they get there?"

"That's where Miss Jefferson comes in." Miss Jefferson. Why not Mrs. Harry Ryder? Why not? Because he was fifty-two and she was twenty-eight. And twenty-four years separated them. And he didn't want any jests from his argumentative brain. When I'm ninety she'll be sixty-six. No, the Arabs had worked it all out centuries ago. With four wives at a time and perhaps a harem or two, they had mastered this age-differential bit. Divide the man's age in half and add ten and that's the youngest possible age a man can look for in a woman. At least, in a woman he wants to be happy with. And on that basis, Terry should be thirty-six. Half of fifty-two plus ten. Well, she wasn't thirty-six. She was twenty-eight. "We'll take two cars in case one breaks down. We'll leave Makati no later than four A.M. and drive to Tagaytay. Miss Jefferson will meet us there. At six A.M. In a plane."

"In a plane?"

"Yes." Of course, Terry at twenty-eight had more experience than most women at fifty-eight. That was not a piece of logic Aristotle would have tolerated, now was it? "She's in Nasugbu. She's sleeping in the plane. She'll leave Nasugbu at five forty-five this morning and land at the big field outside Tagaytay near the P.C. barracks. Do you know it?"

She nodded. "But I don't understand. With a plane there's radar and the military planes. Won't there be danger?"

He looked at his watch. It was twelve forty-five. "I'm going to have a sandwich and a beer. Will you join me?" He helped himself. "Yes, there'll be danger. It's a question of timing. If the escape is discovered before six o'clock, we'll have trouble. If the escape is discovered at six or six-fifteen—that's my hope—then we might be thirty miles out to sea. It all depends. The plane goes over two hundred miles an hour. And at thirty miles out we can dip down to sea level and start dodging radar. We'll swing south and then west before turning north. We have our flight plan registered. Miss Jefferson told the airport people at Nasugbu that we were heading for Sandakan. In Borneo. But we'll report properly to Manila we're on our way to Hong Kong. That's if we get away—well, we'll work it out. There're too many intangibles to predict what's going to happen, not the least of which is where are your aunt and uncle? Come on, let's take up our posts."

They got out and Pilar walked west and he walked east. He stood under a narra tree and tried to hear beneath or beyond the shriek of the cicadas. One good thing, not a vehicle had come along this one-lane dirt road. If José Manzano and Emerenciana had been apprehended in their escape attempt, wouldn't there be M.P.s scouring every corner of Fort Malolos for putative accomplices?

He paced up and down for over an hour and there, materializing with no warning, just as a pelting rain scudded through the leaves, were two dark figures. They took a step backwards. He held up an arm and beckoned. They looked at each other—he sensed this rather than saw it in the dark—and they came forward. Mr. Manzano and Mrs. Darang, I presume. He repressed a giggle.

"I am Harry Ryder, Harry the American, Mr. Manzano.

We met once thirty years ago. You were with your father in Leyte. Your niece is a couple hundred yards down the road. Mrs. Darang."

They all stood there looking at each other self-consciously. Manzano put out his hand. Emerenciana Darang did the same. Ryder cupped both their hands in his. "Thank you, Mr. Ryder. Thank you." Manzano seemed to have tears in his eyes. "We put pillows under the blankets on our beds, didn't we, Emmy?" And she nodded solemnly. "Yes, pillows. And we put the bars back in the window. They were our ideas, Mr. Ryder."

"Good ideas," he said gravely. "I should have thought of them myself. Come, let's go to the car. While I get your niece, you can wipe away the blood on your cheeks and hands. There are towels and Band-Aids in the back seat."

Manzano put his hand on Ryder's arm. "My niece is here? Pilar? Why?"

"She is best qualified."

"Best qualified? Ah. Best qualified. Yes, she is, that was my wife's idea. Pilar is best qualified. Yes. But why here?"

"Come, please come. It's about three. We must get out of here so we can leave Makati by four. We must meet a plane at Tagaytay by six in the morning. We're cutting it fine. Please come."

Emerenciana Darang took her brother's arm, "You heard Mr. Ryder, José. We're sorry it took us so long." She led Manzano beside her. "But the grass was so tall and we got lost. I think we crawled around and around in circles. We finally stood up and followed the stars. If this rain had come an hour ago, we'd never have made it."

They stopped by the car and Ryder put his glasses on the front seat. They were useless in the rain. "Please wait here. I'll be right back."

But Pilar was already returning on her own. She flung herself into her uncle's arms and they both wept. Ryder got the Band-Aids, towels, and snacks and opened the trunk. "Good people, will you please crawl in here? It'll be very tight." Pilar had said forty percent of the Filipinos suffered from malnutrition. Manzano could have been one of them; however, Emerenciana Darang did make up somewhat for her brother's anorexia. "Please, here are the towels and Band-Aids. And some sandwiches and beer. You can take care of yourselves while we drive out of here."

Emerenciana once more guided her teary brother. "We'll be quiet, Mr. Ryder. I promise you. You first, José."

Ryder eased the trunk door down. "Everything all right? Good. Come on, Pilar, now it's our turn."

He got behind the wheel, put his glasses in his shirt pocket, placed the Hush-Puppy under his right leg, rolled down both windows, looked at Pilar. The rain splattered them. "Ready?" She nodded, reached up her right hand and tore her blouse. Her right breast was fully exposed. Woman as actor. How did she come by this talent? "I understand. Here we go."

Lights blazing, they drove east toward Bagumgayan. The guard gate was two kilometers away. Long before they reached the hut, two astonished soldiers were standing on either side of the road, rain bouncing off their ready carbines. He pulled up between them and grinned at the slight, toothy soldier by the window.

"Hi! I didn't realize it was so late." He pointed to Pilar. They leaned into the car to look at her. She tried to pull her torn blouse together, but not enough to conceal her breast. It might have been small, but there was nothing wrong with its aesthetics. So far as he could tell, the soldiers never once looked at Pilar's face. Lucky for them. "You understand?"

They still stood astonished, but the one by Pilar, a round-faced lad of twenty or so, began to laugh. "Yes sir, we understand." He looked across the car at his toothy partner. He spoke in Tagalog. "Let's send this bastard on his way. Hell, we've got five hours yet. How about it, little angel? Five hours, now that's good duty, wouldn't you say? And it's dry in the hut." He laughed uproariously, head thrown back, eyes half-shut. That's why it took him quite a while to see the look of anguish on his toothy partner's face. His laugh choked off, though his mouth continued open, as if in a rictus of death.

Ryder had his Hush-Puppy in against the toothy teeth. He was sliding slowly out the side door. "You explain to your friend if he so much as twitches, you are dead." He spoke in Tagalog. Both men heard him plainly. "Say it!" And teeth said it. "Now tell him to drop his rifle and put his hands over his head and walk around and lie on the hood. Tell him!" And teeth told him. "Now you join him." And teeth joined him. They were really quite young.

"Girl, you go in the hut and see if you can find some rope or something. We'll have to tie up these two. If we can't tie them up, we'll have to kill them. Or does either of you have any better ideas?"

"Handcuffs. They're in the box on the wall. Handcuffs."

"You hear, girl? Bring the handcuffs." He reached in and turned off the car lights. He lifted the pistols from the holsters of his prisoners. Army forty-fives. He should go into the gun-running business. "Don't you turn around. After we blindfold you, we'll tie you up to a couple of trees in that narra grove." He pointed to a lofty, swaying clump about two hundred yards to the north. When they tried to look, the rain made them blink. Ryder had been oblivious to the whistling shower. "And we'll gag you of course. Don't worry about being found. We'll phone in and say where to find you. Now that's better than being dead, isn't it?"

The look on their faces said, "Not much." He had to agree. He consoled them. "You'll find a lot of other people will be looking a lot worse than you do. You'll be lost in the shuffle. Believe me. Be sure to say I hid in the gumamela bushes behind the hut and caught you by surprise. That's the way we'll phone in the story. Does that help? Good."

Pilar said not a word as they drove east to Rodriguez, then south to Donna Julio Vargas, and then on back to De los Santos and south to Urdaneta Village in Makati. Then she leaned back and called to her aunt and uncle. "We are approaching number fifty-five. Do not talk until we come to a stop and I say its okay. Do you understand me?"

"We understand."

And she looked at Ryder. Now her admiration was almost worship. "Thank you, Mr. Ryder. Thank you."

"No thanks yet, Pilar. Guard against hubris. Knock on wood if you can find any. We are a long ways from safe yet."

41

San Vicente, like most of the streets in Urdaneta Village, was as long as three normal blocks. He pulled the Mitsubishi into the curb next to a tree and sat quietly until the night silence was the only noise. San Vicente was a well-lit street with banaba trees and apartment buildings lining both sides. The buildings were about six or seven stories high.

"I don't like this. My antennae smell trouble all around us. Any insomniac could be watching us from those blank windows. I should have gotten your aunt and uncle out of the trunk back in Fort Malolos. And I'm leery of starting the motor again. It might wake someone up. Which apartment house is number fifty-five?"

She pointed. "About two-thirds of the way down. The one with the awning out over the sidewalk."

"Mr. Manzano. Mrs. Darang. We are a short way from your friends. Can you hear me? Knock if you can." They both knocked. The sound boomed like a drum roll. Or pistol shot. Jolly. "We'll watch for a while. From what Pilar's told me about your friends, it's possible Calugas's men may be around somewhere. Please bear with us."

They sat in silence. Pilar watched him not unlike the way Terry Jefferson used to. Used to. Still did! If he was almost twice Terry's age, he was almost three times Pilar's. He had never been aware that young people in or around Orinda, Contra Costa County, California, U.S.A., watched him—with respect or any other way. In fact, they seemed oblivious of his existence. To the youth of Orinda, age fifty-two was no better than a walking death. And if he ever got back to Orinda, he would once again vanish in their eyes. Jolly again. "I don't know what to do, Pilar. Shall we drive up? Shall we walk up? Shall we sit here all night and stare at the building?"

"Why did you say Culuga's men 'may be' around here. Of course they are. They're watching both Mr. Mori and Mr. Frega." Pilar seemed quite relaxed about the whole thing. "They try to keep out of sight, but we know where they stay."

"Ah, thank you, Miss Manzano. That's interesting information. Why didn't you tell me before?"

"I thought you knew." He was the expert, wasn't he? "I thought you knew everything."

She was not sarcastic. The sweet sound of a woman's praise. "Thank you for your confidence." God above, she would have let him drive right to the front door. "I should have asked sooner. Believe me, no, I don't know everything, Pilar. I'm just living by my wits. So please help me. Please."

"Help you?"

He drew five deep breaths. "Yes, if you please. Where are the tails, pardon me, the men watching the building?"

"Why, one's hidden in that bougainvillea by the front door. The other puts himself in the clump of banana trees across the rear alley. Their cars are parked on the street and in the alley. In the morning they are relieved by two men who drive up in delivery trucks and park in the front and back."

"Rear alley? What's that, Pilar?"

"If you go to the corner and turn right, halfway down there's an alley that runs parallel to this street and serves as a trade entrance for the apartments on San Vicente and San Martin. It's also the way you get to the garages."

He weighed the possiblities. "I don't like this business of two men separated from each other." He sensed her surprise. "Yes, we can confront them one at a time. That's good. But inevitably, while I'm facing one, my back is to the other. And that's bad, Pilar, bad. But we have no choice. Let's take the one in the banana clump first. The one in the rear."

She nodded and slid next to him. She put both arms around his neck and pressed against him. No nymphomaniac could have been more wanton. He turned the key in the car and the motor roared. Well, purred. The Mitsubishi was not a Volkswagen. "This is the first time you've ever done this with a man in a car, isn't it?" She nodded. He felt her shiver. The one nymphomaniac he had known had shivered in just the same way—of course for a totally opposite reason. "You should go on the stage, Pilar. You're a natural-born actress. Better than that, playwright. You write the lines as you go along."

"No, Mr. Ryder, I'm just doing what you do. What all Filipinos do. We live by our wits. This will tell the man in the bougainvillea why we stopped, hey?"

"That it will. But please don't cut me off from the Hush-Puppy, the gun. I've got to be able to reach it."

They eased out into the street and drove slowly to the corner. She reached a hand down, shuddered as she touched the pistol but pulled it up and placed it on his lap. "It's so long."

"That's a silencer." He turned the corner. "As soon as we stop, pull away from me, Pilar. Keep your face turned away from the tree. I don't want them recognizing you.

This won't be as easy as with the guards. And no names when we talk. As my friend, Terry, is always telling me, someone is going to get killed here. Sorry, Pilar, but that's the way it is."

"Kill 'em."

Sic semper tyrannis. Except there are an awful lot of tyrants. More tyrants—real or imagined—than time to kill them. Too bad history moves so slowly. Well, right now he didn't want it going any faster.

"Right. Careful now." He pulled up beside the banana clump. Pilar was next to the trees. Was that a darker shadow between the two trunks? "That was a lovely evening, darling. Here, I'll open your door." He got out and walked behind the trunk. A concrete pathway went along the side of the building. It led to the bougainvillea in the front. The pathway was empty. He leaned around the right side of the car, pulled up the Hush-Puppy, and whispered in Tagalog, "You, there, come out. I've got you covered. Quietly."

The pause seemed infinite. But these days, of course, infinity is finite. The bulk came forward, hands up; and then, more by intuition than by actual sight, Ryder sensed a disembodied hand rising toward him—a disembodied hand with a pistol in it. As Ryder fell to his right, the Hush-Puppy and the pistol went off together. But if he hadn't been falling to the right the bullet would have caught him in the heart. As it was he felt his left arm dissolve. The blow knocked him to his right knee, a perfect position for a second shot, but it wasn't required. While the roar of the unsilenced pistol reverberated up and down the canyon formed by the alley, the unseen cop first pitched backwards, hit the tree, then fell forward to the pavement. Bougainvillea bush. Of course the son-of-a-bitch would come back here to goof off with his buddy— or were there three?

He motioned to the cop with his hands up. Obediently, he lay down by his comrade; he was wincing in anticipation as Ryder knocked him out. The exertion sent an agonizing twinge through Ryder's left arm, but on the whole the pain was far from excruciating. A hammer blow on his thumb would have hurt more; but the numbness, the shock, wouldn't last long. In fact, by the time he concluded that no other cop was around—and even more amazing, that not one person had thrown open his window to ask what the hell was going on—the pain hit him and he doubled up. The sight of blood spurting through his mangled shirt sleeve didn't help any.

"Girl!"

She sprang from the car, took a towel, ripped his shirt sleeve and made a tourniquet above the wound. She worked efficiently and silently. She didn't seem the least moved by the wound or the blood. Her placid face could have modeled for the Lord Buddha. He knelt and put the Hush-Puppy on the ground, pulled out a handkerchief and mopped his face. The sweat was busting out in great beads, as if his body was exploding liquid atoms. If this kept on, he would be dehydrated.

"I've never been hit before, Pilar. All those years. Thanks. And thanks again. Look up and down. Do you see anyone watching us?"

She looked serenely about her. "Yes, I see someone."

He wrenched up the gun. "Who? Where? Kneel down, for Christ's sake. Point them out!"

"Up there. On the third floor. That's Frega's apartment. They've been watching us."

He sank slowly till his behind hit the ground. He mopped his face again. "I'm getting too old for this sort of thing. Signal them to come down. Then let's stash these thugs somewhere. Maybe in the garage. In a storeroom. We'll do the usual. Like with the guards."

She nodded. "We'll wait till the others come down and help us." He hurt. He was exhausted. Why did an innocuous, peace-loving Rotarian type like Harry Ryder surround himself with bodies? The women were the bloodthirsty ones. Kill 'em. That's the women's motto. And then he made out it was Pilar's voice he heard, not his own maunderings.

"Shall we kill 'em?" She pointed. "This one's also alive. He's acting unconscious. He might be. But he's not badly wounded. If we don't do something they could sound the alarm. Shall we kill 'em?"

He stared at her. The same inviolate serenity. Would you like the salt and the pepper? Kill 'em? What dress shall I wear today? Kill 'em?

"Did either of them see your face?"

She shook her head. "I kept my back turned like you said."

"Then we shall not kill them."

"They are scum," Pilar was as polite as a nun. "They're all scum. Men like them have tortured my friends. Boys, of course. But girls my age, too. Shall I describe what they do?" She waited. He stood up, said nothing. "My friends are coming. The two cars—in the garage. I'll open the trunk."

"You do that." He knelt by the silent bodies and took their pistols. Two thirty-eights this time. Chow Woon Chung would have real competition at this rate.

42

It was five forty-five. Already broad daylight. And they all saw them at the same moment. The Philippine Constabulary was strolling out onto the double soccer field in T-shirts and shorts. They were getting ready to do their morning calisthenics. Fifty or sixty of them. They were almost three hundred yards away.

The fugitives looked at Ryder. They were crouched

amidst the niog-niogan bushes. A white flower kept swinging into his left eye. By noon the niog-niogan flower would be pink and by evening, red. The Filipinos called it the yesterday, today, and tomorrow flower. Just let there be a tomorrow.

"No problem, my friends." They were reassured. If the American said there was no problem, why, there was no problem. Q.E.D. They looked at his arm. Two skinny Filipinos, Manzano and Frega; a beautiful poet; one tall one, Mori, with the high cheekbones of the mountain Visayan. He could have been another brother to Gemi Mandares. Had they discovered Mandares's body yet? There had been nothing in yesterday's papers. "We'll keep to our plan. When Miss Jefferson pulls up in front of us, we walk—not run—to the plane. And my arm is okay. I'll be right with you."

They nodded. So far everything had gone without a hitch. After trussing and gagging the policemen and depositing them in a storeroom, they had left Makati shortly after four in two cars. He had kissed Pilar goodby. On the cheek. "Thank you, Pilar. You are indeed best qualified. You and your friends will win out yet."

"God be with you," she had said. "And I will have a man make the phone call to the P.C. like you said. 'Here is a message for Colonel Calugas. I will say it once. You will find the Bagumbayan guards two hundred yards north of the hut in the narra grove. Don't blame them. I came at them from the gumamela bushes. You should remove those bushes. And please tell Junius Oakland—O-A-K-L-A-N-D—I'll be in Hong Kong.' And the caller will hang up instantly."

He had nodded. "I knew a girl like you once, Pilar. Her name was Teresa Morgan. In Leyte. Thank you again."

And the two cars had caravaned away, José Manzano driving with his sister and Ryder; Frega driving with Christopher Mori. Pilar was to take the Mitsubishi back to the Intercontinental Hotel and leave it in the parking lot.

The drive to Tagaytay through Las Pinas, Dasmarinas, and Silang had been decorous and uneventful. When they reached Tagaytay at five-thirty, they parked the cars a half-mile from their destination and tipped two boys five pesos each to watch them. "We're going for an all-day hike up to Lake Taal. You watch the cars for us. We want to see all the hub caps on when we get back." And the tykes had nodded solemnly. "We will stay home from school and watch them for you." As they spoke, their ancient eyes were on Ryder—and his arm. Even though it was hidden by the barong tagalog Mori had given him —Mori was now in his T-shirt—there was no concealing the fact he could not move it. "Never show—never tell," he had said gravely to the boys. "That's what a domino-playing friend of mine always says." They had nodded in profound agreement.

Five fifty-five.

By now Terry should be almost here. She would have started the engines, called the tower, if there was anyone there to call, told them they were on their way to Manila Domestic and taken off before they could digest the shock of hearing a woman's voice. Everyone at the airport had seen Ryder pilot the 310 to its parking place. Had they tried to stop her? She was a hard woman to stop. By the time he had caught the Manila bus from Nasugbu, she had begun to fudge on her announced flight from spydom.

"Do you know what I was planning to do when you walked up to me that day at Channel Twelve?" They were having an early lunch at the Nasugbu Restaurant and Lodging House. "I was going to go to real estate school. Can you imagine? Terry Jefferson, Realtor. But why not? I was going nowhere in Hollywood. There are five thousand girls in Hollywood prettier than I am, ten thousand who can act better. Dead End kid, that was me. Once I considered going into banking. One of my friends —he was a bigwig at Wells Fargo Bank—he told me he'd get me into their management training program. He said women were not minorities at Wells Fargo. Yes—don't look at me like that—yes, he was one of my friends. All right, one of my marks. Does that please you more?"

"I haven't said a word, Terry."

"No, but you were about to." And she had leaned back, stroked back her hair in a quintessentially feminine gesture, said, "Oh hell, Peter—see how good I am with that Peter?—I'm sorry. You have been perfect. I didn't think this could ever happen to me. I've known girls like me who married and apparently lived happily ever after, but I didn't believe it. And thank you for not once asking me if I was enjoying myself. Any time a man asked me that I never saw him again. Yes, you passed with all colors flying in every way. Anyway, I thought about becoming a banker, and I would have made a good one. I'm good at mathematics and think I could learn to understand how money works. But when I talked to friends, I learned about the committee system in banks and that was more than I could swallow. I am not a committee. I am Terry Jefferson. And that's why my own little real estate business appealed to me. Real estate is math, too. But then you came along. . . . Well, I don't know."

"The Company has ten times more committees than all the banks in America put together."

"Maybe. But you're not a committee."

"I'm not in the Company any more."

"I don't know, I don't know."

And Manzano grabbed his good arm. "There it is. Out over the lake."

Ryder had been watching the 310 for the last two minutes. Terry was flying low and, as she made her turn to come in over the schoolhouse on their left, she was at rooftop level. None of the calisthenicists had seen her yet. While the fugitives watched her land, he kept his eye on the P.C. They were leaning forward and trying to put the palms of their hands flat on the ground. They didn't even see the plane until it was a hundred and fifty yards away

211

from them. Terry had come in so low she almost scraped the schoolhouse roof and so slowly she almost pancaked. But she did cut the turn-around distance by fifty yards. Good girl.

She taxied back to the schoolhouse, turned, started to pull up beside them. He wished he could have blotted out the identification. But there was no escaping the fusilage-high print. This was, for all to see, plane G AW 2X.

"Now," Ryder said. And the Filipinos rose with him, pushed through the bushes and strolled to the plane. The P.C. were watching them now. The fugitives plunged into the seats. Terry looked at his arm, raised her eyebrows, gunned the motor. Good girl. As they pulled up over the barracks, Ryder said, "Wave to them." And they all waved and the constables waved back. They couldn't have been more blasé. Marvelous fellows. Great cops.

"Head south," Ryder said. The pain in his arm had flared up, his face was white. "Give me the mike. I'll report to Manila. Tell 'em G AW 2X is on its way to Hong Kong. But you head south. As if to Sandakan. Thirty miles out duck down to the water. Head west. Don't hit any ships. Turn north after another hundred and fifty miles. If they catch us, well, we tried. Wake me up when you approach Kai Tak. And thanks. Real estate is not enough for you. I can see that now."

43

The waiter was just pulling out the wings of the breakfast table when the phone rang. Junius Oakland pulled back his bathrobe sleeve. Eight-fifteen.

"Yes?"

"I just resigned. On the private line. You know the one.

I suppose I must thank you for all your help."

"I'm sorry. Truly. It was a ghastly mistake on my part. What happened?"

"Our friends flew the coop. In a private plane. G AW 2X. Piloted by a woman. Terry Jefferson. Our friend goes by the name of Peter McClaren. They were at Leyte. The plane reported it was on its way to Hong Kong. But it headed south. Nasugbu reports they said they were going to Sandakan. We've searched in both directions. Nothing."

"Sandakan?"

"In Borneo."

"Do you believe it?"

Caluga's harsh voice softened, as if he were suddenly pleased with something. "No, not at all. I got a message for you a few minutes ago. An anonymous call."

"And?"

"And the message said, and I quote, 'Please tell Junius Oakland—O-A-K-L-A-N-D—I'll be in Hong Kong."

Oakland signed the breakfast tab and watched the waiter go out the door. From his window on the ocean side of the Philippine Plaza Hotel he could count thirty-eight freighters on the hook in Manila Bay. "On the hook." He hadn't thought of that phrase since 1945. On the hook—did that symbolize something?

Calugas rumbled, "Are you there?"

"I'm here. I was thinking."

"Thinking what?"

"He won't accept your resignation."

"You're smart. Of course he won't. The official line is that we planned the whole thing. I'm to get the word out today to Forbes Park, make a public announcement before our birds alight. Our great humanitarian belief in human rights. And you?"

"Appointment in Samara."

"Pardon?"

"I'll catch the next plane to Hong Kong."

"Cathay Pacific has a flight at ten-fifteen. I'll see that you get a seat. And good shooting."

Junius Oakland replaced the receiver, pulled back his sleeve again. Eight twenty-two. He picked up the phone. "I want to place a call to my wife in Hong Kong. And when that is through, please call Mr. Li Ngor Sheung. Also in Hong Kong. Both calls are person to person. Here are the numbers."

Part Four

44

When the pain became too intense, Ryder had to wake up. The roar of the engine seemed to harmonize with the throb in his arm. For a moment he wondered if he really had awakened. All he could see was grey. Grey mist out the windshield, grey clouds beside them. What was the phrase? Grey death? He leaned to the window and looked out. Palpable grey, above and below.

"Where are we?"

"Two hours or so from Kai Tak."

"No, I mean how high are we?"

"Twenty feet above the waves."

He peered out again. The grey clouds below them now seemed to have occasional whitish glints. Christ, the waves were fifty feet high. How did she know she was above them?

"What is it? Typhoon?"

"No. Class-three signal."

The signals ran 3–8–9–10. Ten was typhoon.

"Are planes still landing?"

"They're landing."

"Good girl." How jolly if they had to turn back to Manila. He leaned back and felt the beads of sweat course down his cheeks. "You can go up now. We're safe."

He turned and looked at the four Filipinos. They had been watching him anxiously. "Sorry to conk out on you, my friends. It's only a flesh wound. I'll be all right." He followed their eyes. They were watching his arm. It was a bloody mass. And getting bloodier.

"Please, Mr. Ryder, we've just been waiting for you to wake up." José Manzano held up a bandage. "The first-aid kit. We've got it set up. It has sulfa, too. Emmy will take care of you. Please."

Ryder nodded. "Okay. But Mrs. Darang, will you please conceal this gun?" He had deposited his arsenal in the trunk of the Mitsubishi. "And Miss Jefferson also has one. She'll tell you what to do. Mrs. Darang, you're an excellent nurse."

"Filipinos learn how at an early age. I daresay you know how, too. The bullet took a piece out of the bone. But not much. Basically a deflection, I'd say. There. How is this sling?"

And the almost professional treatment did make a difference. "The wound must be stitched up. Otherwise you'll have real problems." Manzano held up a bottle. "Pain killers, Mr. Ryder; would you like one? One every four hours or as needed, that's what it says."

"No thanks. And the sling is just right." He was watching Terry. She was following the activity behind her, but only remotely. Her concentration was superb. Like her skill. "Nice going, Terry. My friends, have I introduced Miss Terry Jefferson? We owe our rescue to her, and not just today. The only person as heroic as Terry is Pilar Manzano. Your niece. You should be proud of her indeed."

He pointed to Terry's purse. "If you'll look in there, Mr. Manzano, you'll find your passports. Maricar Macasieb provided them for you. You won't need them in Hong Kong. You might in Tokyo, though I doubt it—I'll explain why in a moment—and in San Francisco they'll be quite superfluous. Macasieb will be waiting for you at Immigration, along with the people from the media. But you still've got to have 'em. And I needed them to get the plane tickets."

Manzano reached in, but came up with the tickets first. Ryder nodded. "Flight number two, JAL. It goes straight through to San Francisco. With a stopover in Tokyo. It leaves at thirteen-fifty." He looked at his wristwatch, glanced at the fuel gauge. Ten-twenty. Plenty of fuel.

"Head winds?"

Terry nodded. "Easier now. I went west far enough to get the winds at least quartering on us."

Manzano laughed when he saw the passports. He studied each one, scrutinized his friends. "Victor, you are Alex Carpiso. Chris, you are Lee Coloma. Except that Mr. Coloma, whoever he is, has twice as much hair as you do. Emmy, you'll do all right. You're Felicia Farlega. And me, I'm Manuel Lugado. But where do I get a moustache?"

"I suggest you stay on the plane in Tokyo. It sits at Haneda for not quite two hours. Tell 'em you're tired after an all-night farewell party. That way you won't have to show your passports." He got up and opened Terry's cosmetic case. "Here, Mr. Manzano. This should be an adequate moustache. And Mr. Mori, how about this for a wig? And this should be enough money to get you to San Francisco or a bit further. I've kept it in twenties."

He went back to the copilot's seat. "Now, here is what we do. Miss Jefferson will park beside a plane that's disembarking. There should be two or three to pick from. We'll all pile out and get into the bus. I'll lead you to the transit lounge. Miss Jefferson will then park the plane and join me at Immigration. Any questions?"

The flight plan recorded only two passengers. If the authorities saw a pilot and five passengers, the fat would be in the fire.

Terry talked to the airport, reported, "We're going in

at twelve-forty. Just behind Singapore Airlines flight five. . . . It lands at twelve thirty-seven. We will follow it in and try to time it right."

She looked at Ryder, reproachfully. "That extra wig you bought. You knew all the time what you wanted it for."

And two hours later, when they finally pulled to the end of the two-mile long runway, they all saw it. Passengers from the Singapore Airlines 707 were heading down the ramp stairs.

"Cessna 310, where are you going? Not there, not there."

"I know, Control. I've got a lazy passenger here. He wants to ride in with the bus."

"Ride in—what's the matter with you? You can ride in with a bus from your berth."

But Terry swung in behind the 707. The tower was out of sight. Ryder took off his sling, gestured and the five scrambled down the wing. He could hear Terry. "Sorry, Control. That was dumb of me." Then she whisked the 310 away.

"Slowly, calmly," Ryder said. "Under the plane by the ramp."

A few disembarking Singapore Airlines passengers looked at them in surprise; but four brown faces and one white—even a Caucasian who held his arm awkwardly and whose face was whiter than it should be—was about what one expected to see in Kai Tak airport, so the interest was transitory. The Filipinos were serene as monks. Brave people. The bus trundled to the terminal, and Ryder led his charges into the transit lounge. The hard plastic chairs felt like overstuffed divans.

"This is it, gentlemen, Mrs. Darang. You were wonderful."

All four of them shook their heads. "You were the wonderful one." Manzano spoke for them. "You and Miss Jefferson. May we ask one question, Mr. Ryder?"

"Ask away."

"Is she a Charlie's Angel?"

Terry had still been wearing her platinum wig. God, would she get rid of it before Immigration? "No, Mr. Manzano. She's an angel, but not the Charlie kind."

Should he ask her to marry him? Jean would love that. He hadn't thought of her in weeks. Did she ever get together with John Sweeney?

Terry was standing at the door. Her wig was gone. Her natural hair fell below her shoulders. Brunette. She was not so glamorous now, but she was prettier. She was carrying a jacket. His jacket. He stood up.

"We won't shake hands, gentlemen. I'll just fade away. Good luck and I hope to see you in San Francisco."

Darang laughed. "Goodbye, MacArthur."

He walked toward Terry. By putting his left thumb in his belt, he managed a sling effect.

"There's still time for you to change your mind. You can go to Tokyo with them."

Terry shrugged and handed him his jacket. "Here, put this on. You might start bleeding again any minute. We'll get you to a doctor before we do another thing. And as to going back to San Francisco, I know the message you gave Pilar. If you're meeting Junius Oakland in Hong Kong, I'm meeting him, too."

"I don't even know he's here."

"Good. Then we'll have a vacation and catch up on all those weeks of missed sex. You do like sex, Mr. Ryder, I believe?"

"Not Ryder. McClaren. He likes it. We'll have to wait on Ryder. I'm not at all sure of him."

45

It was strange to tell the Hilton registration clerk his name. Mr. Harry Ryder. Of Orinda, California. He had the Ryder passport in his pocket. But hotels in Hong Kong never ask for passports. Almost never.

"We happened to stop by Hong Kong for a few days." He pointed. Terry was supervising their bags. "We took a chance you might have an available room."

On July twenty-second, the Hilton had nothing but available rooms. Even with near-typhoon weather Hong Kong was beastly hot. In retrospect the Philippines seemed almost balmy by comparison. The clerk—he might have been all of twenty—glanced at Ryder's stiff left arm, hesitated the barest fraction of a second, then pushed the registration slip forward. He had had a chance to examine Miss Terry Jefferson.

Ryder filled out the form. He spoke in Cantonese. "Will you be so kind as to send a message for me? To Mr. Li Ngor Sheung?"

The clerk's eyes widened. The other Chinese clerks edged nearer. (Not only are there five million Chinese in Hong Kong and the New Territories, but there is also the British committee system. Never have one man do a job when four can screw it up better.) The youth looked at the others. One was in his forties. He spoke up.

"I'm afraid we don't know a Li Ngor Sheung."

All of them knew he was lying.

"You can reach him at the New China News Agency. Just tell him I am registered here. I'll be in all day."

Terry came up. But for once she was not the center of attention. The elder Chinese kept to Cantonese. "Ah yes, the New China News Agency. Yes, we will send a message. We will tell him Mr. Harry Ryder just happened to drop in for a few days."

"Here," Ryder said to Terry. "You'd better sign your name. So you can charge things, too."

The Chinese sighed, shook themselves, returned to humdrum. The clerk crossed out the room he had already assigned them, looked inquiringly at Ryder and Terry.

"Would a suite do, Mr. Ryder?"

"A suite would be fine. With a king-size bed."

The Chinese sighed again.

"I'd also like to send a cable." He wrote out the message to Maricar Macasieb. "Flight two. JAL. Departed Hong Kong thirteen-fifty."

It was now fifteen-twenty. They had watched the plane take off.

In the elevator Terry said, "What was that all about? Chinese, yet."

"Li Ngor Sheung. The Bank of China. The sixth, eighth, and thirteenth floors. Just across the street from here. I've got to find out his place in this scheme of things."

They were alone in their suite—one of the Hilton's best—before she said another word. Then she let him have it. "Why did you go through that Philippine shenanigan if all you really wanted to do was confront Li and Oakland?"

"Ah, but it's never just 'all,' is it, Terry?"

He started to take off his jacket but she shook her head. "No you don't. You're seeing the hotel doctor. The infirmary is on the fourth floor. I set up an appointment. While you were registering. One of the porters went off to do it."

"See a doctor! You're crazy. I can't let a doctor see this gunshot wound. He'll have to report it to the police."

"Tell him you were clipped by a propeller blade. Tell him anything. Toss out some more Hong Kong dollars. I've never seen a town where the dollar talks so loudly."

"But Li might come at any time."

"Leave word at the desk you're out for a few minutes."

She was changing from Levis and blouse to a cheongsam, the same one she had worn so long, long ago at her apartment in the Hollywood hills.

"Now what are you doing?"

"I should be taking a bath. But I'll just rub myself down now. I'm going calling on Mr. David Thompson. I want our pistols back. David Thompson, you remember him?" She saw the stricken look on his face. "Harry. And from now on you are Harry. The Harry who, unlike you, I'm most sure about. Remember I told you before, David Thompson is not Sir Spencer Smith? Let me go further. There are no more Sir Spencer Smiths."

"I shouldn't go to the doctor. I'm too weak. I should sleep for twenty-four hours. And forgive me. I'm still not used to this. To you. To living. To being alive. Three years of quiescent, acquiescent celibacy. I didn't even know I was lamed until you tore up the crutches. But I'm healing. I will heal. You go return the plane to David Thompson. I'll see the doctor."

46

It was only a fifteen-minute stroll from the Hilton to the P. & O. Building, but she couldn't walk down Des Voeux Road Central in this Suzie Wong outfit. She could barely get out of the Hilton without causing a riot. Every Chinese in the place stopped to turn and stare—but not any harder than the Caucasians, Malaysians, Indians, Africans, Japanese, and Semites.

You have goofed, Terry my girl. You should go back upstairs and change to the most demure skirt and blouse you can find. Well, the hell with them. If they all thought her a call girl, why should that concern her? Harry didn't think that. Not any more. On the way from the airport he had almost asked her to marry him. And then backed off.

She got into the cab. She saw the driver grin at the Hilton porters and doormen who had come flocking behind her. Well, the hell with him, too. And them.

What would she say? She was in love with Harry. But in Nasugbu he had made clear that when this adventure was over, it was all over. "I retired five years ago," he had said. "And as far as I'm concerned, I'm still retired. This is just an episode, a confrontation, involving me and Junius Oakland. Obviously he finds me a threat. I really don't know why. The kidnapping of Yong Song Hom was so long ago. Over fifteen years. Why should that concern him now? Or if it's not that, what is it? I've got to find out, Terry. I know he wants to kill me. I think that's why he was talking to Li Ngor Sheung. But if that's not it, then what's this all about? Because, sure as shooting, he tried to have to have me killed in San Francisco. Sure as shooting, he sent that photo of Roger Hiller to Colonel Calixto Calugas."

"What do you mean, when this is all over?"

"Not us. Not you and me. I mean this kind of life. I'm not up to this sort of thing any longer. Spying is a young man's game. And the old man part of it, the management end, that's not for me. I'm into management now. I'm a management consultant. A damned good one. I've got major clients and I make major contributions. That's all the excitement I want."

And then she had said the words that probably made him back off on his marriage proposal. "But I like the excitement, Harry. And I must confess, now that I'm two days away from those policemen in Leyte, I'm not even bothered so much by that any more. Oh, I know this is a terrible thing to say. I've waked up each of the past two nights and seen those round little holes in their foreheads.

And their strange grins. That's no good. I'm sorry I had to do what I did, but I'm not sorry, if you know what I mean."

And he had shivered. The air conditioning wasn't all that cold. "You're still thinking of going into the business, aren't you?"

"With you, Harry. I want to go in it with you."

"It doesn't work that way, Terry."

"Oh yes it does. There are man-and-woman teams." She had carefully refrained from saying 'man and wife.' Not yet. "I saw it on a television show."

"All right. But not in this kind of work. As station workers in some god-forgotten country where we shouldn't even be. Not as spies in the covert sense. Hell, everyone in town knows what you're up to as a station employee. It's like civil service, and just as dull."

The cab stopped before the P. & O. Building. She paid the driver and was very aware of his eyes on her as she went into the tiny lobby. She was also aware that she had resumed her former style of walking; head bowed, shoulders slouched, legs swinging in front of her. Harry's leopard stride. One designed incidentally for a cheong-sam. Damn it, she couldn't help it if she was no Filipina. They were beautiful; they were beautifully mannered, beautifully postured. But she was sexy, had been ever since her freshman year at Chico High. Even then she knew that sexiness had little to do with beauty.

The elevator door opened and she found herself at the entrance to British Empire Aviation. She paused and braced herself. She had no illusions about the coming struggle with Mr. David Thompson.

The middle-aged, horse-faced British receptionist raised an eyebrow. That eyebrow exuded distaste—at having to look at her, at having to look at herself. "Ah yes, I recall you. Hamilton. No, Jefferson. Miss Jefferson, wasn't it? Well, I'm sorry, Mr. Thompson has a visitor. I'm sure he'll be tied up quite a while."

Terry smiled sweetly, stood patiently, tried to look as serene as Pilar Manzano. She wanted to strangle the bitch. "Would you be so kind as to ask him when would be a convenient time?"

"He asked not to be disturbed."

Terry smiled even more sweetly.

"Oh, very well." Horse-face rose and walked into the inner office and tried but failed to beat David Thompson back out through the door. In fact, she was almost flung on her face by the burly Englishman's rush.

"Well, well, well. How good to see you. Naughty girl. 'I want to take this fuddy-duddy on a trip through the islands.' Some trip. Where is the fuddy duddy by the way? My old pal—oh, don't think I'm not burned up the way he treated me. But that's the game, isn't it? So—where is Mr. Harry Ryder?"

Her hand went to her throat. She swallowed until she was able to talk again. "Oh. Harry Ryder. You know then. Well, he's sleeping."

"Of course. The sleep of the innocent and the just. I think I must have slept like that once or twice. But come on in. I've got another pal with me. He very much wants to meet you."

"Oh, I'd love to. But all I want to do is return the keys, pay any charges—I've got a blank check signed by, well, by Peter McClaren. And I'd like to go out to the plane with you to pick up a couple of things I forgot."

"Sure, sure. Plenty of time for that. I see you're a real sport after all. I do think you owe me one, don't you?" His leer was pure David Thompson. "But come on in. It'll just take a moment and we'll be on our way. I do remember your promise, my dear. And I expect you to keep it."

This was going to be a lot more difficult than she had foreseen. She preceded Thompson into the inner office and halted dead in her tracks as she saw the elegant Leslie Howardish man standing by the desk. She stumbled as Thompson knocked into her. Leslie Howard sprang forward to hold her up. He did so by grabbing her left breast to support her. His fingers caressed her nipple expertly and he stepped back. There was no leer in his face, no sign that anything at all had happened. Except that his forehead glistened slightly. Harry had told her about that giveaway. His only overt expression was one of curiosity, as if he was trying to remember something.

"May I present Junius Oakland. Miss Terry Jefferson."

"Hah, I remember. The Polo Lounge. Your way of walking. Catlike. But you weren't dressed like this." And now he let an expression of approval flicker across his face. "You were wearing a white blouse, dark trousers, and marvelous boots. They had no wrinkles in them. Marvelous. And the man you were with?"

"Was Harry Ryder." She wanted to return the praise; she had never seen a man so elegantly dressed. Junius Oakland looked the way a spy ought to look. James Bond all the way. "He told me he recognized you. He told me a great deal about you."

"I'm sure he did. He's known me as long as anyone. I recruited him right here in Hong Kong. Did he tell you that? I'm so sorry he didn't see fit to introduce you that day—or himself. Especially since I was the one who recommended him for the job you pulled off so magnificently. Harry the American. The man of many disguises. Well, he fooled me and I must congratulate him—and you —at your leisure. I'll call you for lunch tomorrow. Where are you staying?"

But she was too thunderstruck to say a word. And he understood. "Oh yes, Miss Jefferson, the word is out. Everyone in Forbes Park . . . you know Forbes Park in Manila? All the Americans who count live there, and they already know how President Raymundo let Manzano and Darang escape. The kindness of their hearts—a very common pattern these days in the Philippines. Good ol' Raymundo, Cruz, and Calugas."

David Thompson had gone behind the desk. He was

leaning on it and listening too intently to the sparring.

She recovered. "He didn't introduce himself at the Polo Lounge because of the man you were with. I believe he is one of the top men in the Chinese Secret Service."

Oakland's face was impassive, but his eyes blinked rapidly. She saw that Thompson had also caught this display. If he had slammed the desk in rage, Oakland could not have revealed his agitation more clearly. His hesitation was momentary. "Ah, Li Ngor Sheung. We're old friends, and as you know, our governments are not so unfriendly any more, Miss Jefferson. Not since Mr. Nixon broke the ice."

Thompson's lips formed voiceless words. If she read them correctly, he was repeating 'Li Ngor Sheung.'

"Of course," she said gently. "And Harry did not want to intrude on any delicate matters you might be settling. But I know he'll be so glad to hear you're in Hong Kong. This is a coincidence, isn't it? We're staying at the Hilton and I'll accept your invitation for him right now. I know he'd so much enjoy talking to you."

"Perfect. I love the Hilton and usually stay there myself. But not this time. Here, walk me out to the elevator, my dear. David, you'll be able to monopolize her for the rest of the afternoon. So spare me this favor, old chap." And Oakland took her by the arm and almost hoisted her out of the office. An outraged Miss Horse-face flared after them. At the elevator he stopped. "If Harry told you about me, I'm sure he mentioned my lamentable peccadilloes. Harry always rather disapproved of me. He's not a prude at all—I've always understood that—but he looks at life differently. Please do not think ill of me, Miss Jefferson, and certainly not evil. I simply admire rarity when I see it. You are so rare you're precious. So Terry—may I call you Terry? Please call me Junius. So Terry, I'd like an opportunity to plead my case. I am not what he thinks I am. I only want to be what you think I am. After lunch tomorrow—well, how about drinks? Or better, supper?

I'm sure Harry won't mind sparing you for an evening. What do you say?"

"Harry always said you are the most elegant man he'd ever met." Oakland's forehead was now glistening red. No Chico High School freshman ever lusted more hotly. But then none of them had worn clothes the way Junius did. "And I can see he's right. Look, we've just got back from a rather strenuous trip. Let me give you a reply at lunch tomorrow."

And he took her hand and bowed over it as if he were about to kiss it. But he didn't. Harry was wrong. Oakland didn't walk up to a girl and ask, 'My dear, will you fuck?' No way. He simply didn't kiss her hand.

47

She was quite defenseless when David Thompson decided to become aggressive. She was kneeling at the door to the Cessna 310, screwdriver in hand, and this turned out to be a most unfortunate position. The slit in the cheong-sam brought the skirt open to the thigh. To the crotch, in fact.

This bothered Thompson. On the way to the airport he barely seemed to look out the Mercedes windshield. His eyes saw only her bare legs. These apparently brought on the usual male fantasies, for which she refused to take any blame. If she had been wearing a nun's garb, David Thompson would still have fantasized. But the privacy of the plane and the opportunity for an animal coupling and his conviction that she owed him one—he referred to her debt a half-dozen times on the way to the airport—drove him to unilateral action. He put his right hand on her thigh, slid it until he was stroking her panties. They obviously wouldn't prove much of an obstacle. His left hand, meanwhile, had grabbed for her left breast. He was not an expert. He hurt.

As his right hand got past the panties and grabbed for her flesh, he paid no attention to her work with the screwdriver. She had told him she had left a few goodies concealed there because she didn't want to confront customs. This had amused him. "Running men and smuggling, too. Harry knows how to pick 'em." Now her hand reached a goody. She gently eased it out and swung it against Thompson's chest.

"David dear," she said sweetly, "I have a Hush-Puppy against your chest. Please don't move a muscle. The Hush-Puppy fires nine-millimeter Parabellum cartridges. Without a silencer, the nine-millimeter Parabellum has a muzzle velocity of about twelve hundred feet per second. I read all this in the company manual. By comparison, this is a good deal faster than the U.S. Army forty-five, Model 1911A1, which has a muzzle velocity of only about eight hundred feet per second. I know that because I am an expert with the Army forty-five. But oddly enough, even with the silencer attached, and with special 158-grain cartridge instead of the 164-grain, the less powerful Parabellum cartridge for the silencer manages a muzzle velocity of nine hundred feet per second. That is quite enough to cause instantaneous death. I know. I've already killed two men with it. Instantaneously. And if you don't take your hands off me, I'll gladly make it three. Harry warned me against growing to like killing.

"So please back carefully away. Make no quick moves. And don't try grabbing my pistol. I am classified as an expert with the National Rifle Association. As you may not know, rapid-timed fire is an important part of that classification. Please, David dear."

He backed away and stood up. His eyes were screwed

up as he weighed his chances. David Thompson was no coward. And he did not complain.

"You fooled me before. You fooled me again. Well, that's the way the game is, no? Harry sure does know how to pick 'em."

"Thank you, David. Now I'm going to reach in here and pull out another pistol. I will put it in my purse. And we'll walk back out through the flying school. And you will not try to stop me or alert the authorities, because, my dear, I'll kill you right there in the flying school."

He rubbed his chin. "Did you really kill two men? In the Philippines?"

She did not answer.

"Oakland told me about them. He thought Harry did it. He said Harry has become quite a killer in his old age. Eight men he knows about. I'm glad to see Harry's not responsible for every one of the bodies he leaves behind him. Come, let's get going. The plane looks fine and I just remembered I have a pressing dinner engagement tonight. I hope you don't mind if I don't drive you back to the Hilton? I'd do it with Harry. He's a professional. But one thing professionals learn very early. Be wary of amateurs. Especially with amateur women who are cock teasers."

When she reached the door to their suite at the Hilton, it was about six in the evening. She could hear voices in the room. She unlocked the door and eased her way in, one hand on the Hush-Puppy in her purse. Maybe Thompson was right. Maybe being an amateur made her jumpy. But the feel of the cool, aluminum-alloy butt somehow did seem to calm her nerves.

48

The handsome Chinese saw her first. He broke off in the middle of a sentence in Chinese and sprang to his feet. He smiled at her—and it was a glorious, happy smile. For once, someone did not automatically lech for her. The Chinese smiled happily because he was a happy man. And maybe because he had marvelous teeth.

"You are Terry Jefferson," he said. His English had a strong accent. "I saw you in Los Angeles. I see now I should have recognized you when my friend described you. Sir Charles Sam. Sam Them Nai. He watched you shoot at the gun club. None of us knew who your escort was. What a surprise to find that Mr. Peter McClaren is Mr. Arthur Twilling who is also Mr. Harry Ryder, and all three of them are also Mr. Roger Hiller, customer of another friend of mine, Mr. Chow Woon Chung. I'm so happy to see you again. Sir Charles, I must say, is a master of understatement."

She blushed. How extraordinary to blush. She sat down and said, "And you must be Mr. Li Ngor Sheung. Harry has spoken of you with the greatest admiration."

She looked at Ryder and sucked her breath. He was terribly white, perhaps feverish, but certainly exhausted past bearing. "Harry, you shouldn't be up. You look like death warmed over. You need at least forty-eight hours uninterrupted sleep."

But his face was suddenly getting color and vivacity. The look of joy in his eyes was exhilarating. And humbling. She was used to many expressions in men's eyes. Joy was not one of them. Her poor dear Rotarian. And he shook his head. "I know. No, I guess I don't know. Mr. Li has been most kind to me. With me. Would you mind if I bring Miss Jefferson up to date, Mr. Li?"

"My English name is Ralph. Ralph Lee. With two *e*'s. Please call me Ralph. We've known each other too long —even if not intimately—to be anything but Ralph and Harry. Yes, certainly, tell Miss Jefferson. I understand from Harry you've played a major part in your strange adventure in the Philippines. I hope you will not be so actively involved in Hong Kong."

"What he means, darling, is that Junius Oakland is very much in Hong Kong."

The darling was something new. And she liked it. She was no cock tease. She was a normal American housewife. Maybe even an Orinda housewife. Darling. "I know. I've met him. At David Thompson's. He sends you his congratulations for doing the job he recommended you for."

"He? Oakland. So Carter told the truth." And Harry began to laugh. He was definitely feverish. "But go ahead. What else did he say?"

"He's going to invite us to lunch tomorrow. I accepted for both of us. He's also invited me for supper tomorrow night. I've not accepted."

The smile slowly faded on Harry's face. Li Ngor Sheung seemed to pluck away his smile. This was plainly not smiling time. Harry whispered, "The bastard." He seemed to be struggling for words, so she intervened.

"We'll discuss all that later. Please go ahead with what you and Mr. Li had to say."

"Ralph."

"Oh, Ralph. I'm Terry. Fire away, Harry."

"I told Ralph about my career subsequent to that day in Singapore—including everything you and I did in the Philippines. I told him the story of David and Uriah. Only this Uriah got out safely. And everything was peaceful until two Filipinos tried to kill me in San Francisco. I told him about the lunch in the Polo Lounge. I told him about my visit to Professor Mok at Cal Tech. I gave him Professor Mok's bibliography on energy." He pointed to the papers on the floor by Li's chair. "I told him if Mok was right, then China need not kill Harry Ryder to get what it wanted. We would give China all the theory it could possibly want or use—with no holding back. I also had some layman's thoughts about Ralph's role now that the Gang of Four is locked up. Presumptive thoughts, surely, since I am not an expert on internal politics of the People's Republic; but I think it's obvious China is taking Japan as its model. Not Russia. This is a vast subject, but Ralph was polite enough to agree that I might have a point.

"And the hypothesis, if correct, has some interesting corollaries and implications. If China is turning to Japan, it will also and inevitably be turning to us. Killing me might be, I imagine, a counter-productive thrust against this new turn. Of course, if killing me gives Li's colleagues a hold over Junius Oakland, if, bluntly, they can make Oakland into a mole in the CIA—you understand mole, Terry?—well, then the People's Republic might have an incalculably valuable asset. Then my death would prove an acceptable trade-off. A real tit for tat. But, as I explained to Li Ngor—sorry, to Ralph—I've taken elementary precautions. Emilio Lanante has a document which he will read if I die, no matter how or where I die. It's a simple document. It will alert the world and the powers-that-be to check into Junius Oakland's role in my death. And once the question has even been raised—no matter if there's no proof of any connection whatever, and I'm sure there would be none, not at the start anyway—then Oakland is finished as a useful source. As a mole.

"Does that about sum up what I've said, Ralph?"

Terry did not realize her face had settled into the obstinate expression Ryder had commented on so many times. She was thinking out—and rethinking—the implications of Ryder's summary. She was so intent she did not notice the look Li Ngor Sheung exchanged with Ryder. Li's glance showed his amusement—and respect. "You are right, she is a force."

And she finished her analysis. "All right, I understand all that. But did Junius Oakland ask Mr. Li—Ralph—to kill you."

Li Ngor Sheung winced, but his smile was as marvelous as ever. And very gentle. "Not in so many words, Terry. Oakland implied to me that Harry had become a threat to his country. He said Ryder was embarking on some personal vendetta to rescue two old friends from Cruz. The U.S. government had heard about it and was terribly embarrassed. That's why they were working with Cruz to have Harry . . . ah . . . taken care of as soon as he arrived in the Philippines. But he, Mr. Oakland, was not sure that was enough. He said Harry Ryder has more than nine lives—and Calixto Calugas would have a most difficult time with a man who could act more Filipino than the Filipinos."

"And what did you say to all this?"

"You are most direct, Miss Jefferson." Li's smile was a bit strained now. "Mr. Ryder told me of your desire to study at the feet of Sun Tzu. Well. What did I say? I said the obvious. Why was he telling me all this?"

"And?"

"And he said we had worked together during the Cuban missile crisis. And perhaps we could work together again."

"And?"

"And I came home and talked to my people and we came substantially to the same conclusion Harry advanced." The happy smile returned with the "Harry." "The mole concept occurred to us, of course, but we rather doubted we would be able to secure a real hold over Mr. Oakland. He's a cute and slippery man. And as for secret information, there is nothing we particularly want from the United States at this time—nothing, that is, that wouldn't be thrust at us if we decide to accept it. You have a phrase: 'Beware the Greeks bearing gifts.' What will be left of China if we accept all the gifts you want to bring us?"

And Terry suddenly laughed, so that both men started. "Gifts. Cokes and MacDonalds and Pizza Huts and deodorants. We'll civilize you, by God."

Li winced again. "I'm afraid so, Terry. Four thousand years submerged in catsup and relish."

Now Harry laughed.

"And computers and nuclear reactors and Com-Sats."

"Yes, well, that too."

Terry frowned. "And so Harry only has to face one front here in Hong Kong? Our rear is secure?"

"Quite secure."

"Why don't you join us? Go to Junius Oakland and tell him you know everything he says is a pack of lies and he'd better bug off."

"Bug off?"

"Get off Harry's back."

"Terry, you can't ask Ralph to do that. He's already done all he can do, more than he should, probably. He's told me that Junius Oakland phoned him for the number of Leong Chak Hom and said Leong met Oakland at the airport the minute Oakland got off the plane. He also said Alison Oakland caught the thirteen-fifty JAL flight to Tokyo. Yes, the very same plane."

"And who is Leong Chak Hom?"

"A man who has accepted various assignments from a number of employees up and down the Pacific Basin."

"A professional killer?"

Li Ngor Sheung broke the silence. "From the People's Republic of China to a professional killer. Mr. Oakland is certainly coming down in the world."

Terry stood up. "Harry, I think we should catch the next plane to Washington, D.C., and we'll have this thing out right then and there. Oakland hasn't got a leg to stand on."

Now Li spoke up. "It's my turn, Terry. You can't ask Harry to do that. He doesn't have a shred of evidence to support any charges he might make. I'm not evidence. I'm afraid I'm a nonperson in this situation. And Harry still is not sure if Oakland is working alone or if he represents Company policy. Or a segment of Company policy. Because if we've learned one thing about your Company, it's that it's so vast no one in it knows what anyone else is doing. I sincerely hope we stay as lean as we are now. But I'm afraid, along with MacDonalds, we'll also accept your Parkinson's law."

She looked at Ryder. "So we have to confront Oakland? And his stooge, Mr. Leong? Okay, then. Mr. Li—Ralph—thank you for all you've done. We'll do our own confronting. And that means Harry has to sleep. Look at him. Nine lives. He's already past eight and seven-eighths."

"I'll go to sleep, Terry, if you phone Hertz in Manila and the Bayview Plaza and take care of the bills. Tell 'em to charge 'em to the Visa card number they already have."

And she and Li looked at each other in astonishment. Terry said, "My God, the man's dying and he worries about debts."

49

"Why did Oakland pick the Jade Garden? Why not the Hilton?"

Terry had her hand on the railing of the Star Ferry, but she did not seem to see the junks and sampans and freighters and destroyers. How much she had changed in two weeks. Where was the wide-eyed innocent inundated with the exoticism of Hong Kong, Taipai, Tacloban? He chuckled and she looked her question.

"I was thinking of the bed bugs in Tacloban," Ryder said. "I never once laughed, did I? But it's all right to laugh now, isn't it?"

"And I never said I told you so about going back and getting the pistol."

"And I never once asked you if call girls like sex."

"Are they—note the 'they,' Harry—are they capable of orgasms, you mean? What do you think?"

"After this morning, you can ask?"

To her amazement he had awakened at six in the morning, fresh and horny as a Cal Berkeley football player. He had looked in dismay at the empty bed beside him, then found her ensconced on the sofa. "What are you doing over there?" "Silly. Letting you sleep. Go back to sleep." "I don't need sleep. I need you." "How disgusting. Before breakfast, too. Do you also realize you haven't eaten in forty-eight hours?" "Good. Order breakfast. We'll have two goes at least before breakfast—and no telling how many more after. Come over here, girl. You phone and while you're ordering I'll take action; isn't that the way to order breakfast?"

And the memories brought her out of her apprehensive gloom and she shook herself and smiled and looked around her as if she saw the teeming harbor for the first time. "You're right, Harry. I mustn't forget the real things. Junius Oakland's just a miasma. This is real. This moment's real. This morning is real. You are real."

"Good. That's healthy. If you really do go into the business, remember this moment. Let it radiate through all future moments. Reality will follow you always."

"Okay. Done. And so, what about the Jade Garden?"

"He said it has the finest Peking Duck in all the territories."

"When you took me there before, I thought it a topflight restaurant; but the finest of anything? I don't get it."

The Jade Garden was on the fourth floor of a building just beyond the ferry terminal and halfway to the Peninsula. He nodded to their former hotel. "Shame that Harry Ryder couldn't register there. Or at the Mandarin or Luk Kwok. Before long we'll be running out of hotels." He looked at her thoughtfully. "You've got sound instincts, Terry. I don't get it either. I happen to know the grill at the Hilton is Oakland's idea of culinary heaven. Well, we'll soon find out if our common suspicions are sound—or just lapses of two sex-besotted minds."

"Are you going to challenge him?"

"We'll play it by ear. If we're right in our low thoughts, he'll challenge us. Somehow."

"My instincts are to attack."

"And mine are to run. We make a good team."

Junius Oakland was waiting for them at the reservation desk and he greeted them warmly and triumphantly. "The conquering heroes!" He looked sharply at Ryder's stiff arm, decided to ignore it. "What a shame the world will never know what you pulled off. My heartiest congratulations. I'm proud of you. The Director, I know, is proud of you. And certain other individuals who are nameless are mighty proud of you. But let me tell you, I've already called Washington and taken full credit for my wisdom. Come, we have a table, a feast is all prepared."

And with that fanfare she couldn't imagine how she could attack the elegant Leslie Howardish civil servant. Oakland babbled almost nonstop.

"My dear," he said—and she saw that he tried not to look at her too often, since if his eyes lingered too long on her barong tagalog his forehead would start to glisten—"I saw that I surprised you yesterday. I thought Harry would have told you about my recruiting him right here in Hong Kong. You were staying at the YMCA, do you remember? The YMCA. That half-block from the YMCA to the Peninsula is a veritable light-year leap, isn't it, Harry? And Harry didn't want to talk to me. He had already turned us down in New Haven. Hah, I see the modest Mr. Ryder has not told you all, has he, Terry? Let me tell you about him.

"Harry's company commander with the RCT in the 32nd Division . . . the man he reported to, I mean, since Harry was still working up in the hills with the guerillas. Harry was liaison. Anyway, this commander took a liking to Harry and when the war ended he pushed and shoved Harry into accepting a G.I. scholarship at Yale. I see he didn't tell you. Modest man. I went to Princeton myself. I'm not modest. Of course, I look my fifty-eight years and Harry still looks thirty-five. But that's the difference between Princeton and Yale, hah-hah. Here, have some more vegetables. And another beer? Yes, he graduated from Yale in three years. Majored in Asian studies and minored in romance languages. The people in New Haven never had a student with such language facility and they wanted him to teach. Failing that, they touted him to us—and he turned us down. He wanted to go back to the Philippines. Don't fidget, Harry. It's quite a story. You know what happened?

"What happened was he got to Manila and stayed in the Binondo district so he could talk Chinese as well as Tagalog and he met an ancient Chinese who said Harry ought to go help the Old Marshal fight Mao Tse Tung and Chiang Kai Shek. Marshal Yen Hsi-shan. One of the really unusual—maybe great—men of this century. From 1911 to 1949 he held off Mao and Chiang Kai Shek and Feng Yu Hsiang and Hsu Hsi-feng and Fan Chung-hsio and God knows how many other warlords who coveted Yen's precious Shansi. Do you know how far Mao was from Yen? Like California to Nevada, Terry. Shensi to Shansi. One mountain range. And Mao could never take over or subvert Shansi. One by one the Chinese provinces fell into Mao's palm, but not Shansi. Mao had to conquer all China to get Shansi.

"So, Harry heard about the Old Marshal in Manila and

headed to Shanghai on the next boat to fight communism. I know he talked to our consul there, John Lowell. Lowell tried to dissuade him from going inland. But Lowell knew a destined Asia hand when he saw one, so he gave him lots of good advice and watched him go to a certain death. Yes, that's what Lowell thought, Harry. He told me this about two months after you left. I followed you to Shanghai after you left Manila. But once you got into the interior, we knew you were going to be roasted in the waffle iron of war. Mao's war certainly. Chiang's war maybe. But you vanished and the next thing I know you're in Hong Kong. And I get a wire from Washington: 'In view of latest developments, resume previous objective re Harry Ryder.' I've remembered every word, Harry, because I didn't know what the hell they were talking about. What latest developments? I didn't dare ask, not in those days. When Yen escaped in his DC-3 to Canton and threw himself on Chiang's not-so-tender mercies, you weren't aboard. I know, I checked. And then three months later you show up at the YMCA. What happened, Harry? Where were you those missing months in 1949?"

Harry had gone into his anonymous look. She whooped when she saw it. "Harry, this is Terry. Remember me? Don't look so self-conscious. Certainly not paranoiac, Harry. This is not the Burauen airfield. Tell me, Harry, I want to hear."

Her Mr. Everyman sipped a cup of tea and then said, "Almost thirty years. God, nothing ever disappears, does it? Murder will out, said the monk. Well, all right. Thirty years should be long enough. Because I promised John Lowell I'd never tell what happened. 'They pissed all over us, young Harry, all the way from Washington they pissed all over us.' That's what he said. 'But if we say anything publicly, we'll really fuck things up. We'll lose our only friend in China. So don't you forget this. He's our only hope. Don't get him killed in his homeland. We have to give him time. Remember this, Harry. We've got to give him time.'

"He was a good man, Lowell. And he was right. It took our friend about twenty-five years to pull it off, but he was a very determined man. And a truly great one. Not half-great like Yen. But he's dead now, so I guess it's okay."

Oakland wiped his lips. "Who is dead, Harry?"

"Chou En-lai." Oakland knocked over a teacup. "Yes, that's where I was. When I got to Marshal Yen, he was more amused by me than anything else. But that devious old bastard knew how to use everybody. After about two months of watching Oriental politics—it's just like Watsonville, only a good deal rougher—he sent me to Shensi. To make a proposition to Chou En-lai. The proposition was just another ridiculous stall—Mao and Chou had a noose around the Marshal's neck and were slowly tightening it—but Chou didn't get upset. He talked a lot to me. Asked me a million questions about America and world politics. Yes, I was a Yale graduate. And I learned I had learned nothing. Certainly nothing about Chinese communism. I never felt so ignorant in my life. But at least I had the sense to say I didn't know when I didn't. And that was almost always. And so Chou made me his messenger boy. He sent me back to Shanghai to tell Lowell that China preferred to work with the U.S., not with Russia. If we would cooperate, he would see that China dumped Russia and became an ally of the United States."

"Chou? You're out of your mind, Harry. China never made any such offer. Why, if we had been China's ally these last thirty years, we'd own the world. If you follow my hyperbole. But it never happened, believe me, Harry. Sorry. I'm not calling you a liar. It just never happened. Maybe your Mandarin wasn't good enough then."

"You reacted just like Lowell when I saw him. 'No way, Harry. They hate our guts. And rightly so after the way we've treated them the last four years.' So I said, 'Talk to

243

Chou yourself.' And a quiet meeting was arranged and Lowell got it from the horse's mouth and sent a formal request to Washington from Chou En-lai for help and cooperation by the U.S. Peace on earth and goodwill to men."

There was a long silence. Oakland suddenly thumped the table. "My God, the China section of volume eight of *Foreign Relations of the United States.*"

Harry nodded. "Exactly."

"What, gentlemen, is volume eight of the *Foreign Relations of the United States?*"

The two men looked at each other. Oakland carried on. He looked as if he had eaten a sour apple. "Every year for a hundred years the State Department has been publishing the *Foreign Relations* series. Part of volume eight covers Chinese events in the year 1949. The year Harry is talking about. It was supposed to come out in 1974. It was skipped. And next year the State Department serenely went on with 1950. That part of volume eight—the 1949 part—still has not come out in this year of our Lord 1977."

"And that's what I was doing in 1949. When Lowell told me to shut up, I shut up and went to the YMCA. Junius here called me from the Peninsula and said, if I signed up with the Company, I, too, could stay at the Peninsula. How could a man refuse that?"

Oakland chuckled. "Don't you believe him. He said he would sign up only if he was posted to the Philippines and the Orient for at least ten years. I thought that condition would finish him but, so help me, the powers agreed. Harry was our old Asia hand for ten years. How about that?"

She couldn't restrain herself. "Harry, you're a hero. Why did you give all that up?"

"Yes, Harry," and Junius did not attempt to conceal his mockery. "Why did you?"

Terry leaned forward. This was the opening. This was

the time to attack. But Harry now not only seemed anonymous, he also looked stupid. He said, "My wife threatened to divorce me."

She wanted to kick him. What was the matter with him? Why didn't he challenge Oakland? By jingo, if he wouldn't, she would. But Harry had been watching her and as she opened her mouth to say "What about those photos of Roger Hiller in the hands of the Philippine Constabulary?" he forestalled her.

"And by the same token, when she did decide to divorce me after all, I accepted this little assignment in the Philippines. And so here we are, friends together. How nice."

Oakland's forehead had started to glisten. But he wasn't looking at her. He was watching Harry with raw malice on his face. "Yes, how nice. Well, thanks for clearing up the mystery of your past, Harry old boy. And I must say it was a wonderful lunch. One that will, I hope, be followed by a charming supper. How about it, Terry? Are we on for supper tonight?"

He still did not look at her. Harry did not look at her. He seemed like a statue. With sightless eyes. Now she could have tipped the table in his lap. After all they had meant to each other this morning, after all they had gone through together, after all her admissions of love—that long-forbidden word—how could he desert her like this?

"You know, Junius, I forgot to check Harry on our plans for this evening." For a moment she almost heard herself say, "And there's nothing I'd rather do more than get away from this dummy," but she couldn't do it. She continued weakly. So weakly she could hardly hear herself. "I'll call you this afternoon."

And she glared at her Rotarian—her Rotarian lover—and thought, "You coward. Wait until I get you alone."

Oakland said calmly, "Fine. I'll expect your call. You can reach me at the consulate. I'll tell them to put your call through."

50

They strode in silence to the Star Ferry terminal. Terry was going to wait until they were aboard before she let her Harry have it. How could a man be so pusillanimous?

But as they paid their fare, he said, "You forgot one thing in that whole lunch. You got so interested in my past, my tiny bit of heroic adventure, that you forgot one thing. Like that time with Pilar. You didn't see her coming across the park. Antennae. Remember the antennae. You must never pull them down."

They stood behind the gate and waited for it to swing open. "You mean I goofed in there? What should I have said to Oakland? Yes, I'm looking forward to supper tonight. I want you to plead your case. I want you to demonstrate for me what a great lover's like? What did I forget to do?"

"No, not that. You handled the invitation just right. You kept your options open. Our options."

The gate swung back, the crowd clumped down the ramp. But no one could hear the thudding feet, not over the babble of Chinese. Harry led her to a seat in the forward closed section. There were fewer people there and they got a whole bench to themselves. Harry flipped the seat so they faced backwards and could look over the entire deck.

He leaned forward to whisper in her ear, "Leong Chak Hom."

He watched a look of consternation cross her face. He sat quietly until she had worked it out. Oakland's hired killer. He waited until she reviewed her conclusions. Then he said, "Do you see it now?"

"That was a set-up?"

"That was a set-up."

"You mean . . ."

"Please, no names."

"You mean the Pacific Basin traveler might be after us right now? Somebody on this ferry? One of those?"

He nodded. She continued. "Then why didn't we take a cab through the Cross Harbour Tunnel? Why be sitting ducks?"

"A cab would only be a temporary evasion."

"But no one can do anything on this ferry. There are too many people. And he could never get away."

"No, of course not. It's when we get off. Oakland will have phoned Leong the second we left the Jade Garden. Look for someone standing alone with a magazine or newspaper or book or briefcase in his hand. He'll expect us to walk through the underpass toward Chater Road. That'll get us about two blocks from the Hilton. Three blocks. There'll be hundreds of people around. If a shot is fired—a silenced shot—no one will have any idea what's going on. Least of all us."

"Least of. . . . How can you be so calm?"

"A few minutes ago you were prepared to throw a plate at me for being so callous."

"Only to me. I know you, remember?"

She grabbed his arm—his good arm—and snuggled against him. "Harry, forgive me. By now you'd think I'd have learned. It was Burauen airfield all over again, wasn't it? When you started looking just the way you did the time you saw Mandares come up to us with his gun out, I should have known. Forgive me."

"Nothing to forgive. Do you have your Belgian pet?"

She nodded.

"Don't use it. The Pacific Basin traveler is not our present target. Be prepared for evasion, not action."

She thought a moment. As the ferry docked, she looked

up at him. "You mean, get behind somebody and stay there?"

"Well, partly that. Remember, our man might be behind us. So we'll keep near people. You look toward the front, I'll cover the rear. Training, you know. Come on, let's get in the middle of all those good folk."

And they went down the stairs into the underpass and it was Terry who saw him. A lean Cantonese who looked exactly like two million other Hong Kong Cantonese. He was leaning against a pillar. He wore a business suit and carried a briefcase. His hand was in the briefcase as if he were fumbling for a paper. And when he saw them, he started to point the briefcase and she gave an inarticulate cry and flung herself in front of her man.

The Chinese threw back his head, turned, and trotted up the Mandarin Hotel exit. Harry swung around just in time to see him disappear. He grabbed Terry and helped lower her stiffly pointing arm. She was trembling. To his surprise, he found he was trembling, too. Maybe because the exertion sent a flare of pain through his arm.

"You jumped in front of me. My God, girl, you might have been killed. Suppose he had fired?"

"Suppose, suppose." And suddenly tears came. "Oh, Harry, this is awful. What can we do? Let's get out of Hong Kong. I don't want you killed."

"Hong Kong. San Francisco. Washington. What difference does a place make?"

"Then we have to do something. Something aggressive, no more evasion."

"Yes, I know. But how? Come on, let's get to our hotel room and have a drink and do some heavy thinking."

51

Ryder parked the Porsche on Bank Street, between the Hong Kong and Shanghai Bank and the Bank of China. The same Porsche Terry had rented before. He could see the entrance to the Hilton from there. He could also see the Jaguar parked five cars behind him. A 320B. The Jaguar had followed his cab to the Watson Street rental agency and followed the Porsche back to Bank Street. He couldn't see who was in the Jaguar. He didn't have to. It had to be Leong Chak Hom.

He looked at his wristwatch and winced. He should have put the watch on his right arm. Ten minutes to seven. At seven Terry would be at the entrance and Oakland . . . ah, there he was, also driving a Jaguar. But naturally an XKE. Oakland got out of his car and went to the stairs to wait for Terry. It was getting harder to see, since a light mist was clouding the windshield. He would have liked to lean out the window to follow Oakland better, but that would give Leong a clear shot. Of course, at this moment Leong might be creeping along the row of cars and just about ready to poke his head over the fender and pot him from five feet. His head was conspicuous, no question about it. Leong had to go, no question about that, either. He hunched down so that he could barely see over the windshield.

And there was Terry. In spite of the heat she was wearing the same outfit she had on that day in the Polo Lounge. She greeted Junius with a gay gesture, flounced into the left seat. He carried her purse for her. The son-of-a-bitch. He already knew Terry was unarmed.

Ryder started the engine and the windshield wipers and crept out into Queen's Road Central and swung in

249

behind the XKE and followed it from two blocks' distance along Queensway. He should have gotten an automatic shift, not this stick job. Pain was constant in the Porsche. They were headed out toward Shau Kei Wan district—out Queensway, Hennessy, Yee Wo, Causeway, King's, and Shau Kei Wan. Same street, but—London fashion—constant metamorphosis by name incantation. Behind him, also two blocks distant, trundled the 320B. As he had told Terry, "To get at Junius, I've got to get rid of Leong. That's the name of this game. Let me alone and in private with Oakland and I'll get the guts out of him. There's no need to kill him. He'll sing. He's a Princeton man, remember?"

"What is that I stuff? Haven't you learned yet? This corporation is 'we.' We will kill Leong. We will make Princeton sing 'Boola, Boola.' Okay?"

And he had kissed her. "This is foolish, Terry. Madness. But I can't head you off. If you want to die for me, that's every woman's privilege. Male chauvinism cannot disappear so long as women like you are around."

The final plan was her idea. They had had their drinks and done their heavy thinking and never gotten past their starting point: There must be a shoot-out at Hong Kong Corral. And then her face had illuminated.

"I've got it, Harry. I'll do it again. Oh, I know I said I never would, but what's a never? I'll pull another Sir Spencer Smith."

"Like hell you will. Junius Oakland will never put a finger on you. Never. And that's a never that is a never."

"Of course it is, sweetheart." Sweetheart and darling. A new vocabulary, new world. "I'll get him alone in the bedroom and pull out General Duquesne's High Power and hold him until you arrive. That means you'll have about five or ten minutes to handle Leong Chak Hom. Of course, if you don't arrive in time, or not at all, I'll have to kill Oakland myself on general principles."

And he had backed away speechless.

"Why do you stare at me like that? I am not becoming a hit girl. You're my man. Anyone who tries to kill you deserves to be killed first. Isn't that logical?"

"It's logical, yes."

"Oh, I see what's wrong. It's too simple. You like complicated plans. Rube Goldberg creations."

"Terry, there are three logical reasons why your generous offer to sacrifice yourself is not the way to go. Because *sacrifice* is the right word. First, Oakland knows you've already killed. Second, the minute you are alone he will take your purse and confiscate your gun. Third, Oakland will know you're in love with me, and I with you. He saw us at lunch together. So he'll capture you as bait for me. He'll kill you the minute he thinks he's got me."

"Sweetheart, you don't understand Junius Oakland, do you? You and me in love—that won't bother him at all. He's a professional lady killer, can't you grasp that? He's had too many women in his day who professed to be—thought themselves to be—in love with their man. He's a picker-upper of the overflow at love feasts. No, he won't suspect me, Harry. Not Junius Oakland."

"All right—and I'm not being invidious—I defer to your superior judgment on that score. But not about the gun."

"And now I'll defer to you. I'll go unarmed. I think you're right. It's better to let him be suspicious, but not certain."

And in spite of his nonstop protestations, she had phoned Oakland. "Junius, you know how it is. I had to wait until Harry went out. He's got an appointment with some Chinese fellow at the New China News Agency. I didn't know Harry was a publicity hound. He'll be back about ten. I told him I'd go to a movie. Is that all right? You'll come get me? At seven? That late? Well, I guess three hours will have to do. Let's skip the supper part. I'm not that hungry. I can't wait, Junius, pet."

Ryder was aghast. "Did he really swallow all that?"

"How do I know? But what choice does he have? His

forehead glistens every time he looks at me. Just like you said it would. He doesn't care if I'm lying through my teeth. He's got Leong to take care of you. And while you and Leong are playing out your little games, he'll take care of me. Life is really quite logical, Harry, once you learn to accept the mad premises it's based on. Only one thing I ask. Get there soon. Don't linger too long with Leong."

And the three-car parade swept out Shau Kei Road into Chai Wan—still the same street—and as Ryder saw Oakland dart up Tai Tam to go over the mountain, Oakland's destination came to him. Probable destination. Just over the mountaintop, past Tai Tam Reservoir and the Tai Tam Bay isthmus, a short dead-end lane turned up the hill and led for a quarter of a mile or so to an estate hidden behind a four-foot stone wall and a heavy iron-reinforced wooden gate. Beyond the gate a circular driveway led to the mansion door. The Company safe house. Two elderly Chinese servants maintained the thirty-room establishment. They lived in the basement. When the house was being used, they were confined to their quarters and stayed there until the basement door was unbolted for them.

He braked the Porsche to the curb on Chai Wan and parked before a Chinese restaurant. Traffic poured past him in both directions. The Jaguar also parked a block behind him. Its hesitant maneuvering revealed a puzzled man. Good. Always keep the bastards off balance. He got out, pulled up the hood, shook his head dubiously and leaned forward as if to fiddle with the motor. His Hush-Puppy stuck so far down his belly that he couldn't really bend over until he had pushed it away from his scrotum. A phallic symbol somehow, no doubt. He straightened up, pulled down the hood, got back into the Porsche, started the engine, and swung out into the street. By this time Oakland should be at least a mile ahead of him. When he reached the Tai Tam intersection he shot up the hill, accelerated, went through the stop sign two blocks up the street, and roared up the mountain road.

He had a four-block lead on the Jaguar. Ryder did not pilot the Porsche up Tai Tam as skillfully as Terry had done two weeks ago. He couldn't, not with an arm that felt like a diseased tooth. However, he did all right. Once when he had to pass a lonely bus on a curve he didn't even slow down, but zoomed right past it around the curve. The pursuing Jaguar was long out of sight—and though it was still daylight the low clouds and the mist made visibility difficult. The infrequent cars going the other direction all had their headlights on. As his unlit Porsche hurtled past them, he saw their white, startled faces and heard their enraged horns fade away in the distance. What was that called? The Doppler effect? To them he must seem a doppelgänger.

Once past the reservoir, he slowed a bit. Now he risked switching on his lights. The Jaguar was nowhere in sight, but it couldn't be more than a half-mile behind. And he saw it, the lane to the safe house. Swinging up the hill he went beyond the first curve, stopped, parked the Porsche broadside in the middle of the lane. The small car was still lengthy enough to block the lane effectively. He turned the motor off, got out and walked five feet back to a tree overhanging the lane. He stood behind the trunk and listened. His ears adjusted to the silence and he began to notice the rain drops patter on the leaves. And then he heard the Jaguar. It slowed for the turn, came up the lane and at an accelerating rate sprang around the corner and went into a shrilling, skidding slide. Leong was a good driver. He brought the Jaguar to a halt just as the bumper thudded into the Porsche. At the moment of impact the 320B wasn't going very fast—no more than five miles an hour—but the blow knocked the Porsche two feet up the hill and placed the driver's head against the windshield.

It didn't linger there more than a second, but when Leong pulled back and looked up, he was staring into Ryder's pistol. His eyes recognized the nature of the pistol and he sucked in his breath.

"Out," Ryder said in Cantonese. "Keep your hands in sight and get out and turn around and assume the position. I'll take your gun and then, Mr. Leong, we'll go calling on your employer."

The round Cantonese face had only betrayed surprise for a fraction of a second. He nodded and eased himself out the door, face impassive, body relaxed. He turned around, put his hands on top of the roof and started to spread his legs. Ryder hit him on his head as hard as he could. Leong Chak Hom collapsed to the ground, bumping his face along the door so that blood spurted from his nose. It kept on spurting. Good, he was not dead. Ryder didn't want him dead. Not yet. Blotting out—trying to blot out—the pain in his arm, he picked up the unconscious body, carried it to the Porsche, placed it spraddled over the back of the seat, face down, took off Leong's belt, and tied his hands behind him. Then he searched the pockets. He found two pistols, one of them the same ugly assassin's weapon from the People's Republic that Chow Woon Chung had offered—the PRC Type 64. He put it in his belt, threw the other away, went back to Leong and found two knives—one strapped to his right arm, one to his right leg—and a stiletto in the sole of his right shoe. He took off the shoes and threw them into the brush along with Leong's pencil, pen, wallet, key ring, and money clip. These things might be innocent, they probably weren't.

"I'm sure I've missed something, my friend. I should probably take off all your clothes. You are a walking killing machine. But we haven't time for your full repertoire. The lady said get here soon and soon it's going to be."

He got behind the driver's seat. The pain in his arm was

so intense, tears flooded his eyes. He started the Porsche, drove up to the gate. It was unlocked and open. He got out, went around the car and slapped Leong's cheeks until the Chinese shook his head and muttered something.

"Climb out and lead the way up to the house. Go to the right. Stay under the trees. When the house comes into sight, go into the trees and go to the side entrance. The kitchen door. We'll go in there. I'm sorry about the belt, but you have a formidable reputation, Mr. Leong. And to save you any worry—or anticipation—I've removed your tools of trade. So let's go. I, of course, will have the pistol at your back."

It took them five minutes to reach the kitchen door. The house was unlit except for a hall light downstairs and a light in an upstairs room. A bedroom. Harry gave a windowpane one tap with his Hush-Puppy. The crack and tinkle were reasonably muted; certainly they could not be heard upstairs. Not if Terry was talking as he had told her to. How far behind was he? Five minutes? No, nearer ten, maybe even fifteen, with all the delays. He reached through the hole, turned the doorknob, waved the pistol at Leong. "One more thing, my friend. Open your mouth. I'm gagging you with this handkerchief. We can't have you giving some heroic shout. Not that I think you will. Professional, no? But why take chances? Now, go through the kitchen out to the front hall and up the stairs. I see you know the way. I'll follow."

They went upstairs, turned to the left, halted before the bedroom door. The hallway was lit. It was really quite attractive. Lovely grass wallpaper, thick carpets, handsome Chinese vases, and a magnificent Chinese scroll at the end of the hall. Now he could hear Terry. She was talking fast and loud—and there was no mistaking the tension in her voice. Tension? Or terror? He shoved the pistol in Leong's back and whispered, "We're going in together. Don't do anything foolish. If you do, you'll get any bullet aimed at me, because I intend to stay right behind you."

And he started to reach his left arm around Leong to turn the knob—the paining arm, but what was pain now? —and Leong did something foolish. He kicked the door and tried to hurl himself to the right. Even in his stocking feet the kick made a mighty bang. And as Harry wrestled with Leong to prevent him from falling away, there came a simultaneous explosion of a pistol and a tearing sound in the door. A bullet hole. A forty-five bullet hole. For the door had not been much of an obstacle, Leong proved that. The bullet slammed Leong against Ryder so that they were both knocked to the floor, Leong on top of him. Had the bullet gone through Leong's body, too? Was he hit? Dead? Hardly, if the screaming and shouting from the bedroom was any criterion.

He recognized some of Terry's epithets. Louse. Scum. Bastard. Followed by the sound of bodies thudding to the floor. Followed in turn by another pistol shot. And silence.

Ryder struggled from under Leong and picked up the body. Leong was quite dead. Foolish man. He reached around Leong, wrenched at the doorknob, and flung the door open.

Junius Oakland and Terry—both of them half-naked— were grappling on the floor. They could have been copulating. Oakland's leg was flung over Terry's thighs; her hands were at his throat. Neither gesture was tender. And Terry's rage-contorted face was, in fact, hideous to see. More hideous because it was immobilized, statuelike. A face in death. Unmistakable death.

Harry let Leong's body crumple to the floor. He stepped inside the bedroom, started to bark a command to Oakland, cut off his cry, so that only a gargling sound escaped his mouth. For Oakland was disengaging himself from Terry and pulling himself to his feet. If he had seen

Ryder, he ignored him now. His horrified eyes could not look away from Terry. He backed up and stood on his feet. His hand went out as if to push her away from him. Or push the sight of her away, the sight of the hole between her breasts and the blood seeping from the hole and trickling onto the carpet. And his hands were empty. The pistol was half-buried under her ribs.

Oakland backed away from Terry until he was only a few feet from Ryder. Then he turned and pointed a finger at Ryder.

"It's your fault."

Ryder raised the Hush-Puppy and pointed it at Oakland's chest. The bullet hole location would match the one in Terry. He started to squeeze the trigger. The Hush-Puppy held eight cartridges. One hole would not be enough. He would put eight of them into Oakland's scrawny but surprisingly well-muscled body. He couldn't miss.

And as he let his arm fall, Oakland whispered, "Shoot, you son-of-a-bitch. Shoot."

"Why, Junius?"

"Why! Because you've ruined everything. Ruined me. Ruined all I've lived for. Shoot, like the low-down Watsonville dirt you are."

"Not that, Junius. Why did you do it? Why kill her?"

"Kill her? I didn't want to kill her. She was giving me a hard time, but I wasn't going to kill her. Hell, lots of women have tried to give me hard times. But she went for the gun as soon as I yanked it from under the mattress. I didn't kill her, she killed herself. She wouldn't let me shoot at you again."

And then he saw Leong on the floor and his hand went to his mouth and he stepped back toward Terry.

"Yes, Junius, you killed Leong. You killed Terry. You tried to kill me. Why?"

"I didn't want to kill them. Just you. You deserved it."

"Why did I deserve it, Junius?" Ryder heard his voice as if in an echo chamber.

Oakland stared at him as if he could not comprehend Ryder's words. Then he laughed and laughed. "Why did you deserve it? You can ask? You who have taken my life away from me?"

"How did I take your life away from you?"

"I could have been director—do you understand that? Director. But suppose you were to talk about Yung Hom Sung? No one ever knew I was responsible for kidnapping the professor. I should have told the truth fifteen years ago. But now? With the witch hunt that's going on in Washington? Eight hundred field men fired, congressional investigations—laughing stock of the country, that's what we are. What would have happened to me if you told about Yung? What's happened to Kenworth, Murcredy, Arlett, Swanson? Shamed and booted out. The way I'd be shamed and booted out. How can you ask?"

"Junius, you'd never have made director if you were the last man in the Agency. A lecher can become president of our country, but he can't become director of the CIA. Never."

Ryder took Leong's assassination weapon from his belt and tossed it on the floor. "For you Junius. This is Leong's gun. I'm not going to kill you. You understand?" Oakland looked at the ugly weapon and pulled his shoulders together. Ryder nodded to Terry, a final benediction, a last ineradicable vision, and turned and went downstairs to the living room. He sat by the telephone and waited. Fifteen minutes went by. He thought of Terry and he saw her on the floor and he wept. Great flooding tears. And with each memory, a new torrent burst out until, even though he still wept, no more tears came.

And thirty minutes went by and then it sounded. The faintest of phuts. No more than a sigh. Leong's gun. Terry was wrong. She played the Sir Spencer Smith game once too often. And whose fault was that? Terry's?

He looked in the phone book, dialed a number. "American consulate? Put me through to the watch officer, please."

"Watch officer? We have no one by that title here, I'm sorry."

"Listen. I'm tired. I can't argue. You give the watch officer this message. Tell him that Junius Oakland just died in the line of duty. He was killed by a notorious Chinese assassin, Leong Chak Hom. So was the girl he was with. Killed. But Oakland managed to kill Leong before he died. At the safe house off Tai Tam. Tell him Oakland was a modern hero. Tell him Harry Ryder said so. Tell him I got here too late to help and I'm leaving this place—I don't care what the law says—and when they want me they'll find me at the Hilton. Tell him."

And he put the phone down. There was not a sound from the Chinese couple in the basement.

Epilogue

San Francisco Bay was totally covered by billowing clouds. Fog. He stared down at the fog, noted it, noted that he was without emotion. Nothing new there.

Pan American flight six was on time. The plane plunged into the fog, and through it and landed. He waited until every passenger had exited, then he got up and labored down the aisle. He walked like an old man. He went through the red-carpeted tunnel and came out into the lobby and didn't see the man until his arm was grabbed. The good arm fortunately.

"Oh, it's you."

"It's me. Come on, I've got everything taken care of. You don't have to go through Immigration or Customs."

And James Carter gave one strange look at Harry Ryder and he was almost tender as he guided him out of the airport. They did not say a word until they were in Carter's car, a nondescript grey Plymouth. Carter sat and looked at Ryder. "You were magnificent, Harry. We're all proud of you. The Director—all of us. You're a hero."

"You've got your heroes mixed up."

Carter sighed. "Poor Junius. I've heard your tape to the watch officer. You handled the whole thing masterfully."

"The whole thing? José Manzano and Emerenciana Manzano Darang, you mean?"

"Yes, that. And Oakland, too. The Hong Kong police accepted our story. Your story. Dead in the line of duty. Killed by Leong's gun. Masterful. And Oakland is getting full honors. A modern hero indeed—and fortunately a posthumous one."

"Oakland?"

"We all knew about Oakland. He was an embarrassment to the Agency. We've known about his unauthorized kidnapping of Yung Hung Som for ten years. One of the Mafia goons sang. And with all the current investigations and freedom-of-information and Senate committees, it was only a question of time until the truth would come out. Who could face that? We couldn't."

Ryder turned to stare at Carter. "Look," the latter said, "we have the highest regard for you. We knew you could handle him, just like you handled those thugs in Frankfurt and Syria. You have amazing survival talents. You showed that before you even took on the assignment. With those Filipinos on Montgomery Street. We knew Oakland would try to kill you, but he never had a chance."

"You mean, you wanted me to kill Oakland? Expected me to?"

"Of course. You're not usually this dense, Harry. We know how good you are. We want you back. On a special consultant basis. For real emergencies only, Harry."

"I didn't kill him."

"No, you didn't kill him."

"You want me back? What about all the cracks you made about me? Goof-off, expense account leech?"

"Your profile, Harry. You're quite phlegmatic until you're threatened or annoyed. It's all in your profile."

"You forgot to mention Terry Jefferson, James."

"Everyone in Hong Kong knew Junius Oakland, Harry. Including the police. Miss Jefferson was an unfortunate victim. Sorry about that, Harry. Real sorry. I've gathered she was something special. But we had enough clout to keep her out of the report. Sorry, Harry, but that's all we could do. You can't blame us for what happened. We want you back. Okay?"

Ryder got out of the car, leaned in. "Come back to you? Come back to the company? After all you've done? You're incredible, James. You're all incredible. You're so incredible there's no point even to try to tell you what I think of your offer. But I do have this one satisfaction left. I'll never have to see you again. That's something, anyway, isn't it, James?"

And he closed the door gently and walked away.